THE

DANCING
GIRLS

ALSO BY M.M. CHOUINARD

Taken to the Grave
Her Daughter's Cry
The Other Mothers

THE
DANCING
GIRLS

M.M. CHOUINARD

GRAND CENTRAL
PUBLISHING

NEW YORK   BOSTON

Copyright © 2019 by M.M. Chouinard
Reading group guide copyright © 2021 by M.M. Chouinard and Hachette Book Group, Inc.

Cover design by Ghost UK. Cover photos by Shutterstock.
Cover copyright © 2021 by Hachette Book Group, Inc.

Grand Central Publishing
Hachette Book Group
1290 Avenue of the Americas, New York, NY 10104
grandcentralpublishing.com
twitter.com/grandcentralpub

Originally published in the UK in 2019 by Bookouture, an imprint of StoryFire Ltd., Carmelite House, 50 Victoria Embankment, London EC4Y 0DZ

First GCP Edition: May 2021

Grand Central Publishing is a division of Hachette Book Group, Inc. The Grand Central Publishing name and logo is a trademark of Hachette Book Group, Inc.

The publisher is not responsible for websites (or their content) that are not owned by the publisher.

The Hachette Speakers Bureau provides a wide range of authors for speaking events. To find out more, go to www.hachettespeakersbureau.com or call (866) 376-6591.

Library of Congress Cataloging-in-Publication Data has been applied for.

ISBN: 978-1-5387-5446-7 (trade paperback)

Printed in the United States of America

LSC-C

Printing 1, 2021

For Mrs. Israel, and other teachers who encourage young writers to reach for their dreams

THE
DANCING
GIRLS

PART I

Jeanine Hammond

November 2012

CHAPTER ONE

The man adjusted his fedora as he collapsed into the hotel room. The woman with him stumbled and laughed as they pushed through the door, unaware she'd finished their bottle of Cabernet Sauvignon alone. He pulled her into an embrace, teased her with a long kiss, then whispered in her ear, "Where's the switch?"

Her hand slid along the wall until light filled the room.

He gauged her lack of coordination. She tossed her purse onto the laminate nightstand a little too hard, then teetered and almost fell while kicking off her heels. He nodded to himself, loosened his tie, and eased toward the bed.

"Come here." His most charming smile slid over his face and he extended his hand. "I can't wait anymore."

She met his gaze through lowered lashes and reached back to the zipper of her dress.

"No, my love, I want to undress you."

She ambled toward him, head tilted, and raised her hand to his.

Humming a snippet of the last song they'd danced to at dinner, he twirled her in a slow circle, then drew her into his arms, her back to his chest. A soft moan escaped her lips as he kissed her neck and ran his hands down the sides of her body, then trailed a hand back up the smooth aubergine silk to cradle her breast. She gasped as he caressed her nipple.

He pulled his tie past her cheek, smooth fingers stroking her skin as they slid by, and his teeth tugged at her earlobe. He gathered the thin, blond hair off the nape of her neck with a single finger, brushed his lips against her exposed skin, then paused to drink in the woodsy notes of her perfume mingling with the floral scent of her hair.

His hand slipped from her breast to her elbow, and he pressed her closer, closing his eyes to relish the softness and warmth of her abdomen.

"Ouch, darling, that's too tight." She gave a throaty laugh.

He made no move to loosen the grip. With a pickpocket's light touch, he wound the tie, now draped around her neck, through the fingers of his free hand.

Then he twisted, with one fierce, swift pull.

She tried to call out but only managed a hoarse hiss. His wrist wrenched the joined ends a second time with a practiced swivel, then a third, driving the fabric deep into her flesh.

Her body tensed and jerked, seeking any escape. First, she tried to pull away, then pushed back against him—futile movements, with her arms pinioned against her sides. When she tried to kick backward, he smiled—he'd positioned her mere inches from the bed, without enough distance to gain purchase and damage him. She tried to push off from the bed frame, desperate to angle enough leverage, and failed.

A sublime sense of power surged through him.

He pulled his attention from her struggle to the side of her face. He memorized her expression, the panic in her brown eyes, let the faint sound of her stifled grunts imprint their melody on his brain. Then he shifted to the delicious tension in her muscles and waited for it to drain away, his signal that her oxygen had run out and her world had dimmed.

He remained in place for several minutes after she went limp, to make sure. He closed his eyes again and used the time to savor the weight of her limp body in his arms and his complete control of her fate. *You danced at my command. Ate and drank according to my whims. Rose to a fever pitch of desire because I willed it. And now, finally, you die.*

And you never suspected.

His erection pushed against his trousers.

He twirled her body around to face him and held her right hand up and out. Cursing her extra pounds, he lifted her slightly and placed his feet under hers. He whistled the opening strains of "Roses from the South," then glided forward, swaying her through the steps in his makeshift ballroom.

Dance, my marionette, because I will it. Compliant. For my pleasure alone.

Her head lolled back, a grotesque caricature of a traditional closed hold. The accident delighted him, swelling his erection so painfully he was forced to stop.

Laughing, he brought her back to the side of the bed, dropped his arms and stepped back, allowing her to slide down the bed and onto the floor. He untangled his tie from her neck and smoothed it out, then put it back under his collar. He knelt beside her, slipped off her wedding ring, and put it into his breast pocket. Then he pushed her right arm out at an angle, left hand back toward her body, and re-created the accidental loll of her head. He stood back up and considered. She could just as easily be a ballerina as a ballroom dancer—but it would do. He captured a freeze-frame into his mind.

Then he scanned the room, running his mental eye over every movement he'd made since entering. He hadn't touched anything. He hadn't dropped anything. Nothing to clean up.

Satisfied, he pulled a tissue out of the box in the bathroom, used it to open the door, and stepped into the hallway. As the lock clicked into place behind him, he tucked the tissue into his pocket on top of the ring, then pulled his fedora down again and angled his head so the security camera wouldn't capture his face.

*

The man kept his face down and his hat angled even after reaching his rental car. The parking lot had no cameras—he'd done his research—but the devil was in the details.

He laughed at the accidental irony of the cliché.

He slid behind the wheel of the car and eased out of the parking lot. Under the cover of darkness, the cloyingly quintessential New England college town was far easier for him to stomach—this way, the gabled Georgians and flat-faced Colonials held an air of mystery as they clung to the splotches of street light, stretching away from the inky woods that crept up on them. But the university was better lit, and as he drove through the mixture of quaint redbrick Federal buildings and clashing uber-modern architecture, he fought the temptation to hunch down. Students were far more likely to notice a bent-over creeper than someone simply going about their business. He watched a student pick up a leaf from the sidewalk, twirl it to show off the golden-red color, and hand it to the girl holding his hand. She smiled, then thanked her beau with a long kiss.

His eyebrows rose in admiration. A simple, easy trick for charming a girl—he'd stash that away for future use.

He turned onto the highway leaving Massachusetts, then glanced at his watch. Just before midnight, right on schedule. The drive to Syracuse should take about four hours this time of night, even with a long enough detour to safely fill up the tank. Then he'd return the car, grab something to eat at the airport, and sleep on the flight home.

He double-checked the timing and ticked each step off his mental list. When the car pulled onto the nearly empty highway, he tossed the fedora over to the passenger seat and ran his fingers through his squashed brown hair.

The delay was agonizing but vital. No matter how much he assured himself the police would never know his actual name, he'd be haunted by flashes of it listed on flight manifests and Avis rental records. His mind was a terrier that couldn't release that type of bone—a blessing and a curse—and he'd toss and turn for weeks, covered in sweat as he tried to sleep. Driving the entire way was also out of the question; it would take days and exhaust him. Either way, he wouldn't be able to savor the kill properly after the fact.

This was the compromise. No records left in the target area but fast enough to get home within a day. Tomorrow he'd be safe, everything would be tended to, and he'd linger over the reward in his own bed.

CHAPTER TWO

Lieutenant Josette Fournier stepped out of the elevator cradling her latte, the closest she could get to an old-fashioned café au lait this far from New Orleans. She'd only managed three hours' sleep the night before, and it was hitting her like a meteorite trailing a wrecking ball. When she was twenty, even thirty, she could get by with next to no sleep for days, even work two or three days with no sleep at all. At thirty-seven, her days of consequence-free all-nighters were behind her. She took a deep draw from the Starbucks cup, let the warm liquid glide down her throat. *God bless caffeine.* She looked down and sighed as a drop landed on the front of her gray suit. *And dry cleaning.*

What else could she do? The work didn't stop because she needed sleep. Once she'd mastered the rhythm of the new position, this intense phase would pass. But for now, it left little time for anything other than work, including sleep. She pushed her hand through the layered chestnut hair overdue for a cut and rubbed the brow above her tired green eyes.

Jo strode down the long hotel hallway toward the group of officers standing near the target room. They nodded and stepped aside to let her pass. Detectives Bob Arnett and Christine Lopez stood just outside the door while the forensic team examined the crime scene. Arnett, whose graying black hair was always just a little longer than looked good on his round face, was checking his notes against the scene. Jo had partnered with him for years before her promotion and trusted him implicitly. Lopez, a new transfer, bent forward in a squat, her long black hair piled into a protective cap, directing the team to take specific pictures. In the short time she'd known Lopez, who was ten years her junior, she'd come to admire her attention to detail and her computer savvy—but worried about her intensity. Jo glanced at the tech next to her, a man she'd never seen before—broad-shouldered, with blue eyes and black hair, he was just the type her mother always tried to match her up with. Oppressive fatigue washed over her at the thought of both her mother's fix-ups and the effort involved in dating. Her mind flashed to the romantic dinner her boyfriend Karl had scheduled for later that night.

She peered into the open room, past the entry bottleneck. A blond woman lay collapsed on the floor, limbs askew. No blood or other evidence of a struggle. From this distance, she might simply have passed out, suffered a heart attack or stroke.

"Catch me up," she said.

Arnett looked up and lifted his chin in greeting. "Woman found strangled in her room. Maid found her during routine housekeeping this morning. Noticed marks on her neck and was smart enough to leave her alone, except to take a pulse. Victim was strangled with some sort of thick cord, no other marks. No murder weapon yet."

"Do we know who she is?"

"License says Jeanine Hammond, thirty-five. We're pulling her information. Home address is listed as Green Rapids, Ohio." Arnett didn't glance at his notes; he rarely needed to.

"What brings her to beautiful downtown Oakhurst?"

"No idea yet. Checked in yesterday around 4:15 p.m., alone, room booked in her name only. Looks like very little has been touched. She left again shortly after she arrived, and the log shows her key opened the room again at 11:39 last night. Medical examiner's first estimate is she was killed shortly after that. The door opened one final time fifteen minutes later."

"Did anybody see her come in?"

"Not sure yet. We need to talk to the night clerk and check the surveillance tapes."

"Burglary?"

Arnett shook his head. "Doesn't look like it. Cash and credit cards in her wallet, and she's sporting a diamond necklace. Laptop on the desk, bags nearly pristine."

The bottleneck cleared, and Jo stepped forward as far as the tape would let her. "She was strangled on the floor, but there's no sign of a struggle. That seems odd."

"She wasn't strangled on the floor. The ME said the bruises and ligature marks indicate she was strangled while standing up."

"Really." Fournier craned her neck left and right. "Mind if I take a look myself?"

Arnett smiled—they both knew she didn't have to ask for permission. He gestured to the protective gear. "Help yourself."

She suited up, ducked under the tape, and followed him over to Jeanine. Over fifteen years on the force, and she still felt the same anger, desperation, and fear every time she faced a dead body: anger at the distorted egos that fueled such callous disregard for life, desperation that she couldn't prevent such tragedies, and fear that she'd be unable to find justice for this victim. Even so, this one hit her harder than they normally did. The woman's face, flushed red from the petechiae spreading angrily across her cheeks, mouth open and tongue slightly swollen, had an unusual expression that tugged at Jo—there was an element of sadness to the expression, like the woman had died realizing that none of her hopes and dreams would be fulfilled.

Jo stooped for a closer look at the red welts encircling her neck. "Fairly even ligature marks. Do we know what he used to strangle her? No way he used his bare hands."

"Not yet. We'll take in any possibilities we find and test them out."

She nodded and straightened up, then took a step back, taking in a bird's-eye view. "The ME's sure she wasn't strangled lying down?"

"Seemed to be. Why?" He followed her glance to Jeanine.

"The angle of her neck feels odd to me. And that left arm, would it fall like that otherwise?"

Arnett shrugged. "No idea. I'll ask him."

She bent down again. Jeanine's left ring finger was dented where a ring had been, the line clearly demarcated as though something invisible were pushing the skin back. That didn't last for very long once a ring was removed if it had been worn for any length of time—as Jo knew too well. She pointed to the finger. "Have you found a wedding ring lying around?"

"Nope, and we've looked."

"Recently divorced?"

"Maybe. We'll know soon." Arnett's brows drew together at an angle, an expression Jo recognized. Something wasn't sitting right with him.

"Met the wrong guy at a bar?"

"Could be. But there're no signs of sexual assault we can see."

"We can't be sure yet, so we'll have to put a pin in that. Anything you need from me before I head down for my chat with the manager?"

"Not as yet."

"Then I'll go do the drill." She nodded to acknowledge Lopez, who was still talking to the forensics team.

Jo walked back down the hall, deep in thought, her fingers toying with the diamond necklace nestled into the base of her neck. Oakhurst was deceptively big, despite a carefully cultivated small-town feel, and murders had been increasing the last few years. Still, she shared Arnett's feeling; there was something odd about this one she couldn't pinpoint. Just an uneasy sense that something wasn't right, like when you walk into a room filled with silent people and can taste the tension.

Didn't look like she'd be making that dinner with Karl tonight after all.

*

Jo flipped the dead bolt on her door well past midnight. She dropped her keys onto the coffee table and winced as they clanked against the glass. Light flooded the hall from the bedroom; Karl was still awake. She hung up her coat to the sound of his feet thumping the floor—not his normal relaxed tread, but a pointed, angry clomp. She looked up to find him glaring silently at her, arms wrapped across his chest.

"What'm I supposed to do, Karl? It's my job. You know that." Her eyes pleaded with him.

"A phone call, maybe, rather than a text. Or take a half-hour break to touch base with me, I'll come to you. You have to eat one way or the other."

She crossed the living room to his side and tried an apologetic smile. "I haven't eaten, actually, and you know how rare that is for me. But you're right. I should have called you."

"Why didn't you?"

Her smile faltered. The truth wasn't going to help, but she was too burned out to come up with a way to finesse. "Honestly, because I knew you'd be upset and I was avoiding it for the moment."

"We've been waiting on those reservations for three months, *Josette*. Three months." The words jerked out.

"I know. I'm sorry." She slid her hand onto his arm.

He remained motionless and silent.

The fatigue washed over her again, bleaching out her normally abundant tact and good sense. She turned and crossed back through the living room to the kitchen. "I know, I know, you've heard it before. I'll see if I can't convince the next killer to pick a better night." She registered his shocked silence, followed by his footsteps back to bed.

She sighed. There was such a thing as too much truth, and she knew better. She'd apologize in the morning.

She started some soft jazz playing through her Bluetooth speakers and turned to pour herself a drink. She grimaced—the counter was covered in coffee grounds. As she wiped it down and pushed the coffee maker back into its place against the wall, her therapist's voice echoed through her head, reminding her not everybody felt the need to be as freakishly clean and orderly as she did.

She reached into the cabinet and pulled down a bottle of calvados and a snifter. She worked too hard, she was never home, she always disappointed him. And despite all that, she was struggling to get a handle on work too, even after two months as lieutenant. Maybe she wasn't the right person for it. The saying claimed you rose to the level of your incompetence, promoted until you sat forever in a job you weren't good enough to be promoted out of. She used to laugh at the cynicism of that; now she wondered. She'd been a damned good detective, by every measure. She'd made detective faster than anyone in the history of the Oakhurst County State Police Detective Unit, had the highest rate of solved homicides in each of her eleven years as detective, and had received three commendations over her fifteen years of service. Not just because she loved what she did, but because it was what she *had* to do. She shook her head to clear the painful memories, one in particular, from her visits back to New Orleans as a teenager. She hadn't been able to get justice for Marc's death, and she'd never allow another criminal to go free on her watch.

So she'd hesitated when Assistant District Attorney Rockney came to her, and only considered the promotion to lieutenant because he'd assured her she'd be allowed a hand in investigations. But until today, that hadn't happened, and her anchor to the work she loved slipped further and further away. And while she'd always been good at managing a team, this was different. Her choices now affected people's careers, and someone's nose was always out of joint. She'd believed a moral person who always tried to do the right thing for the right reason would ultimately be respected for her choices. She was wrong.

And more and more, a voice whispered to her that maybe the promotion had been a mistake, that it wasn't what she was meant to do. Maybe she should just quit, go back to detective. Make everyone happier.

Her phone rang. Arnett.

"Do you have a minute for me to catch you up on the hotel strangling?"

She poured two fingers into the glass. "I'm at the house. Fill me in over a drink?"

"You know me, never turn down free booze."

Five minutes later, Arnett's brisk knock broke the silence. Jo motioned him into the living room, where a gin and tonic waited. Arnett settled in and leaned back on the sofa, drink in hand.

"How's everything coming with Laura?" Jo asked.

He took a long sip. "She moved back home, but she's sleeping in the guest bedroom for now. We're walking on eggshells, trying to figure it out."

Jo studied the mix of emotions on his face. "That's a step in the right direction."

"Yeah, funny how it works. She cheats, and I'm the one that's hard to forgive."

"Nobody ever said marriage was easy."

He raised his glass in a toast. "Truth."

Jo clinked with her snifter. "So, what's the news with the case?"

"Information's coming quickly about Jeanine Hammond. She's married alright, not divorced or separated, and her husband was expecting her back at the end of the week. *With* her wedding ring.

No kids. She was here for a management training retreat. You know, motivation and team-building skills. She worked for Gelarking & Scribes Inc., a paper goods company specializing in high-end stationery. Oversaw her own small department. I contacted the company and they confirmed the purpose of her trip. So did the company heading the retreat."

"Anybody else missing?"

"Nope, otherwise all present and accounted for."

"How was the relationship with the husband?"

"Here's the thing. They informed him and got the basics, took the computers, all that. But I don't want to probe too much until we can talk to him in person, and I'd like to do it myself. I'd prefer you to come if you can break away. The missing wedding ring is bothering me—seems significant, with no other theft. We can do some digging while we're there."

"Why not Lopez?"

"Her mother's in the hospital, had a nasty fall. Stable for now, but Lopez doesn't want to leave town. So, I thought you and I could put the band back together for a day." Arnett met her eye over his drink. He knew her well enough to read her restlessness.

Frustration stabbed through Jo. She didn't just *want* to conduct these interviews, she *needed* to. Needed to sink her teeth into something, feel herself making a difference the way she had when she was a detective—and glossing over official business with the hotel manager hadn't been enough. She glanced toward the bedroom and tried to shut out the thousand responsibilities sitting on her desk at the station. "How long do you think it'll take?"

"From what I can tell, we should be able to handle it in a day. The husband's the main thing, maybe the boss."

Karl was pissed anyway—maybe space for a day or two would help. And dammit, the only promise she'd made to herself when she took the job was that she'd stay hands-on with cases.

Screw it.

"Rockney can keep the wheels on for a day. Make the arrangements. Anything else come back yet?" She sipped the calvados.

"I talked to the ME. He confirmed there was no sexual assault of any kind. Cause of death was asphyxiation; she was strangled with some sort of cloth. The marks on the neck suggest that something was wrapped around and twisted at the right front side to tighten it. No fibers left in the wound that they can see, but they'll take a closer look. Some bruising on the arms around the elbows. Their guess is that she was held in place by someone standing behind her while she was strangled. And, while he agreed that the positioning of the limbs and head was odd, he couldn't rule out it could have happened just from her falling."

She nodded but remained unconvinced. "Any clues from the room?"

"They're still working on it, but it doesn't look good. Plenty of fingerprints—don't get me started on how bad the maids clean—so we're eliminating those that have a reason to be there. But even then, any good defense attorney can make a good case for why a print's in that room unless we come up with something else to go along with it, and we got nothing so far. It doesn't look like she spent any real time in the room before she was murdered, hadn't unpacked, nothing. She used the toilet, and there are a few hairs in the bathroom; we're waiting for the tests, but they looked like a match for the ones in her brush. I don't see us getting much unless we get extremely lucky."

"What about the surveillance tapes?"

"Good news is, camera caught her coming in the north side entrance with a male companion in a fedora. He came back out the same entrance, alone, seventeen minutes later. Bad news is, camera's angled up so high, we can't see his face. I'm having Renny take a look at it, see if he can do some enhancement to pick up anything useful." Arnett's index finger tapped the side of his glass.

Jo registered the tapping. Something was on Arnett's mind. He was an excellent detective, with good skills and good instincts; if he was bothered, there was a reason. "Want to throw some ideas out?"

"Not yet. Let's talk to the husband and take it from there."

CHAPTER THREE

As Roger Hammond led them into his living room the next day, Jo glanced around, soaking in Jeanine's personality. The subtle mint greens and pale blues didn't match Roger or his careless appearance; his brown shirt and black pants were clean but ill-fitting, and his chosen haircut accented the receding middle-aged hairline. The furniture wasn't new, but it was well kept and strategic. The larger pieces were neutral shades while less expensive touches, mostly in the form of throw pillows, brought color and style to the room. A single framed wedding picture sat in the middle of the mantel.

When Roger sat on one end of the couch, Arnett claimed the matching love seat at the other end. Jo smiled to herself—old habits were hard to break, and without a word they'd slipped back into their old dynamic. She'd take the lead, and for the most part he'd observe—because, he claimed, she was far more intuitive when it came to reading and connecting with people. And without a doubt, he was near computer-like in his ability to store information for later retrieval, at least when he was allowed to observe the conversation rather than guide it. So, she perched on the armchair kitty-corner to Roger, closer to him, searching his face as she settled. Dark circles under his blue eyes paired with the rumpled clothes to give an air of despondence, of a man getting through the day as best he could.

Roger lurched halfway back up. "I'm sorry, I didn't think to ask. Can I offer you a cup of coffee?"

"No, thank you. We drank a pot between us on the plane." Jo smiled as Arnett took out his notebook. "We'll be fast, I know this must be a hard time for you."

Roger sat back down. "I just want to know what happened. You always see these senseless killings on the news, but you never think—" He choked and broke off, staring down.

A vision of Jo's uncle Michel flashed through her mind—he'd never recovered from the death of his wife, and the neighbors found him six months later, dead in his RV, where he'd been sleeping outside the house he'd shared with her. A wave of compassion flooded her, and she placed a gentle hand on his arm. "We're going to do everything we can to get you some answers, Mr. Hammond."

He nodded, then turned back with teary eyes. "What can I tell you?"

She withdrew her hand. "Why was your wife in Oakhurst?"

"She went for a company retreat. A team-building workshop that was supposed to help her motivate people or be a better leader. Hopefully get her a promotion."

"Was she excited about the trip?"

"Sure. She was enthusiastic about learning new techniques for work. And we don't travel much, so she was looking forward to seeing fall in New England. That's why she went early, on Saturday."

"Why weren't you with her?"

"I would've had to take off work. I'm an air-traffic controller, and it's not easy to arrange time off outside of our preset bids. Fine if it had been a vacation, but it wasn't. She was going to be busy during most of the days, and probably would have been invited to dinner with colleagues. Why waste the vacation days and the money for that?"

Arnett's eyebrows lifted. "Are you having troubles with money?"

"I wouldn't say troubles, exactly."

"What would you say?" he asked.

"Just that there always seems to be less money than things you need to spend it on."

"Like what?" Jo took back over.

"Well, we could use a new refrigerator. The one we have is ten years old. And we need to replace our pipes. The water pressure in the house can be almost nonexistent if we have several things running at once."

"And you don't have money to replace them?"

"Well, technically, we have the money. But if we spend it on that, it'll cut our savings in half, and then where will we be? That's one of the reasons I was glad she was going to this retreat. I was hoping it would light a fire under her to get that promotion, so we wouldn't have to worry so much."

Jo ran the numbers in her head. If pipe repair and a new fridge only cut their savings in half, they were sitting far prettier than most families. "She wasn't enthusiastic about a promotion?"

"She loved what she did and didn't want to go to the next step. Which was frustrating. She was very cavalier about money."

Jo shifted in her chair. As nice a man as Roger seemed to be, how could he not understand that there were more important things than money?

Arnett's radar zoomed in. "Racking up debt? Credit card issues?"

"Not *exactly*. We always paid our bills, balances in full every month. But we should have been *saving* more than we were. I told her time and again, but she would just brush it off, say we were saving plenty. So I figured, if she got promoted, there'd be more money coming in. And she was finally making a move, and then this happens." His face crumpled.

Jo exchanged a look with Arnett. No debt, plenty of savings, no children to plan for—where was the problem, exactly? "Was there anyone at work who might have resented her for any reason?"

"No, she got along well with the people she worked with. Sure, sometimes someone would get ruffled about something, but that happened to everyone."

Jo made a note. "Did she have any close friends there? Or favorites among the employees, maybe?"

"Not that I'm aware of. She felt managers had an obligation to keep work and personal life separate."

"So, nobody there we should talk to?"

Roger leaned forward. "Why? Do you think someone from her work killed her? What makes you think that?"

"We have to check all the possibilities, that's all. Eliminate what we can. Speaking of, for the record, I need to know what you were doing that day and evening." Jo watched Roger's face.

His voice flattened. "A group of us got together to barbecue and watch the Blue Jackets game. We do it all the time, with two couples we know. I can give you their information, they live about ten minutes away."

"I'd appreciate that." She paused for a moment, but it had to be done. "Were there any problems in your marriage?"

His eyes flicked to Arnett, then back to Jo. "Absolutely not. We had a great marriage. Sure, there were issues we fought about, mostly money, but all couples fight about those things. Nothing out of the ordinary."

"No big fights recently?"

"None."

She put a drop of honey into her voice to give it a soothing edge. "Any affairs, now or in the past?"

"Never. I would never do something like that to her." His throat seized again. "I would never have done anything like that to her. I loved her. She was my entire life. I don't know how I'm going to…" He trailed off, gesturing around the room, words evaporated.

"And what about her? Would she have done something like that?" Jo's voice stayed gentle.

"No, I don't believe that. There's no way."

"Why do you say that?" Jo studied him.

"I don't see how. She never did anything even remotely suspicious. She never worked late or on weekends. She was a loyal employee, but always said nobody ever wished on their deathbed that they'd worked more overtime. She hardly went out without me, only once a week with her friends Paola and Lorraine. Even her hobbies were home-based."

"What were her hobbies?" Arnett asked, face blank.

"She loved to read. She loved to draw. She played a lot of computer games and we watched a fair amount of TV, although she's been watching less lately. That's it, really."

"And what about her mood? Any unusual changes, good or bad?" Arnett asked.

"Nothing unusual... Well, I guess she was a little happier recently. She got depressed a lot, it runs in her family. It always passed sooner or later." His eyes darted between them, and his face tightened. "No. I'm sorry, Detectives. I don't believe she was cheating on me, not for one second."

Jo met his eyes with a well-practiced, reassuring smile. "We have to ask, that's all. Cover the bases. I'm sure your wife loved you very much."

Roger looked at her for a moment, then nodded and looked down into his lap.

"Her family, any issues there?"

"She didn't really have any family. Her mother and father are both gone, and she didn't have any siblings. She doesn't have much extended family either, and what she has, they aren't close. They live on the West Coast and weren't in contact. I don't even know any names."

Jo closed her notepad and stood up, Arnett following suit. "Thank you, Mr. Hammond. I know this wasn't an easy conversation."

"I want you to find who did this to her. Please. If there's anything else I can tell you, let me know. It's just so—I mean—she was staying in a good hotel, with good security—I don't understand how this happened."

Uncle Michel flashed through her mind again. She put her hand on the man's shoulder. "We'll do everything we can to get answers for you, Mr. Hammond."

*

Arnett automatically headed for the passenger side, giving Jo her turn to drive. "*That* brought home Laura's point about passive neglect. Might be a good idea to bring her some flowers when I get home." He tapped a dour reminder into his phone while Jo started the car and programmed the address for their meeting with Paola Lowell, one of Jeanine's two close friends, into the GPS unit. Paola had agreed to meet with them between client appointments at a Starbucks about a mile away.

"Passive neglect? I thought the issue was empty-nest syndrome, now that the girls are gone?"

"Turns out she felt like I'd left the nest, too, emotionally speaking. She wants us to find some activity we can do together to try to reconnect." He rubbed his brow.

"Well. It never hurts to make an effort." Jo pushed away the memory of a dead bouquet of flowers on her mantel and Karl's grumbled complaint that she hadn't been home enough to enjoy them alive. Her mind replaced it with another, of her father, chastising her for not visiting more. She banished that one too, before the guilt could take hold of her. "And at least we can drink some coffee now; I need all the mental lubricant I can get. I never have a problem wrapping my mind around people, but I can't get my brain to construct who Jeanine Hammond was."

He took a deep breath. "Dedicated employee and boss. Cared about the people she worked with, but kept a distance. Homebody—solitary hobbies that kept her to herself."

Jo watched a pedestrian cross the street. "I don't doubt the husband loved her, but I just can't figure out the relationship. There's a lack of nuance to it that bothers me. On the surface I'm getting a picture of ordinary, typical. But something feels off."

"What rings for me is the obsession with money, and the focus on the promotion. That pushed the limits of ordinary, and she clearly didn't share it."

"Mmm. But doesn't every couple fight about money?"

The turn-signal click punctuated a long pause before Arnett answered. "Maybe."

They arrived ten minutes early. Arnett ordered at the counter while Jo scanned the room for a table that wasn't set flush with the others near it, eventually settling for one in the corner. She sat facing the entry, crossed leg bouncing, and watched for a woman matching Paola's description.

Paola was also early. She pushed through the door with gale-force purpose, already scanning the room for them. Jo raised her hand in acknowledgment and Paola maneuvered over to her.

"Detective Fournier?"

"Paola Lowell?"

She nodded confirmation. "I need caffeine to face this. I'll be right back."

Jo watched her walk up to the counter. She was dressed professionally but attractively in bold, eye-catching colors—a red blouse over a full white skirt with large black-and-yellow flowers. Her makeup was minimal but still striking, full auburn brows set off by bloodred lipstick. She ordered drip coffee and returned to the table with Arnett just behind her.

She sat stiffly, with legs crossed at the ankles. Closer now, Jo could see that her eyes were shot with red and were surrounded by puffy shadows. She took a sip from her cup and left a red slash on the lid, somehow without marring her lips.

"Thank you for taking the time to meet with us on such short notice. I know it can be hard to get away during the workday." Jo sipped from her mocha and realized most of the wine-colored lipstick she'd swiped on that morning was already long gone.

"One of the benefits of working in real estate. I can usually carve out an hour here or there if I need it. The downside is, clients are demanding. Other buyers aren't going to wait to put in their offers while I lie in bed crying all day." Her lips trembled as she attempted a smile.

"Still, it's much appreciated."

She leaned forward. "Of course. I want you to find the rat-bastard-son-of-a-bitch who killed Jeanine."

Jo's brows shot up and she swallowed a smile—Jeanine had good taste in friends. "Let's get down to it, then. How do you know Jeanine?"

"I met her about ten years ago at a book club organized by a mutual friend. We were the only two people who seemed to get that when you meet to discuss a book, it's a good idea to read the book and have something to say about it." She shook her head at the memory. "Everyone else wanted to talk about the newest recipe they'd found, or which diapers were less likely to leak. Neither of us were domestic goddesses, so we ended up talking about the book while everyone else did whatever it was they came to do. No surprise, the 'book club' quit meeting after a few months, and she and I formed a book club built for two."

"How would you describe your friendship? Were you two close?"

"Mm-hm. We talk every other day or so, see each other at least once a week." She winced. "Saw each other. We had the same outlook on life, politics, most everything. She was an introvert, but had a wicked sense of humor, and we always made each other laugh through our problems."

Jo latched on to the emotion. Finally, some sense of vitality, of something dynamic in Jeanine's personality. Why hadn't she felt any of that coming from Roger?

"What problems did she have?" Jo asked.

"Typical problems, really. I know where you're going with this. How was her job? How was her marriage? Right?"

"That's as good a place to start as any." Jo took another draw from the coffee and noted Arnett's eyes fixed intensely on Paola's face. Jo felt the same draw, didn't want to look away, like at any moment Paola would turn into some sort of mystical creature before their eyes. A fairy queen? No, more like a fierce master of dragons.

Paola leaned back in her seat and crossed her legs at the knee. "She loved her job, and they loved her. There was always an employee here or there that would test the boundaries with her, but for the most part, she worked well with her team. She believed in giving her people space to do their job. Most of her employees appreciated that."

Arnett spoke up. "What about when she had to fire someone? Any hard feelings there?"

Paola's gaze swiveled to him. "Not that I know of. She hated doing it, even when the person deserved it, and I think they could sense that. It helped stave off bad feelings."

"So she never complained to you about threats or anything like that?" Jo asked.

"Never."

"How about her marriage?"

"Her marriage was good. They loved and respected one another. The relationship wasn't perfect, but whose is?" She shrugged. "Her complaints could have been interchanged with just about any married woman's on the planet. He didn't listen to her, would tune out when she talked about work and other things. She didn't feel appreciated. Their sex drives didn't match up. You know the drill." She took another sip from her cup.

"Did they fight over money?"

Paola grimaced. "Not as much as they should have, in my opinion. Roger can be ridiculously tight-fisted, it's really bizarre. She said his whole family is like that. No matter what they have, they can't ever take any joy in it, like it will all disappear any second. If she bought a pair of shoes, he asked her if she really needed them. She loved shoes, to be sure, but didn't have nearly as many as most women have. And it wasn't just that kind of thing. He made her feel guilty for buying a twenty-five-cent bulb of garlic once, because he was sure there was some at home. Right in the middle of the grocery store, in front of everyone, like she was a child asking for a toy she didn't need."

Jo winced. "How did she react to that?"

"She told him that if she wanted the garlic she'd get it, and she didn't appreciate him always making her feel that way. But it hurt her."

"Was that common?"

"Oh yeah, standard operating procedure for them. It was really weird. She'd always feel guilty about every penny she spent, and then she'd be annoyed at feeling guilty about it and take a stand. Then she'd feel guilty about taking the stand. Every month he'd tell her she was spending too much, and every month she told him to make up a budget so she'd know what the issues were, and how much she could spend." She punctuated each "every" with a finger slash through the air. "But he never did it. I think because there wasn't any actual problem, he just didn't want her to spend anything at all. So the cycle just repeated. It would have driven me crazy. I mean, it's not like they were poor, and she earned her own money, for heaven's sake! But I guess you never know what works for other people."

Jo nodded. People made mistakes, put their marriage at risk all the time and in all sorts of ways, but still stayed together. Lying, cheating, even abuse. Where did humiliating a spouse over a bulb of garlic fall on that continuum? *That* depended on who you were asking. Any man who tried to control her spending or who chastised her in public would find the door slamming him in the ass. But then, nobody'd ever mistake her for a relationship guru.

Arnett took over. "You mentioned their sex drives weren't equal."

"Oh, that was straight out of the sitcoms. He always wanted more sex, she always wanted more romance, and neither of them ended up getting what they wanted."

"Did either step out?" Jo asked.

"I don't know, maybe Roger looked for it somewhere else, but I'd be surprised. He's really a good, loyal man, despite the weird money issues." She paused. "But Jeanine? I can't see her doing that. She loved Roger."

Jo kept her face passive and avoided looking at Arnett. In her experience, the relationship between love and cheating was rarely straightforward. "Would she have told you if she met someone?"

"I think so. I mean, I guess I don't know. If she told anyone, it would have been me." Paola hesitated again, stroked a fringe of hair away from her eyes. "But every once in a while, just when you thought you knew everything about her, she'd come out with something that would make you look at her like *wait, who just said that*, you know what I mean?"

Jo nodded. "So, it's possible she might have been involved in something but didn't tell you?"

"I don't see how, honestly. None of her behavior changed, nothing new. Logistically, I have no idea how it could be possible." She thought for a moment. "But if you're asking me if she could keep things to herself, then I have to say yes. She could be very... *private* when she wanted to be."

Jo leaned forward, sensing an important shift. "How so?"

She ran a red nail around the lid of her cup. "Well. About a year and a half ago, maybe a little less, she had some problems with her niece, Teresa. She's Roger's niece, actually, Jeanine's by marriage. They were close, and it meant a lot to her. They never had children of their own, and although she was fine with that, I think Teresa became almost like a daughter to her. They spent a lot of time together, and even played online video games with each other when they weren't hanging out in person. She'd always looked out for Teresa because Teresa had a lot of problems adjusting, from her tween years and beyond. Always at odds with her parents, few friends, barely managed to graduate from high school, that kind of thing. Jeanine took Teresa under her wing and put up with a lot of bad behavior because she wanted Teresa to have a safe place she could come." Paola leaned forward, eyes flashing. "Then Teresa turned on her, made her into this big enemy, accused her of some really horrible things, like emotional abuse. But Jeanine didn't mention it to me or Lorraine, our mutual friend, until about six months after it happened. And I'm not sure she would have then, except her brother-in-law called while we were all on a weekend getaway to Vegas. She disappeared talking to him for over an hour, so there was no hiding something was wrong. She said she hadn't told us before because she didn't want to bias us against Teresa if the whole thing blew over."

"Did it blow over?"

"Depends on what you mean. They haven't spoken since."

"When did this happen?"

"She told us about a year ago, so several months before that."

"And nothing happened to reawaken the situation?" Arnett asked.

"Not that I'm aware of. But maybe she just didn't want to mention it again."

Jo considered. Maybe, but maybe not. Either way, Jeanine kept the situation hidden well for quite a time before it came to light. "So, if she had an affair, it's possible she didn't want to involve you in something that could compromise your relationship with her husband, since he's a part of your circle? The same way she didn't want to bias you against Teresa?"

Paola's brows knit, and she shook her head once. "Maybe. I don't know. Lorraine and I were her friends first, she knew that. But still, maybe." She held Jo's eyes. "Even so, I just don't see how she would have worked it. She never went out."

Jo moved on to her last question. "Is there anyone you knew of that wanted to hurt her? Any grudges anyone had against her from her past, anything like that?"

"Not that I can think of. It sounds horrible, but she just didn't have a very exciting life, you know? She didn't go out much, and never without Roger or us. She didn't interact with all that many people. She didn't even have a Facebook page."

Jo stood and pulled out a card. "This has been very helpful. Thank you again for your time. Will you contact us if anything else occurs to you?"

Paola took the card. "Of course. I know you're busy, but will you keep us updated?"

Jo met her eyes. "When we catch the bastard, you'll be the first to know."

A wan smile crossed Paola's lips.

Jo and Arnett stepped through the crowd toward the entrance. As Arnett held the door for a pregnant woman heading inside, Jo glanced back and caught a last glimpse of Paola, staring down at the lid of her coffee with an expression of puzzled concentration on her face.

CHAPTER FOUR

The man's real name was Martin, although Jeanine had never known that. His tension drained away when his front door clicked into place behind him. He paused to draw a deep breath of the familiar scents—fresh-linen Glade inserts and Pledge—and let his eyes slide over the dark hardwood floors and the black-and-white desert print in the hall. Reassuring markers.

He carried his bag into the master bedroom at the rear of the house. As he removed his hat and coat to hang them on their hooks, a button flew off. He retrieved the cracked halves and swore under his breath; he'd have to have it replaced. With practiced movements he unpacked the rest of his few belongings, restoring them to their proper places, careful to set aside the plastic bag containing Jeanine's ring and the tie he'd used to strangle her.

Once finished, he crossed into the living room and built a fire. He took the ring into his study while the fire caught, pulled open a small drawer in the sleek black desk, nestled the ring with four others hidden there, and locked the drawer in place. He returned to the hearth and stoked the fire, coaxing the flames to burn hotter and brighter; when he was satisfied, he lifted the tie out of the plastic bag and tossed it on the center. He watched the flames lash up around the sides, licking the edges like a child determined to make a Popsicle last. For several moments, the fire and tie stood in stalemate, until several dark spots blossomed on the golden sheen of the silk, and flames broke through from underneath. The fabric curled up at different angles and hissed, then broke apart and disappeared into ash.

Martin removed his shirt and added it, along with the plastic bag, to the flames. A good wash would likely get rid of any possible DNA transfer from the tie, but he saw no need to take the risk. He closed the glass doors against the chemical smell and waited. When it too had disappeared, he poked around to make sure no scraps remained. Tomorrow when the fire had cooled, he'd double-check the ashes and add them to the trash.

Fatigue lapped at him—there was a screaming baby on every red-eye—but before he could nap, he had to attend to the remaining details. He wouldn't sleep well until he finished, regardless. He washed his hands, then made himself a strong cup of Earl Grey and a ham sandwich. He brought them into the study and ate while his computers booted up.

First, he deleted the e-mail address he'd used with her, then created a new one to replace it. He discouraged e-mail communication, so she'd never used it, but who knew where she'd jotted it down? Next was the Skype account. There wasn't much to find there either, other than decoy information and two or three lines of text chat, but the fewer links in the chain the better. Then only one crucial step left, and he could fully relax. He logged on to his Battle.net account and clicked into his *World of Warcraft* information. He paid for a realm transfer and a name change for his main character, a level 90 rogue. If anyone thought to look into Jeanine's account, his rogue would no longer appear in her friends list, and even if she had scribbled his information down, the character would no longer exist. Since he never gave out the Real ID information that allowed players to track one another across different servers, there would be no evidence left that he had ever interacted with her there.

He shrugged off the standard warning that the transfer might take several days to go into effect. It never took more than a few hours, and any attempt by the police to access her account would take days, if they even thought to check it.

As he confirmed the final transaction, he yawned, fatigue settling over him like a leaded blanket despite the caffeine. Now he could spend the evening enjoying the kill. He stretched and let the shiver of anticipation and elusive sense of peace wash over him. For a while, he could feel normal. At least until the hunger started to demand again.

CHAPTER FIVE

"Where next?" Jo hit the button for the GPS display.

"Lorraine Barnott can only meet before her daughter's ballet class, exactly during the only time Debra Chen has free between client meetings. Both are adamant they can't reschedule anything."

"So we'll split up. That'll give us more time anyway."

"Who gets the friend and who gets the boss?" Arnett started the car.

"You talked to them, you have the lay of the land better than I do."

Arnett grimaced. "Chen gave me attitude, so maybe she'd relate better to another female higher-up trying to get through the day?"

Jo grinned. "Not sure what that'll buy me, but it's worth a shot."

Ten minutes later, Jo walked toward the three-story white building that housed Gelarking & Scribes Inc. as Arnett headed out to his interview with Lorraine. The angular lines and minimal blue accents were stuck in the strip-mall style that dominated the early 1990s, but the paint and landscaping were well maintained. The doors opened to a marble-floored lobby decorated with glass and chrome accents. She examined the guard at the desk as he called up to Debra Chen. Middle-of-the-road looks, average height, air of eager-to-please.

She made a show of glancing around. "Snappy place. Are the people as pleasant as the surroundings?"

The guard laughed. "They treat us well, we even get profit sharing. Most people are happy."

"Nice. Did you know Jeanine Hammond?"

His face clouded. "I did. Just to say hello and goodbye to, but she was always friendly."

"The people that aren't happy here, were any of them not happy with her?"

"Not that I know of. But then, I don't hear very much out here."

Jo doubted that was true, but as she opened her mouth to call him on it, Debra Chen appeared through the metered door. Her gray skirt and beige blouse were well tailored, but Jo's eyes were pulled by a faint stain just above her right breast. Splatter from brushing her teeth?

"Lieutenant Fournier?" she asked.

Jo waved her thanks to the guard and stepped over to introduce herself, impressed that Debra remembered the title—maybe Arnett was right about her attitude. "Is there a private place we can speak?"

"Right back here." She slid her badge through the reader, and a green light clicked on.

Jo followed her down a short hall that opened into a large space divided by tall cubicles. While each had the same basics—computer, phone, filing cabinet—they were differentiated by internal color and personal touches. At the far end of the space, Debra opened a door into a conference room and pointed toward the table in the center. "Please, sit anywhere you like."

Jo scanned the chairs, all covered in the same blue upholstery, and sat in the second-closest one. "Thank you for meeting with me, Ms. Chen. I appreciate you taking the time."

"Debra, please. And, of course. We're all still in shock about the news. I can't believe it's real, I just saw her a few days ago." She shook her head, face tight with emotion.

Jo waited as Debra settled in across from her. "Were the two of you close?"

"We didn't spend time together outside of work, but liked each other and got along well." She glanced down at her hands, then back up at the table.

"You just didn't click on a friendship level?"

Debra's eyes came up to hold hers. "I think it's important to keep proper boundaries in the workplace. It keeps things simpler, don't you think?"

Jo grinned and gave a quick yes-and-no wag of the head. "I can see the benefits. And she didn't mind working under those boundaries?"

"On the contrary, she insisted on keeping her personal and professional lives separate. It's one of the reasons we worked so well together, we had the same outlook on team management."

Jo kept her face friendly and adjusted her approach in light of Debra's defensiveness. "Ah, of course. My understanding is Jeanine Hammond worked directly for you?"

"Yes. I'm the head of my division, and she was one of three managers who work under me. She oversaw our sales outreach team." She looked down again, and Jo's eyes followed. Debra's hands were shaking.

"Was she good at what she did?"

"Very." Her voice caught. "She was warm and genuine. She connected easily with people, and they trusted her. Our customers say she makes them feel they're important to us. That also has a lot to do with how she managed her team. She knew that most people think once they sign on the bottom line, attention and service will wane. She saw herself as the protection against that."

"Sounds like she took her job seriously. I'm sure that must have put her in conflict with some of her employees."

Debra held eye contact. "Not really. She took the same care of her people. Made sure they were rewarded for good performance, worked with them when they needed time off. She even bought them pizza once a month as long as they met their team goals, out of her own pocket."

Jo's mind flashed to Roger Hammond—he must have loved that. "So, she never had any conflicts? How about the people she fired?"

Debra cleared her throat. "Fewer than most managers had. It's always unpleasant when you deal with those issues."

Jo scanned her face, unsure which tack to take. She was doing a dance of some sort, but why? Jo decided on sympathy, and wrinkled her brow. "Tell me about the unpleasant parts."

Debra's eyes flitted quickly to each side, then back. "There were two firings that didn't go well. One was fairly clear-cut—Jon Renke. He failed to show up at work repeatedly without calling in. The other, Ronald Craig, was more complex. He skated a lot of lines and was written up several times for different complaints. He'd straighten up for a while, then as soon as enough time had passed, start up again."

Jo's frown deepened. "What was the final straw?"

Debra shifted in her chair. "He called a co-worker a bitch. He thought they were alone in the break room, but a third person walked in and witnessed the incident. He claimed the witness was also lying, but in light of his past history and the one open letter in his file, we had to fire him. Jeanine agonized over it and brought it to me for a second approval, because she wanted to make sure there was no question of bias. But he still claimed conspiracy, and that Jeanine was a part of it."

Jo widened her eyes. "I'd say that goes beyond unpleasantness."

Debra's posture stiffened. "He never threatened her, nothing like that. And that was three years ago, and we haven't heard a thing from him since."

So much for sympathy—Debra's resistance wasn't on Jeanine's behalf. Jo leaned back and shifted her approach. "But did Jeanine hear from him?"

"Absolutely not. She would have come to me, filed a complaint."

"Or maybe she tried to handle it herself."

"She wouldn't have done that, she wasn't stupid." Debra's eye contact held firm.

Jo narrowed her eyes. "And yet, she was murdered in her hotel room."

Debra didn't respond.

So, it was going to be like pulling a hen's teeth. "I'm going to need his contact information and anything else you can tell me about him. I'm also going to need to talk to the two co-workers involved in the incident."

"Why do they need to be involved?"

The last piece clicked into place. Debra wasn't that naive; she was toeing the company line, and the company was terrified of a lawsuit. "We'll need to interview them. And what exactly happened with Jon Renke?"

"I told you, there were a number of occasions where he didn't show up for work, and Jeanine had to let him go."

"And he fought it."

"Not exactly." She shifted in her chair.

Jo held her gaze and waited.

"The thing is, she suspected he had a substance abuse problem. And she tried to, uh, advise him."

Bingo. "Advise him?"

Debra's eyes flicked to the side again. "She confronted him about it, said she thought he was addicted to his painkillers. He'd been in a car accident about a year previously and had back surgery. He'd been a very good employee, very reliable, did excellent work. Over the year, he started missing deadlines and making mistakes. He missed several appointments with clients and called in all of his sick time. Then he started missing work without calling."

"And he didn't like her suggesting there was a problem."

"No. He denied it. Strenuously. At that point she should have let it go. But she pushed the issue, urged him to get help. He bristled and demanded to talk with me. When I asked her why she hadn't let it go, she said she had a friend who recently went to rehab for alcoholism, and she couldn't bear watching Jon also throw his life away. I told her we couldn't force anything on him."

Jo calculated the liability. "So, she backed off and he left quietly?"

Debra nodded.

"You think he was worried Jeanine would tell other employees about it?"

"No. Jeanine was very discreet, and everyone knew that." Her jaw tightened and released. "If you ask me, it's more likely that Jeanine contacted him again after he left, and he didn't like it."

Jo's eyes narrowed. "You think it disturbed her enough that she'd step out of her carefully maintained propriety?" Or was Debra trying to deflect fault from the company?

"I don't know." Her eyes flicked away.

"Wouldn't Renke have contacted you if she'd done something like that, filed a complaint of some sort?"

Debra met her eyes again, her tone icy. "I have no idea how he would have handled something like that. I just know she was surprisingly intense about the issue."

Jo quickly considered whether to press and decided there was nothing to be gained. Debra's position was clear. "Did she have issues with anyone else?"

Debra relaxed. "No. She didn't have to fire many employees. But I can get you a full list of names."

"I'd appreciate that. You said she was good at her job. Would you say she was above average in that respect?"

"Certainly. She was probably the best I've worked with. She'll be missed, both personally and professionally." Her eyes glistened—she was sincere about that, at least.

"Office politics what they are, it's hard to be that good at your job without professional jealousy. Did anyone want her job, or worry she'd take theirs?"

Debra's neck flushed. "If you're asking if I was threatened by her, I wasn't. Jeanine was happy where she was. She wasn't interested in moving further up the corporate ladder. Even so, she was the type of person who would have waited for an opening, not tried to finagle someone else out. And if anyone else was jealous of her, I didn't know about it."

"Just the same, we'll need to talk with everyone on her team and everyone lateral to her, confirm they have an alibi for the time in question. And I'll need to do the same for you."

The flush reached Debra's ears. "My husband and I were out to dinner at Panache that night with friends. They can confirm, and my husband paid the check with a credit card. I'll add their information to the list."

Jo stood up. "Thank you for your assistance. I'd like to talk to the other employees and get that list from you before I go."

She nodded her assent and walked Jo out to Jeanine's section. "Everyone in these cubicles worked on Jeanine's team." She stepped into the first. "Cory, this is Lieutenant Fournier, she has some questions to ask you about Jeanine."

*

"So that was the sort of afternoon that kills your faith in mankind," Jo said as she climbed into the waiting car.

"Men strangling women in hotel rooms isn't enough for you?" Arnett asked, expression skeptical.

"Nope. That's aberrant evil. Corporations covering their ass is cold, systemic evil. What's that smell?"

"I stopped for burgers. Figured you'd be hungry, too. Not as good as a meatball sub from Sal's, but it'll do."

"You're a god."

"Tell it to my daughters."

Jo turned around and grabbed the bag. "What did you learn from Lorraine Barnott?"

"Not much. Mostly confirmed what we already got from the husband and Paola, and even that was a chore. Haven't wanted a cigarette so much in months."

"Resistant?"

"Not exactly. More hostile. Made it clear I was wasting her time since the killing was *random*. Took it as a personal insult that I was *putting Jeanine's personal life under a microscope*." He paused around the quoted words for emphasis. "Until I mentioned the fight with Teresa."

"Ahh. Do tell."

"Her entire demeanor changed. Called Teresa a *self-centered, spoiled brat* who didn't appreciate having someone in her life that cared for her and tried to help her. Called Teresa's boyfriend Philip a *cocky snot* and corrected me when I downgraded her description to *jerk*. Then it got really interesting. Said he wasn't respectful, treated the older generation like *beer buddies*. And he constantly had his hands all over Teresa, right in front of the girl's parents, like he was trying to prove something."

"So, no sense of propriety?" Jo's mother flashed through her mind. She'd have kicked any boyfriend who did that right out of the house.

Arnett wagged his head. "More than that. She said he was odd, but she couldn't put her finger on exactly how. And when I asked if she thought he might have it in him to hurt Jeanine, she said it was possible. And not just like she was happy to bash him, but like she was struck by the possibility."

"And she wasn't just taken by surprise?"

"No way. The shift was night and day. She'd been insistent before that the murder couldn't be related to anything in Jeanine's life. Adamant that there were no problems at work, with her marriage, no ugliness, period—until she considered Philip."

Jo glanced at her watch. Paola's description of the argument had bothered her, and Lorraine's reaction ratcheted the chorus of warning bells up to high. "We need to talk to the niece."

"Agreed."

Jo pulled out her phone and called Roger Hammond for Teresa's contact information, then plugged the address into the GPS unit.

"Looks like she's about fifteen minutes away, do we have time?"

Arnett considered. "It'll be close."

"I don't see that we have much choice. I have a couple of leads from her work, but the time frames are odd; both possibilities have been gone from the job for quite a while. This is the only hint of discord in her personal life, and two of the people closest to her have had strong reactions to the memory. I don't see a phone call cutting it for this one."

CHAPTER SIX

Jo checked her watch again as Arnett eased into traffic. "What I really want to do is show up unannounced, get a really candid reaction from her. But I don't think we can risk missing her at home." She entered Teresa's number into her phone, and Teresa answered on the second ring. Jo could feel her weighing her options, but after she made clear how put out she was to have to cancel a coffee date with her friend, she agreed to talk with them.

Traffic was on their side. They arrived a few minutes early and surveyed the area. The house had the neglected, worn-down look of a residence that was lived in but not loved. The landscaping was minimal, the paint and roof were pushing their expiration dates, little problems here and there needed fixing. Probably a rental Teresa shared with roommates.

A vision of a surly mouse flashed through Jo's mind when Teresa answered the door. She wore jeans and a shapeless gray sweater, her brown hair tied back into a wild, frizzy ponytail that made her look younger than her twenty-four years. Her eyes were dark and could have been striking, but their effect was ruined by features that were too small for her face; her teeth looked like they belonged in a toddler, and her nose came to a tiny point. She carried about thirty pounds too much weight, and acne scars dotted her skin. Not hard to believe she'd had a difficult time in her teen years.

She turned her back on them without a word, clomped into the living room, and threw herself onto the worn couch next to a man Jo presumed to be her boyfriend, arms yanked across her chest. The boyfriend—a misnomer, since he looked nearly a decade her senior—put an arm around her and kissed her forehead while maintaining eye contact with Jo.

Teresa cut Jo off as she started to introduce herself. "I don't understand why you need to talk to me about this. It has absolutely nothing to do with me."

Jo took a deep breath and reminded herself to stay polite. Something about this girl banished all her patience. "We appreciate you making the time. We're talking to everyone your aunt was close with."

"We weren't close." Teresa glared at her.

Jo met the boyfriend's eyes again. "I'm Lieutenant Josette Fournier, and this is Detective Arnett, Oakhurst County SPDU. Are you a friend of Teresa's?"

He lifted his chin and matched Teresa's glare. "I'm Philip, her fiancé."

"Congratulations on your upcoming marriage."

His eyes narrowed. "Can we get on with this, *darling*? Teresa and I have plans for dinner, and then I have work to finish."

Arnett froze for a brief second at the overt condescension, then pulled over a wooden chair from the corner. Jo kept her expression blank and sat on the edge of the torn La-Z-Boy next to the couch.

"Hard at it late into the night. What sort of work do you do?" Jo asked.

"I'm a freelance web designer and software engineer, and when you freelance, time is money."

"Please don't let us keep you. We only need to talk with Teresa," Jo said.

"I prefer to stay," Philip said.

Jo nodded and shifted her gaze back to Teresa. "Can you tell me about your relationship with your aunt?"

Philip answered. "There isn't much to tell. The last time they saw each other was well over a year ago."

So, it was like that. Jo looked Philip up and down. His tawny hair surrounded his blue eyes in hipster waves; he had the sort of face that you might call "chiseled" or "old Hollywood," except the proportions were off, like a caricature. He wore a wrinkled dress shirt, and corduroys half a size too tight across his thighs. *Don't suppose you own a fedora, do you kid?*

She kept her voice low. "I'd like to hear what Teresa has to say, if you don't mind."

"I do mind. This is very distressing for her. You don't seem to *get* that there's nothing she can tell you that will help, and you're harming her well-being for no reason. If I were here when you called, I'd have told her to tell you to get lost."

"Your concern for your fiancée is admirable. However, someone choked the life out of her aunt, and whether you mind or not, we have an investigation to conduct. Now. We can ask the questions here, with you holding her hand, or we can bring her into police custody and conduct the interview there, where you won't be allowed in the room. Your choice. Frankly"—her eyes flicked back and forth between them—"I'm starting to be a little concerned that the two of you are so unwilling to answer a few simple questions when a family member has been brutally murdered."

Philip's face flared red and he leaned forward. Then he seemed to think better of it and leaned back, forcing a smile on his face. He pulled Teresa slightly in front of his chest. The view of her small features under his wavy mane made Jo think of a small animal caught in the paws of a lion.

"Of course, you're right, Detective. I apologize if it seems we're being difficult. The whole situation has been such a shock. Of course we want to help you in any way we can," Philip said.

Her face professionally blank, Jo turned back to Teresa and started again. "Thank you. Now, tell me about your relationship with your aunt."

"Like he said, there isn't much to tell. I haven't seen her in over a year and a half."

"And before that?"

Her face tightened. "I used to visit her now and then, and we'd talk sometimes."

"I'm told you were very close."

"What do you mean by 'close'?"

Jo looked at her without blinking. "What I mean is this. Your aunt used to be an important part of your life and now she isn't. Why is that?"

Teresa's face tightened again and she glanced back at Philip, whose jaw was clenched.

"Because she was a controlling bitch, that's why," she finally spat out.

"How did she try to control you?"

"I'd ask for her advice on something, and she'd tell me what to do. If I didn't do it, she'd get pissed off. She didn't like Philip and was trying to break us up."

"What did she say her reason was for that?"

"Oh, she never *said* it. But she implied it. And she implied horrible things about me. And emotionally blackmailed me."

"How so?"

"Like, Philip and I were fighting. I made Philip uncomfortable. I wasn't taking responsibility for myself, and when he got frustrated and called me on it, I got angry at him. He told me to leave until I'd calmed down, so I went to my parents' house. He told me he'd call me when he was ready to talk to me. She didn't like that."

"What did she say?"

"That he could have handled it differently, that he hadn't taken my feelings into account, and that she didn't like how upset I was."

Oh, the horror. "How did she tell you to handle it?"

Teresa fidgeted in her seat and pulled her arms closer. "Don't you get it? That's not the point."

"Humor me."

"She told me to give him a few days and write out what I wanted to say to him, so I wouldn't get flustered and freak out. But that's not the point. She didn't like him and she wanted me to leave him."

"She said that?"

"She said it seemed like we handled stuff very differently, and we'd have to learn to compromise. And that if he didn't want to do that, I should think carefully about whether he was the *right person* for me." She twisted her face to mock the words.

"And you didn't like that she criticized him," Arnett said, face hard.

Teresa's eyes flashed to his. "She was totally unfair to him! She was jealous because for the first time I had someone in my life other than her who had a say."

"And so she emotionally blackmailed you? How?" Jo asked.

"Well, I got angry with her and decided not to talk to her for a few months, so she'd get the message that if she treated me that way, I wasn't going to let her into my life. Then I texted her one day about a fight Philip and I were having, and she texted back that she *didn't feel comfortable* giving me advice because of *what had happened*." She made air quotes around the phrases. "So basically, unless I do what she tells me to do, she's going to refuse to talk to me. Total bullshit. I was so upset it took Philip forever to make me feel better. We talked about it for hours, about how completely fucked up it was of her to emotionally blackmail me like that, and that I can't have that in my life."

"And that was the last time you talked to her?"

"Philip helped me write her an e-mail telling her what she was doing wasn't right, and that I wasn't going to let her get away with it. She replied saying she didn't think it was me talking, it was Philip, and she wasn't going to talk to me through him. She said to call her when I calmed down and we'd talk without Philip there. I told her to go to hell."

Teresa beamed adoration up at Philip, and he leaned down to kiss her. Pavlov's salivating dogs flashed through Jo's mind.

She cleared her throat to dislodge the vision. "I realize you hadn't seen her in a while, but back when you were in contact with her, what was her relationship with your uncle like?"

Teresa rolled her eyes. "They bickered like crazy, all the time. It drove me nuts, especially when I was younger. Now that I know the truth about her, I feel bad for him. It must have been horrible for him, married to a control freak like that."

Jo felt rather than saw Arnett shift in his seat. "So, it was an unhappy marriage?"

She started, and her eyes widened briefly. "No, I think they loved each other, just, you know, they bickered a lot. They never talked about, like, divorce or anything."

"But underneath it, you think they were unhappy?" she pushed.

"No. It was just their thing. I mean, they were affectionate and all." She shrugged. "My uncle Roger loved her."

"Do you think she loved him?"

"Sure, I guess."

Jo considered. Judgmental gossip from a disgruntled relative, or something more? She switched gears. "Do you know of anyone that might have wanted to hurt your aunt?"

Both Teresa and Philip seemed to relax. "No, not at all. But I'm not really the person to ask about anything recent."

Jo nodded and closed her notebook. "I think that's all I have for now; I'd appreciate it if you'd give me a call if anything else relevant occurs to you." She handed the girl a card as Arnett moved into the doorway.

"Thanks, *Officer*, we will," Philip said, stressing the title.

Jo suppressed a laugh. *It's "Lieutenant," you little fuck. And we both know you know it.*

They left the house in silence. When Jo circled around the car, she saw Philip watching out of the window, his expression pointedly neutral. Jo watched him stare after them as they pulled away down the street.

*

"I can still smell the bullshit from here." Arnett flicked on the radio as they pulled onto the highway.

One corner of Jo's mouth curved up as she merged into the fast lane. "Definitely a different perspective. The truth is somewhere in the middle, no doubt, but I suspect Jeanine's would have leaned heavily away from Teresa's version, and I'd like to check on that with Paola."

"I don't have her number in my phone."

"It can wait until we get to the airport. I'd like to handle it, anyway."

Once safely through airport security, Jo called Paola's cell. She picked up on the second ring.

"Hello, Lieutenant. Is something happening?"

"No, sorry to alarm you. We're heading back to Massachusetts, but I've got a couple of quick follow-up questions, if you have a moment."

"Of course." Curiosity hovered on the edge of her voice.

"You mentioned that Jeanine had fallen out with her niece. Can you tell me why?"

"From what I can remember, her boyfriend, Philip, kicked Teresa out of the house and wouldn't have contact with her in any way for a week. Teresa freaked out because she couldn't handle that he wouldn't talk to her by phone, text, anything. I remember that for sure, because it really pissed me off. That's abusive."

Jo's jaw tightened. "And Jeanine was angry, too?"

"She didn't like it, of course, but tried to give constructive advice. Jeanine told Teresa that if Philip didn't want to talk right then, she should give him that space, and write out what she wanted to say. That way she could sort out her thoughts, figure out what she really wanted to say when they did talk."

More reasonable than I would have been. Jo plugged her free ear and raised her voice against an announcement going over the PA. "Why would that upset Teresa?"

"I think the part that upset her was, Jeanine encouraged her to talk to the boyfriend about how much it hurt her to be thrown out and given the deep freeze. She stressed the importance of finding a more constructive way to communicate with Philip if she wanted the relationship to last."

Jo nodded. Also reasonable.

"Teresa said that's just who Philip was, and Jeanine said if that was the case, Teresa would need to decide if that was something she could live with in a life partner. I think that last part really freaked her out, the idea of not being with Philip, of losing him somehow."

"And Jeanine was angry when she didn't follow the advice?"

"Oh, god no. Never once did Teresa follow her advice the whole time I've known the family. She'd come to Jeanine, and if she didn't like what Jeanine had to say, she'd verbally attack her, tell her she was wrong, then ignore her."

"Attack her?"

"Oh yeah. Once, Teresa had a huge crush on this guy, right? They went out a couple of times, but he was acting weird. Couldn't schedule anything in advance. Couldn't talk when she called, either didn't answer or needed to call her back. Anybody with half a brain could see that he had a girlfriend he was hiding. When Jeanine suggested that to her, she lost it. She told Jeanine that only a cynical, bitter person would think that, and it was *vicious* to accuse *normal* people of things like that. She even said someone must have really 'fucked her up' in her past." She emphasized the words with indignation.

Another set of announcements went out over the PA. "Hang on a minute." When they ended, Jo started up again. "Sorry about that."

"No worries. No such thing as a quiet spot in the airport."

"How did Jeanine respond when Teresa said that?"

"She was so hurt by it, she cried for half an hour. But the whole time, she made excuses for Teresa. Said she didn't know any better, that she was young and girls her age are insensitive and act that way. I called bullshit. At that time, Teresa was a few months short of twenty-three, and I told her, no, thirteen-year-olds act that way, not twenty-three-year-olds. Jeanine held fast, said that because she'd been so sheltered by her parents, she was still figuring those things out." She paused and laughed. "The kicker is, of course, it turned out the guy had a fiancée the whole time. Teresa was devastated but never seemed to remember Jeanine had warned her."

"And Jeanine didn't get angry, confront Teresa for not listening to her?"

"Are you kidding me? She helped Teresa write a letter to the guy explaining her feelings so Teresa could get closure and move on. Every single time, the situation would blow up in Teresa's face. And every single time, Jeanine would be there to pick up the pieces. Held her hand through everything. Even when it was the exact opposite of what Jeanine had advised her to do."

Jo pushed and listened for a defensive edge. "And it never bothered Jeanine, even though it happened repeatedly?"

"I mean, of course she got frustrated when Teresa never seemed to learn from her mistakes. But no, she never got angry."

"So why was this last time different?"

"Mainly because Teresa turned on her so fiercely that Jeanine couldn't make excuses for it anymore. Accused her of some unacceptably nasty things, like 'emotional blackmail,' and used information she thought she knew about Jeanine to hurt her."

Jo's brows shot up. "Like what?"

"She knew that an old friend of Jeanine's, a mutual friend of ours named Marlena, had dropped out of contact with her. Teresa lashed out, said it was because Jeanine was a controlling bitch that drove people away. Completely untrue—Marlena had developed into an extreme alcoholic and went away to rehab in California. She has family there and decided to stay close to them when she got out. Jeanine hadn't told Teresa that, because it's not the sort of thing you spread around."

"No," Jo said.

"I think Jeanine finally saw that this wasn't some adolescent phase that Teresa was going through, it was just her personality. Teresa'd been so nasty and attacking that she couldn't ignore it anymore. So she didn't reach out to her after the fight."

"Was Jeanine normally the peacemaker?"

"Oh, yes. She was always the one to smooth the waters until Teresa's tantrum passed. It was like something clicked in her, I even remember the words she used. That she was just *enabling* Teresa by putting up with it, allowing her to think it was okay to treat people that way. Don't get me wrong, if Teresa had needed her for any reason, she'd have been there in a flash. But she said the relationship couldn't be one-sided anymore, that Teresa had to take responsibility for her own words and actions like any other adult. And, of course, *that* was never going to happen."

"Got it. You said that was 'mainly' why you thought it was different? Was there more?"

"Well. Okay. Jeanine was careful about how she put it, but I got the sense it had to do with Philip as well. She said something about him literally taking over the conversation. I know she wanted to talk to Teresa alone, one-on-one without Philip, but Teresa refused. I think that really worried her."

Not unassuming little Philip! "Sounds like a complicated situation. Anything else I should know about it, or her niece?"

"Not about that so much, but I will say this. I met the boyfriend a few times, and he gives me the creeps. And not just because he's so much older, although that bugged me, too. He seems nice enough at first, but then, I don't know, I got this feeling like he was marking territory. Sorry, I know that doesn't help much or even make sense."

"It helps. Thanks."

"No problem. Please call again if there's anything else I can tell you."

Jo hung up. Arnett grunted and attempted to adjust his torso into the black plastic airport chair. "This is what I hate about flying. We have to Indy 500 it to get here in time, and now we just sit because the flight's delayed." Arnett checked his watch against the posted flight information.

"No, what you hate about flying is being stuck in a confined space for hours at a time. You get all antsy and fidgety." Jo waved her hand up and down.

"Pot calling the kettle black," he said, pointing at her bouncing leg. "Never seen you do that before."

Jo halted her leg. The bouncing was a bad habit she'd broken years ago—or thought she'd broken—after her traumatic return to her hometown of New Orleans when she was sixteen. Her mother had noticed it, and several other signs of anxiety, and insisted Jo see a therapist. Only after she'd banished the bouncing had her mother let her stop the sessions. She told him as much.

He examined her face. "Sounds like stress from the new job to me. What have you been doing to relax?"

She shrugged. "I go shooting on the weekend when I can squeeze a few hours off between the job and Karl."

He paused for a moment. "You need a non-work-related hobby."

She rolled her eyes at him. "Sure. With my abundant free time, maybe I can build an ark."

"I'm serious."

She sighed. "I know you are. But I've never been a hobby type of person. I do one thing, and I do it well."

He stared at her without blinking.

"Okay, fine, I'll look into stamp collecting or something."

Arnett nodded and shifted again in his chair. "Who do they make these chairs for, anyway?"

"I think the primary design goal is to keep people from sleeping in the airport. You know, save money by spending the night between flights. Anyway." Jo gave up trying to balance her coffee on the angled armrest, set it on the floor, and pulled out her notebook. She recapped the conversation with Paola and the interview with Debra Chen for Arnett. "I made a quick attempt to contact Renke and Craig at the last known numbers Chen had, but struck out. We'll need to track them down," she finished.

"You don't sound enthusiastic."

She ran her teeth over her bottom lip. "She was trying to help Renke, too aggressively maybe, but do you kill someone for that? The other employees never found out about Jeanine's suspicions, so what harm was done? He was getting fired either way, unless Jeanine convinced the company to give him another shot if he went to rehab. And the other one, Ronald Craig, I don't see him coming back three years later to kill her. That's the kind of motive you act on when it's fresh."

He tilted his head. "I don't know. Sometimes those things build up for years, especially if they're the start of a chain of bad luck."

"But then, why do it when she's half a country away at training?"

"Maybe he happened to see her, and the old wound opened back up?" Arnett offered.

"I checked the roster, he wasn't one of the attendees. Plus, she seemed very palsy-walsy with the guy in that video. Hard to believe she'd go from I-fired-you-for-shitty-behavior to let's-do-the-horizontal-mambo over the course of a day."

"Maybe it wasn't that fast. Maybe they'd come in contact somehow, he'd reached out to her or something? Maybe he found a way to get back in her good graces. Then, he arranges to stumble into her when she's at the conference—it's a yearly one in the industry, so it's not like it would be hard for him to figure out she's there—and then a few drinks later, horizontal mambo."

Fournier considered. "Sounds more plausible when you put it that way. We'll need to check his alibi to be sure he wasn't in Oakhurst for some other reason."

He wagged his head. "Stranger things have happened. How do you feel about Chen's claim that Jeanine wasn't interested in moving up the company ladder? Directly contradicts what the husband said."

"That part doesn't surprise me. Even he made it sound like this was the first time she'd shown interest in that brand of upward mobility. I suspect it was more about being the best boss she could be, not about being the next boss up the hierarchy." Jo checked the posted flight information again and rubbed her eyes.

"Bothers me that after talking to everyone close to her, I still can't get a clear picture of who she was, on a personal level. Like she's Invisible Personality Woman. Like when you don't realize someone has left the room, and you look up and you're surprised they aren't there."

"Mrs. Cellophane," she said.

Arnett tilted his eyebrows. "Yes, exactly."

Jo smiled. Arnett's unlikely love of Broadway musicals always brought up visions for her of him dressed to the nines, dancing around a stage, completely at odds with his beer-and-football demeanor. "Anytime someone's that astoundingly nondescript, I assume they must have something to hide," she said.

"Or something buried in their past." He took a long draw from his coffee and glanced up at the computerized display at the gate. "Shit, another half-hour delay."

Jo rubbed her eyes again. "Want to run through a bullet-point recap?"

"Might as well. Marriage—typical, no red flags. Husband has strange issues with money, but his grief seemed real."

Jo nodded. "No evidence of an affair, although my mind keeps returning to that."

"Mine too. The fact that she could keep a secret like a clam near an iceberg makes me reluctant to give up that angle."

"So, we'll dig hard into her phone and computer records for anything strange there. Same with the credit cards. And we'll see if we can find any connection with Renke or Craig." Jo shifted to avoid a nearby speaker spewing static-filled boarding announcements. "And no recent promotion or ambitious behavior to cause jealousy if we believe Chen, and I'm inclined to. We still have a few previous employees to talk to, maybe someone not still with the company will have something else to say."

Arnett nodded. "And I really don't like the situation with the niece-in-law. They were so close, hard to believe that would just end without rancor. Especially after meeting the girl and the fiancé. How do you feel about his role in the fight?"

"I think he's responsible. Jeanine gave advice Teresa didn't like all the time, so what changed this time? Don't get me wrong, I think the girl's a self-centered brat with severe angst and personality issues." She punctuated by jabbing the air with her coffee. "I don't think he caused the fight exactly, I just think he took the opportunity to twist the knife. My bet is he saw someone with influence over Teresa, a threat to his control over her, and took the opportunity to put a stop to that."

Arnett nodded. "He's definitely controlling and I don't see manipulative very far behind. The only question is what lengths he'd go to."

"Exactly. And there's evidence Jeanine came to that conclusion herself—Paola said Jeanine told Teresa she'd only talk to her one-on-one, not through Philip, or with Philip there."

"I just don't see any reason for him to kill her. I damn sure don't like the kid, and if he were dating my daughter, I'd get her as far away from him as possible. But he already had Teresa exactly where he wanted her, adoring and supplicant. I don't see any reason to go further, especially a year and a half after the falling out."

Jo rubbed her palm across her eyes again. "Maybe Jeanine had reached out to Teresa, tried to get her to stop seeing him? Maybe the engagement spurred her concern?"

"I'll check phone and e-mail records for any contact." He jotted down the note. "You think he feels good for it?"

She shook her head. "No, I agree with you, it doesn't feel right. And the tape just doesn't play out. I don't see her being as cozy with Philip as she was on the security footage, no matter how drunk she was. I can't find a scenario that gets me there."

The static-overlaid voice announced the mechanical issue on their flight had been rectified and asked them to make their way to the gate.

Jo slapped her boarding pass against her leg. "Still, we should do some digging on him. We also need to check out the baggage and the alibis for everyone at the retreat; it's possible something will turn up there."

CHAPTER SEVEN

By the time Jo turned off the highway into Oakhurst city limits, it was well past midnight. Still, she slowed to a few miles under the speed limit to enjoy the streets gliding past her. Both because she was in no hurry to face Karl, and because she'd been energized by her day back in the trenches even more than she'd expected to be. She'd lived in Western Mass most of her life, and there was a quiet peace to it that always soothed her, especially this time of year. Something about the way the houses nestled into the trees and bushes, and how the foliage slowly caught fire as autumn progressed, until every street and hillside shone like burnished metal. Two weeks ago, Karl'd gotten fed up with the burgeoning drifts of leaves in the yard and had blown them into a bonfire. When she noticed the unblemished expanse the next morning, a strange sadness had settled over her.

She shook the memory away, replacing it with a smile for Hill of Beans, her favorite coffee shop, half wishing it were open despite the hour. She loved sitting inside, sipping a mocha and listening to *musique acadienne* or zydeco through her headphones, watching downtown go about its business. The area, filled with small, independent shops, could have been lifted from a 1960s musical, and it was an anodyne for her soul. Despite knowing too well the ugliness that pervaded the world, she could lull herself for a time into pretending life was as idyllic as it appeared there.

Ten minutes later, she trudged across her porch. She knew something was wrong as soon as she stepped through her front door. No warm glow of lights greeted her, no residual citrus from Karl's cologne in the entryway.

She paused, closed her eyes, and tried for a brief moment to convince herself he'd just gone out for a beer with friends. But she didn't have to weigh the silence to know it marked a different sort of empty home—the sinking resignation in her stomach told her. She knew people too well and was too proficient at reading the smallest of signs to steep in that denial.

Not that there was any overt visual sign in front of her. For whatever reason, very few of Karl's personal belongings had found their way anywhere other than the master bedroom suite. Maybe he'd dropped hints she hadn't picked up on, or maybe they'd both sensed all along there was no point. A memory tugged at her mind and she glanced over to the rolltop writing desk in the corner, where a framed snapshot of his deceased sister normally stood.

Gone.

She looked away. No warning text, no e-mail. At best there'd be a note somewhere. Most likely not.

Her throat tightened and she shut her eyes, tried to keep the constriction from spreading. She knew he was pissed about the missed dinner, and she'd known he wouldn't be pleased by her sudden day trip, but really? Wasn't this a bit dramatic? She'd learned from her previous mistake and sent him an e-mail explaining why she was going and that she'd be back the following day. What should she have done? Woken him up when he had to work the next day, disturb his sleep and piss him off more than he already was? He'd have been just as pissed off about that.

That's bullshit and you know it.

The e-mail had been easier, plain and simple. So she didn't have to deal with the anger and waste time on a fight. So she could sleep well herself and escape for a day in the vain hope he'd be over it when she got back. Denial, procrastination, cowardice.

She'd known damned well there'd be consequences and she'd done what was easiest for her, regardless.

Or maybe you just didn't care.

She threw her keys down. She was upset, yes, but something was off about what she was feeling. She cared about him, not all-consuming love to be sure, but headed in the right direction. He was intelligent, he was kind, he was funny. He was sexy. So why let this happen? He could've been the one, and she'd fucked it up. Again.

She was angry at herself, yes, but it wasn't the right kind of anger. She was angry about failing again, not about losing him. She hadn't been upset about losing any of them, not since Jack.

She closed her eyes against the rush of Jack's memory. One of only two loves of her life, the only love of her adult life, and she'd never been engaged again since. Not even close. Her therapist would have quite the field day with that.

She opened her eyes, glanced toward the master bedroom, then made an abrupt turn toward her study. The bed could stay cold a while longer.

CHAPTER EIGHT

Martin placed a high level of importance on self-awareness, believed it was vital to be fully conscious of one's strengths and weaknesses. And without a doubt, the greatest of his few weaknesses was the hunger, the never-ending need to kill. He could slake it, but could never satisfy it completely.

For a short time after a kill, it would recede almost entirely. With the details still fresh in his memory, he could put himself back into the moment, savor the sights and smells and tactile sensations as if they were still happening, linger over his body's response. But all too soon, he acclimated to the details, the way your nose becomes blind to the smell of dinner cooking, and the hunger would creep back. First, as an annoying hum hovering around the edges of his consciousness, then as tentacles reaching and intertwining through his core. Ignoring it was pointless. He'd feel light-headed and weak, get hot flashes and migraines so bad he'd pass out. He'd become increasingly anxious, more on edge, have sudden bursts of anger. Sometimes even violence. If he didn't feed it, it slowly drove him insane.

But he had two tricks to delay it.

The rings helped as long as he didn't use them often. He'd hold them, slip them on his finger, bask in the feel of something so central to his victims now belonging to him, penetrated by him. The thrill of power came rushing back, the dominance of ownership, and the rush took the edge off. A quick fix, calamine lotion for a mosquito bite that was momentarily unbearable, but effective when needed. The other—the only way to truly contain the hunger for any length of time—was the hunt. Drawing a prospect into his web, shaping her into what he needed her to be, plotting and planning, every word chosen with deliberate precision—all of that ebbed the hunger. Not completely—it was always there, pulsing in the background—but the chase was an appetizer that kept it at bay while he prepared the full meal. Every conversation fed it. Every trust he gained was an amuse-bouche to be savored.

So, he lingered over the chase, squeezed every drop out that he could. It was his moral responsibility to kill as few as possible, and to take as much as he could from each. Like the Native American philosophies about hunting bison or elk. You paid proper respect to the kill by using every part of the life you'd taken. Even if he deliberately chose women who deserved to die, it was only right that he make the most of them when quelling his need.

After all, he wasn't a barbarian.

PART II

Emily Carson

November 2012–April 2013

CHAPTER NINE

Martin stretched and felt a vertebra in his neck crack. He looked at the time on his screen: 6:00 p.m. No wonder he needed to move.

Had he eaten lunch? He couldn't remember. He saved the code he was working on, ran through a series of several more stretches, then headed into the kitchen to find something for dinner. He opened the refrigerator and considered. He was in the mood for something hot but not in the mood to cook. Frozen pizza would be perfect. He pulled one out and flipped the dial on the oven, then went back to the study and brought up *World of Warcraft* on his desktop while he waited for it to preheat. He turned Daft Punk up on his laptop.

Jeanine's ring wasn't working anymore. He needed to start the next hunt.

The beauty of freelance software engineering was the flexibility. As long as he maintained standards and kept deadlines, he could work when and how he wanted. Perfect for his needs and his binge-working tendencies; besides, whatever project he had in front of him swarmed his mind until he finished regardless. Hence his reputation for producing high-quality work with unusual efficiency and speed, one that guaranteed his services were in demand and enabled him to set his terms. One large ongoing project with a company in the Netherlands ensured a regular income, and he added smaller projects when so inclined, to keep things fresh and interesting. And scheduled it all so he had as many free days or weeks off as needed.

The log-in finished. He'd left his main character—an undead rogue now named Porrthos—on the thatched roof of the large hut that functioned as the main bank in Orgrimmar, the orc city. Porrthos popped into view, ready to do business in the trade chat channel, surrounded by the omnipresent crowd of orcs, trolls, tauren, and other races bouncing periodically as their players conducted invisible business. He chose a rogue for his main because they could pick locks; there was a constant stream of players with goods they needed opened. Good for earning gold, but mostly an excellent excuse to sit back and talk to people, to attract the lonely women he was looking for. Because they couldn't all be like Jeanine—she'd been a delicious exception to his standard methodology—usually he had to search for them. Methodically. Patiently.

He hit the macro to send out his standard bark:

[Porrthos]: Chastity belt getting you down? I have an app for that. Porrthos' Lockpicking: making love possible since the days of vanilla. Tips happily accepted.

Within seconds, he had several responses.

[Bubblee] whispers: haha, that's funny
[Pendor] whispers: ROFL
[Grathra] whispers: where r u

Sorting through the responses was almost automatic now, with the help of a quick character check. You never knew for sure if someone was male or female from the gender of the character they played, but it was a reliable indicator. Women were more likely to play female than male characters, so unless he got a response that was particularly compelling from a male character, he'd give them polite treatment and nothing more. Names could clue you in on a lot, too. Some people took the role-playing aspect of *WoW* seriously, threw themselves so far into their character that they'd only speak as their avatar in-game. But mostly, the character names people chose simply revealed something about themselves and why they played the game. Names that played with silly humor were most often younger people, and names that played with scatological humor most often young men, so he never bothered with those. Anything from *Twilight* or *The Hunger Games* was instantly out. He wanted someone with a few more years on the planet than that.

"Bubblee" sounded like a girl, although probably not the kind he was looking for—it hinted at someone younger and a bit flighty. Probably a bimbo. Still, it was worth checking out.

To [Bubblee]: lol, thank you. :)

Pendor was a male character, and the response he'd sent was pretty typical. To make certain, he'd send a reply that implied Pendor was male—if the player wasn't, they'd typically object to that.

To [Pendor]: Thanks, bro.

Grathra was also a male character, and seemed to just want him to pick locks. He threw up a group invite and a response:

To [Grathra]: Bank roof.

He was right about both Pendor (who didn't whisper again) and Grathra (who turned out to be a bad tipper). He focused his energy on Bubblee.

[Bubblee] whispers: Ooo, you're a rogue! Is that fun to play?

To [Bubblee]: I like it. Lots of fun moves. How do you like wizard?

[Bubblee] whispers: So fun! But I wanna pick pockets, haha

To [Bubblee]: Why don't you roll yourself a rogue and see how you like it?

[Bubblee] whispers: Yeah, maybe. I dunno.

He could practically hear her gum smacking. *Still, give her a chance.* Not like anyone else was biting, anyway.

To [Bubblee]: So, what are you up to?

[Bubblee] whispers: Just hanging out, thinking about heading over to the tavern in Silvermoon City ;-)

Nope, that settled it. Players in the Horde, the faction orcs sided with, went there for erotic role-play. He couldn't stomach that, couldn't understand the appeal of pretending to engage in sexual acts with strangers in a video game. He wasn't even sure how that worked, logistically speaking—how did you even type and manage anything else with your hands at the same time? Regardless, she wouldn't do for his purposes.

To [Bubblee]: Well, have fun. :)

[Bubblee] whispers: Awww, you don't want to come?

To [Bubblee]: I'll pass. Night.

[Bubblee] whispers: Jerk

Ah, yes, with an insult like that, she was either chronologically or mentally fourteen. Decision confirmed.

He kept on for an hour and a half, working his way through his pizza and barking at regular intervals and passing time in trade channel. Trolling trade was like cherry-bombing fish in a barrel, always so easy to get pedestrian people worked up into some frenzy or other, just mention the president and then sit back and watch the drama unfold. When he tired of that, he ran a few daily quests, then decided to turn in.

No luck tonight.

*

Unhappily married women, that's what Martin was searching for. For two simple reasons.

The first logistical—they didn't want to be caught any more than he did.

Single women couldn't wait to tell the world about the new man they'd met. Pronouncements and relationship-status changes on social media. Hours spent analyzing their exciting find over coffee with friends, every potentially deadly detail about him passed on to anyone who would listen. And when the time came to meet, more intense consultations to choose outfits for the trip, based on all the information about where they were going and all the romantic activities they hoped would be included. Hell, they might even want their friends to meet him, want to show him off. He couldn't risk a surprise traveling companion.

But married women were blessedly reticent. They didn't *want* texts or calls from strange numbers on their phones. Didn't *want* to friend him on Facebook. No e-mails for a nosy spouse with a keylogger to hack into. He didn't have to convince them to avoid those things—he just sat back and let them wrangle those details, even let them feel guilty about treating *him* that way. They weren't going to press him for information and behaviors they couldn't engage in themselves.

Skype made it all possible, paved the golden brick road for them to skip down. Voice chat, webcam, as easy as the phone, but with nothing traceable. No call logs or identifying numbers on phone bills. Even if a nosy husband hacked in, his "name" in their contacts was easy to explain—so many people used Skype to run dungeons and raids in-game.

Best of all, they needed a cover story for an out-of-town trip just as badly as he did. Their own motivation for creating a convincing reason to go away for a few days without their husbands. They'd put the plan together themselves, with subtle suggestions from him. Real work events were the best cover: business trips, corporate meetings, conferences. A married woman wouldn't want his name on the hotel room or any other records; far too risky for her, which was perfect for him. And the final touch, the coup de grace: a quick call to her husband during their dinner out, and a request to talk to the children (if she had any). Once that call was placed, he could rest assured there was zero chance an angry husband would be waiting for them back at the hotel.

And married women were so desperate to please. The affair was a delicious secret they'd been given, a bright star on the horizon of their desperation. Their grand romance, something to help them face a life that hadn't gone the way they'd hoped. They wanted it to be more, needed it to turn into something, and didn't want to risk losing it. So, they did the things he asked, didn't ask the inconvenient questions, and didn't think too much about any of it, because they were afraid it would all fall apart. And they missed the warning signs that would have made other women turn tail and run.

The second reason was moral. Women who cheated on their husbands and risked destroying their families, risked depriving their children of stable homes and fathers and normal lives, needed to die.

Simple.

CHAPTER TEN

"I want you to change the F on my son's paper."

The muscles in Emily Carson's neck tightened and her pale blue eyes narrowed. *Not again with this.*

"I'm sorry, Mrs. Morgen. The assignment was to write a three-page paper about how Tennessee became a state. You can see that the paper is under two pages long, and it's not on topic. Eric wrote about his favorite vacation."

"His favorite vacation *in Tennessee.*"

Emily did a mental facepalm. *Really?* "That wasn't the assignment. The students are required to write on the assigned topic."

"But he wrote about Tennessee. He turned something in. That should count for something, he shouldn't get an F. He should at least get a C."

Emily looked at the ferret-faced woman sitting across from her wearing the same vacant expression the ferret-faced son wore daily. What was wrong with these parents? They should want their child to learn something, to get the skills for future success. Instead, they fought her on everything. They didn't want their children to have to do homework, write reports, or have assigned readings outside the classroom. They certainly didn't want to lift a finger to *help* with those things. And if their children got low grades, it couldn't possibly signal that they needed to work harder! No, it meant she was a bad teacher. No wonder so many educators simply gave up and passed children regardless of performance.

She pushed her thin brown hair behind her ear and took a deep breath. What she wanted to say was, *Try that in the real world, lady. When your boss asks you to write a report on your department's profit for the fiscal quarter, write him a story about how fun your company retreat was. See if you have a job the next day.* Instead, she explained again, while keeping her speech measured and enunciating carefully. "Your son's paper didn't address the assignment. Papers get an F if they don't meet the minimum length, or if they aren't on topic. Those are the class rules. We feel that by fifth grade, children should understand the importance of following the requirements of an assignment." She pushed the paper back toward the woman.

Mrs. Morgen leaned away from the paper as though it were a venomous snake, and her dull expression turned to stone. "He turned something in. He deserves some credit."

Emily glanced at her watch. The woman wasn't listening, and Emily didn't have time to repeat herself ad nauseam. "I'm sorry. Changing his grade wouldn't teach him anything or be fair to the students who did their assignment correctly."

Mrs. Nancy Morgen leaned toward Emily again, now inches from her face. "Listen to me, you fucking bitch. My son turned in his assignment. He deserves some credit for that and you're going to give it to him. If you don't, I'll make sure you're very, very sorry. I know where you live, Mrs. Carson."

Emily's hair fell from behind her ear as she stood up and crossed to the phone on the wall. "I think it's best we discuss this matter, and your threat, with the principal."

Mrs. Morgen stood up as well. "You're half right. If you don't change that grade, I'm sure I can come up with a story about how you verbally abused my son that she'll be interested to hear. How about if I tell her you yelled at him, called him a 'retarded dumbass who'll never amount to anything,' and tack on that he's been depressed ever since? Oh, I know, how about, when he tries to do his homework now, he throws up and cries?"

The blood drained from Emily's face. She thought she'd seen everything, but this was new.

Stay steady now. Don't let her see she's getting to you.

She opened the door and motioned toward it. "After you."

*

Mrs. Morgen transformed into a soggy morass of crocodile tears the moment the principal's office came into sight. Emily belatedly realized her mistake. She should have left the woman waiting in her classroom, come to report the threat alone, and sent Joyce back to deal with the viper.

Mrs. Morgen's lies were obvious, and she contradicted herself as her story built. But it was good enough, as she'd known it would be. Joyce waited until she'd talked herself out, then confirmed she wanted to file a formal complaint. Joyce assured Mrs. Morgen that her son would be transferred to another classroom the following day, and took her to the assistant principal to officially record the details.

When she returned, Joyce's face bore an impassive mask. "Let's hear your side of it."

She couldn't possibly believe that crazy story? Emily explained why Mrs. Morgen had come to see her. "This is the fourth time she's come to me this year about a grade change, and we're barely into December. She's also sent me nasty notes claiming the homework assignments are too much, and I'm pushing my job off onto the parents." She handed Joyce the paper. "When I explained to her why I couldn't change the grade, she threatened me. Told me she'd make up a verbal abuse claim and said she knows where I live."

"So, you're saying she made up this complaint against you because you wouldn't change Eric's grade?"

Emily blinked. This was insane. "That's exactly what I'm saying."

Joyce's face remained blank. "You know we have to take any such allegation very seriously."

Emily felt a flush wash over her face. "Oh, come on, Joyce. You can't be serious. You know me better than that."

"I'm not sure I do. Sometimes you can be impetuous, and you don't always think things through before you speak."

Emily stared as the implication of the words sank in. She was an idiot—she should have known this was coming in some form. Mrs. Morgen had just given Joyce an opportunity for payback on a silver platter.

Emily was a talented teacher. She'd been a rising star, hired on approval before she'd finished the last of her certification program. She had a way of making her content fun and easy to understand, and a gift for adapting her approach as needed when children were struggling. But, she had no skill for politics or diplomacy, and she'd put more than a few noses out of joint. Including Joyce's.

She'd come into teaching with the naive view that other teachers and administrators would make students their first priority. Those illusions were blasted during her first faculty meeting, when she'd watched two fellow teachers nearly come to blows over a potential new hire. Everyone had their own agenda and students were often an afterthought. Education seemed to be the lowest priority on every funding totem pole, and there was never enough of anything. Which meant there were constant battles over allocation of resources to one department over another, who should be hired and when, who should get access to space and equipment. Alliances were formed to put people into administrative positions over others vastly more qualified, because of promises to allocate resources to those who had supported them. Few cared where the actual need was, and those who did were the ones left on the sidelines alone and without support. They were punished for "making things difficult" and were passed over when it came time for any merit-based rewards—despite having the highest success rates in the classroom. Her graduate school mentor's advice had been to keep her head down and focus on her teaching, but even that was perceived as taking sides. When she tried it, her department chair became angry with her for not actively campaigning for department resources.

Everything had reached an apex when, six months ago, an external auditing team came in from the district to do a routine investigation. When asked about the vague allocation of several controversial "pots of money," instead of feigning ignorance, she and two other teachers had been honest about how the funds were used. The principal and the department chairs hit the roof, and the three of them became pariahs. Still, until today, she'd clung to the hope that even if they didn't respect her moral choice, certainly her skilled teaching and dedication to students would maintain a baseline of respect and support from her superiors.

But maybe she was being paranoid, maybe Joyce hadn't meant it that way. She took a last hopeful stab, her words small and tinny over the pounding of her heart. "No, wait just a minute. That woman threatened to make up a report and come to my house. I'm the victim here."

"We'll get your union rep in tomorrow and you can file a complaint against her. But as far as I can tell, it's your word against hers. And our ultimate responsibility—a value I know you share—is to always protect the children first." Joyce stood.

Message received. Naive she might be, but she could read the writing on the wall when it was written in blood.

CHAPTER ELEVEN

Emily banged through the door an hour later than usual. Nobody bothered to look up. She set down her briefcase along with the stack of books in her arms and peered into the living room. Her husband, Eddie, was mesmerized on the couch by some hockey game, as usual. Susannah, her oldest child, was splayed across the love seat, texting. Her son, Wade, was nowhere to be found, probably out with his friends.

"Hello?" Emily said, not sure who she was asking.

"Hey." Eddie's gaze didn't waver from the screen. Susannah was silent.

Emily walked into the kitchen to help with whatever they'd started for dinner. No pots or pans on the stove, nothing in the oven, only the breakfast dishes still in the sink marred any surface. She turned on her heel and marched back to the living room.

"Eddie, didn't you get my message?"

"Huh?" Eyes superglued to the game.

"I said, didn't you get my message?"

No response.

Emily positioned herself between him and the screen. He tilted to the left and she stepped with him. He tilted to the right and again she followed. *What is this, some comedy routine?*

"What message?"

"The one saying I was going to be late and that you should start dinner."

Finally, he looked directly at her and his scrunched face cleared. "Oh, yeah, I got it. I forgot." He looked over at the clock. "How is it seven already? I guess we can just have spaghetti or something." He leaned back to the left to see the screen.

Translation: I can make spaghetti or something, while he sits on his ass.

"Are you going to ask why I was late?"

His face tightened. "Honey, can it wait? This is an important game."

Right. They were *all* important games.

She returned to the kitchen and put a pot of water on the stove. She added salt, then grabbed a box of spaghetti and a bottle of sauce from the pantry. She fumed while she waited, her thoughts laced with resentment and profanity. When the water boiled, she dumped in the pasta, set the annoying oven timer for eight minutes, and locked herself in her den.

When the timer went off, they could check on it or not. *I don't give a damn anymore.*

*

Emily stared up at the crowded bookshelves that lined the small room without seeing them as her computer booted up. How did she turn into one of those women, the ones whose lives were space ages away from where they thought they would be?

Nothing had gone wrong, that was the confusing part. She'd done everything she was supposed to do to get the life she wanted, worked damned hard, in fact. Got good grades through college and graduate school, got her certification. Got her dream job and busted her ass for her students. She'd dreamed of falling in love, of having a partner to face life with, to ride out the daily ups and downs. To gently share each day with a meal, a glass of wine, and cuddles on the couch. She'd been smart about her choice, found a good soul who had mostly the same outlook on life. She'd been a beautiful bride in a beautiful dress, with a beautiful cake in a beautifully decorated reception hall. They chose not to honeymoon so that they could put the money toward a down payment on a house. And she'd dreamed of children. Ideally a boy and a girl, and that's just what she got.

Nothing had gone wrong.

But nothing had gone right, either.

Teaching turned out to be about politics rather than education, and now she faced attacks by angry parents and losing her job. The fixer-upper that was supposed to become their dream home, à la the Old Granville House in *It's a Wonderful Life*, languished largely untouched. She did what she could herself, but anything that required more than common sense was beyond her, and they didn't make enough for her to hire contractors. Every year the house came closer and closer to becoming a crumbling museum piece, stuck in a prewar time warp.

Her marriage wasn't a partnership, it was a joke. When they were dating, Eddie took her to restaurants, to the beach, to plays, all sorts of places. Now she couldn't pry him away from the TV, not even for sex. She was lucky if it happened twice a year, and when it did, she swore he was racing the commercials. She tried telling him she needed more from him, physically and emotionally. Calmly, at first. Then by yelling and screaming. She tried ignoring him. Tried marriage counseling. Now, she'd just given up. What was the point?

In light of it all, she might have made her children the center of her life. But Susannah had been difficult and unhappy from the moment she was born, colicky and prone to illness; the mother-daughter bond Emily dreamed of was preempted by a pattern of mutual discomfort engraved into their relationship. Wade had been better but was a solitary child, even as a baby. He'd lie awake in his crib and play with his mobile, never crying for anyone to come in unless he was hungry. When he got older, he favored his father, and she supposed that was natural for a boy. But the upshot was she felt like an outsider in her own life.

The password screen lit up her monitor and pulled her out of her thoughts. She logged on, then clicked the *World of Warcraft* icon. She dug out her authenticator while the game started up.

She'd contemplated divorce, had even made an appointment with a divorce lawyer. But with the custody issues and the cost of running two households, she couldn't see how it would improve anything—she'd be a single mother shepherding even surlier children from her tiny apartment to her ex-husband's, struggling to make ends meet. How would that be better than what she had now?

So, it was what it was. Her life was set, and for all intents and purposes, it was over. She was thirty-six and looked every bit the aging mom, with a little too much extra weight for her frame, thanks to the glasses of wine that replaced her husband. The wrinkles were spreading their webs over her face, and gray strands were starting to weave through her hair. There would be no great romance for her, no fulfilling career, no loving children, and no beautiful house.

But when she played *World of Warcraft*, she could be whoever she wanted to be. She was beautiful and powerful, traveled through the magical world of Azeroth fighting horrible monsters and completing important quests. She favored magical classes like druids and paladins, who were forces for good and whose lore included learning. She could immerse herself in a world where good could win over evil, goals were simple, and people fought for high ideals and a better world. She could play out an exciting life filled with passion and adventure. It wasn't real, but it was something.

She entered her information and waited for the welcome screen.

CHAPTER TWELVE

Three weeks without even the hint of a prospective kill.

Martin felt continually restless, like he'd had too much caffeine. He'd caught several inane errors in his code earlier in the day, and now he'd botched an entire section. Completely unacceptable.

He pushed back his chair and paced the room. *I need to flush my system.*

He glanced out the window into the darkness. No rain, he could go for a run.

He pulled on a tracksuit and strode out the door, letting it slam behind him. The brisk air jolted his nerves and broke his thoughts out of their spiral. He cut across his yard toward the high school track down the road and was far around the next corner before he realized he'd forgotten his iPod. He swore under his breath and considered going back for it. No, it was just as well. He needed to think things through anyway.

He'd never gone this long without at least one possibility on the line—if his greatest weakness was his need to kill, his charm was his greatest strength, and it had never failed him. Women were drawn to him, even over the computer when they'd never laid eyes on him or even heard his voice. He'd augmented his natural gift through a meticulous study of seduction. He read books, watched countless seasons of *The Bachelor* and similar drivel, studied couples in cafés and restaurants, listened to women's conversations about men. Whenever he heard a man complain that women were impossible to understand, he scoffed. It wasn't even *hard*, let alone impossible. You just had to pay attention.

He became a master of vulnerability and of holding back just enough at the right time. He sniffed out what they needed to feel special, seen, appreciated. He became whatever they wanted him to be, and then molded them into what he wanted *them* to be.

He did have limits, however; he could only keep it all up for a few months. Any longer and the lies became hard to track, especially if he was working on more than one woman. Worse was the insipid nonsense he had to endure, the stupid jokes he had to laugh at, the pretense of sympathy over insignificant problems. Half the time he wanted to tell them to shut the hell up, and he could maintain the meticulous facade for only so long before the mask disintegrated. Skype helped with this in the short term; he could go off-screen for a moment and release the emotions when he'd had too much. He couldn't conceive of how anyone managed courtship face-to-face.

Was he losing his touch? He considered the possibility while pulling his muscles through a series of warm-up stretches. No, that wasn't the problem. He wasn't *losing* prospects after meeting them; he just hadn't met anyone in the first place.

During his second lap, he hit his stride. As his body's rhythm turned automatic, his mind cleared, and he analyzed his options. It was the holidays, after all—lots of people spending more time traveling and with their families, not as much time for gaming. Perhaps the answer was simply to cast a wider net. He'd been playing Thursday through Sunday, in the late evenings. He was far enough ahead on his work, he could play every night and start up a bit earlier. Maybe spend more time chatting in the trade channel rather than relying on his lockpicking bark? And if push came to shove, if he didn't have at least one prospect in the next week, he could try a different server.

He had a plan, then. That eased his mind, and the tension dissolved out of his muscles. There was no reason to panic. Everything would come together.

And yet, a warning of dissent tugged at the back of his consciousness. The hunger didn't care about the plan, it only cared about the kill. It would wait for now, but only for so long. No amount of running could distance him from that.

*

Martin knew he wasn't a psychopath. He'd done his research, so much so that he probably knew more about serial killers than most profilers did.

In many ways, he did fit the standard picture of a serial killer. Yes, he lived alone, and no, he didn't have many friends. He kept to himself, avoided drawing attention to himself—no flashy car, no bright clothes. But that was one of the benefits of being a "computer geek." People expected you to be a bit reclusive, a bit strange. If anything, he was far more normal than most of the other coders he knew.

Severe abuse as a child? Check. Yes, he'd been a nonentity to his mother, a non-being who existed only as her ego permitted it, to do whatever pleased her when it pleased her, blah blah blah. So what? There was no point dwelling on it. He won in the end.

And, as with many serial killers, he was physically average. He looked older than his thirty-two years and was routinely taken for between thirty-five and forty. Not young and not old. He wasn't handsome, but he wasn't ugly either; he had unremarkable brown hair, average blue eyes, and was only slightly taller than average at six feet. Nothing about him stood out. No distinguishing marks, no scars, no tattoos. You could have an entire conversation with him in line at the grocery store and not recognize him five minutes later. That was the blessing of his face.

But some important hallmarks of psychopathy were missing. He had never tortured or killed animals; even thinking about that made him nauseous. He had no desire to dismember his victims, to torture them, or to have any form of sex with them. Sex with other people disgusted him, men or women, alive or dead. He could barely read about other serials having sex with their victims or ejaculating on them. Foul, base, inferior actions for foul, base, inferior minds.

Possibly more telling was the issue of conscience. That was a big one for psychopaths, who had no conscience, no empathy or remorse. That most certainly was not him. True, he felt zero remorse for the women he killed, but that was because their lives deserved to be taken. They were destructive, disloyal, evil women. *They* were the ones with no conscience about cheating on their husbands, no thought for the families they were willing to destroy. Nobody made them do that; they made their own choices. He was simply the vessel that carried their consequences.

The husbands and families? He felt joy for them. He was doing them a favor, because they were better off without the succubus who would betray them—it was only a matter of time. He was helping them, liberating them, allowing them to move on with their lives more quickly.

In fact, wasn't that the very hallmark of conscience, knowing that what those women were doing was wrong, and helping the world by getting rid of them? That was morality. A code of ethics.

No, not a psychopath—more like an alcoholic, or an addictive gambler, just with a compulsion to kill. Like them, he knew what he was doing put him at risk, in his case, at risk of being locked away or put to death, but also like them, the risk would never stop him. He was compelled to look into their compliant faces, see them twisted to his whims, see them move as he told them to move, eat what he told them to eat, burn with their sick, carnal desire. And when he brought them to that apex, fully revealed them for what they truly were, he needed to feel the life leak out of them, drop by drop, needed their vital energy to recharge his. But there was no twelve-step program for his compulsion, no therapist that could help him even if he were interested in changing.

Not that it mattered. His superior intelligence gave him an advantage, an edge over other killers and a leg up on the ordinary-minded detectives who'd probably never come looking for him anyway. So far, nobody had even figured out he existed. His crimes were random, independent, impossible to link. His outstanding brain had seen to that, and would continue to keep him safe while he used the next cheating whore to keep the hunger at bay.

CHAPTER THIRTEEN

Emily's level 90 Blood Elf Paladin, "Vyxxyne," was everything she wanted to be: a fiery, long-tressed redhead with a perfect body and a seductive, glamorous face. After playing Vyxxyne for a few months, Emily told her stylist she wanted to grow her hair out a few inches, then color it auburn. Moran, her stylist, had explained to her why the look wouldn't work with her skin tone and eye color, but she'd stuck to her guns about it. Moran had been right. The auburn washed out her eyes and gave her skin a permanently nauseous look, while the longer length called attention to how limp and thin her hair was. She had it redone two weeks later.

Vyxxyne appeared inside a cave in Un'Goro Crater, one of her favorite zones in the game, surrounded by neon-colored crystal rock formations. Her guild held a rave the night before to celebrate several guildie birthdays, since the neon rocks and twisted passageways had the perfect atmosphere for it, and they'd passed a fun evening playing with fireworks and trick potions of all sorts. She smiled at the memory of several orcs trying to perfectly time their projectile vomiting potions, to disgusting and hilarious effect.

What did she want to do tonight? She didn't feel much like running dungeons, and the guild wasn't raiding. Un'Goro was an excellent place to farm ore for her blacksmithing, and she could use the materials. She filled up the bag space she had left, then used her hearthstone to return to Dalaran, the easiest major city to raise her skill level.

She went into her bank to swap the nonessential contents of her bag for more ore she'd stashed away the previous week, then headed over to the city's smithing center. As Vyxxyne automatically smelted bar after bar, Emily watched the conversations rolling through the chat channels. There was always some craziness going on; the trade channel was most often populated by hormone cases who made her students look mature, but some days it was downright entertaining. She came in on the end of a Chuck Norris joke binge and was smiling at one of the contributions (Chuck Norris has already been to Mars, that's why it has no signs of life) when a lockpicking ad caught her attention:

[2. Trade][Porrthos]: Chastity belt getting you down? I have an app for that. Porrthos' Lockpicking: making love possible since the days of vanilla. Tips happily accepted.

She laughed out loud and typed in a response.
Finally, something positive in this vast wasteland of a day.

CHAPTER FOURTEEN

Martin logged on Porrthos while saying a silent prayer to a god he didn't believe in that luck would be with him today.

He'd logged off in the Orgrimmar bank. He sorted the items from his bag into storage, then hurried up to the rooftop to throw out his bark. The typical responses came and he dealt with them in the typical ways. For an hour he accumulated tip money he didn't need and watched Chuck Norris jokes roll by in the corner of his screen. Then he got a response that interested him.

> [Vyxxyne] whispers: Lol, funny. Thanks for that, I needed a good laugh today.

Okay, this had potential. Vulnerable. Definitely looking to connect with someone.

> To [Vyxxyne]: I'm glad it made you laugh. Sounds like you're not having the best day. I can relate.

There was a careful line to walk when it came to sympathy. Nobody wanted to be pitied, but they wanted to talk to someone who understood. And it was always best to let them initiate, instead of looking too eager to pry.

> [Vyxxyne] whispers: I'm sorry to hear that. What's wrong?

To [Vyxxyne]: Some problems with work. I freelance, and the contract I'm working on looks like it might not get renewed. You?
[Vyxxyne] whispers: Oh, nothing important. Also some problems with work, and my husband's being a jerk. I should be used to both by now.

Bingo. She didn't just want to reach out, she wanted something she wasn't getting from her husband. She might not even realize it, and certainly couldn't let it go far, at least for today. For now, it'd just be a comforting, sympathetic chat with someone she could connect with. But it would open a channel for future communication.

To [Vyxxyne]: I'm sure he loves you, but men can be insensitive asses. At least, that's what my ex-girlfriends tell me.
[Vyxxyne] whispers: ROFL. Sounds like they know what they're talking about. >.<
To [Vyxxyne]: I have my moments, 'tis true. But I'll say this—if it's because you told him something important during a football game, I may just have to take his side.
[Vyxxyne] whispers: Ha! You're all alike! >:O
To [Vyxxyne]: LOL

Okay, this part was crucial—he had to get her to take the lead here. She seemed reasonably smart, so she knew there were creepers here, and he couldn't risk seeming like one of them. He had responded. If she wanted to talk further, she'd follow it up.

Two minutes ticked by. Then the message came.

[Vyxxyne] whispers: Seriously, though, I wish it were that simple. But you've got your own problems—any idea when you'll know about your work contract?

Winner, winner, chicken dinner. She wanted to keep talking, and he could be less circumspect now.

> To [Vyxxyne]: Not for a few weeks yet. I was hoping to get some sort of word about the next phase of the project, if they want to keep me on, but they've been agonizingly silent on the subject.
>
> [Vyxxyne] whispers: Argh. :(
>
> To [Vyxxyne]: Ah, such is the life of a freelancer.
>
> To [Vyxxyne]: And it's kind of you to ask, but if you need someone to talk to, don't worry about boring me. I've been told I'm a good listener…
>
> [Vyxxyne] whispers: By those same girlfriends? :P
>
> To [Vyxxyne]: I refuse to answer that on the grounds that it might embarrass me, lol.
>
> [Vyxxyne] whispers: ROFL.
>
> [Vyxxyne] whispers: Well, thank you, I appreciate it. I guess it wouldn't hurt to unload on a stranger who can't hold it against me later, lol.
>
> To [Vyxxyne]: Happy to help! Hold on a sec, have to open a couple of boxes.

He didn't have to, but also didn't want to seem too eager. He'd wait a minute or two, and then find an excuse to wait a little longer. Let her sit with the possibility, and then come back to it.

> To [Vyxxyne]: Dammit, a friend of mine needs some quick help. Will you be on for a few minutes?
>
> [Vyxxyne] whispers: Sure, take your time. I'm just working on some blacksmithing, and then I might grind some more ore. I was thinking about queuing for some instances, but I'm not really in the mood for pickup groups right now.

To [Vyxxyne]: Know what you mean, PUGs can be a nightmare. BRB.

He added her to his friends list and then flew Porrthos on his mount up to the zeppelin platform and waited for one to Undercity. He exited the city and flew around Tirisfal. The zone had a semi-Halloween feel he found appealing, with its population of skeletons, zombies, wolves, and bats wandering its fields and hills. And, this way, his location would match his story if she checked. He took his time, enjoying the scenery.

After about ten minutes, he used his hearthstone to transport back to Orgrimmar and threw out another bark.

To [Vyxxyne]: All done. How's your smithing going?
[Vyxxyne] whispers: Ugh, boring. I'm at that point where it's endless smelting and trying to make whatever I can potentially sell that will skill me up.
To [Vyxxyne]: Ah, yes. When I first started playing I changed professions about 4 times, and had to go through the skill-up anew. Not my idea of a good time.
[Vyxxyne] whispers: So true, lol.

Time to get back to the matter at hand. *Said the spider to the fly, tell me all about the problems with your sad life and your mean husband.*

To [Vyxxyne]: So tell me, what happened at work that made your day so bad?
[Vyxxyne] whispers: Well, I'm a teacher, and I had an unpleasant conference with a parent that ended in threats.

Cue sympathy and concern.

To [Vyxxyne]: WTF? Did you talk to the police?

[Vyxxyne] whispers: Oh, the police won't do anything about it unless they can verify the threat. I let the principal know, though, and won't meet with the mother alone again.

To [Vyxxyne]: Hell no. Can you get the student out of your classroom?

[Vyxxyne] whispers: Already done, because the mother claims I was abusive to him. But they aren't taking her threats on me seriously.

To [Vyxxyne]: That's ridiculous! Don't they care about your welfare?

[Vyxxyne] whispers: It's complicated. The principal has a grudge against me, and she made it clear where she stands. It's political. My school is really screwed up.

To [Vyxxyne]: Sure sounds like it. That's completely unacceptable.

[Vyxxyne] whispers: See, your reaction makes me feel a bit more sane, though.

To [Vyxxyne]: What do you mean?

[Vyxxyne] whispers: Well, I was upset about it all, and then the principal just played it down, you know? And then my husband didn't even care enough to ask about how my day went.

Martin leaned forward in his chair as a rush of warmth spread through him. *Ah, here we go. Your husband didn't give you the attention you wanted.*

To [Vyxxyne]: Wait, your *husband* doesn't know you've been threatened?

[Vyxxyne] whispers: No, he's watching some game or something, doesn't want to be disturbed. But something similar happened about a year ago and he told me I was overreacting, that parents just have to blow off steam.

He sipped his tea, enjoyed selecting each word, flirting with the line. Time to ease in, give a polite disclaimer, then start to pry open those cracks.

To [Vyxxyne]: Look, I don't want to speak out of turn.
[Vyxxyne] whispers: No, it's okay, go ahead.
To [Vyxxyne]: Okay, then. I'm sure your husband is a wonderful man. But, I'm sorry, that's just bullshit. Please excuse my language.
[Vyxxyne] whispers: Oh, stop it, I hear worse things from my fifth graders every day, believe me, lol.
To [Vyxxyne]: I'm serious. I don't understand that reaction, I just don't.
[Vyxxyne] whispers: I don't either. I don't know, I guess he just doesn't want me to overreact.
To [Vyxxyne]: Overreact? Someone threatened his wife, and he didn't care? No, I'm sorry, that's bullshit. If someone threatened my wife, there would be hell to pay.
[Vyxxyne] whispers: To be fair, that threat was a much more vague one.
To [Vyxxyne]: I don't care. I'd be down at that school dealing with that problem as we speak.
[Vyxxyne] whispers: Not every man feels that way, I guess. Your wife is a very lucky lady. I hope she knows it. :)

This part was almost too easy. He'd figured out long ago that the best way to disarm even the slightest suspicion was to tell women he was a widower. A thirty-two-year-old single man, and especially a divorced man, was on the prowl and probably flawed; either nobody wanted to catch you in the first place, or you'd been soundly thrown back. But if you were a widower, someone had wanted you, and you'd still be in a blissfully happy committed relationship if fate hadn't intervened and tossed you onto the jagged shore of life. With no work at all, the word "widower" pulled down a woman's defenses and replaced them with sympathy and a desire to heal.

To [Vyxxyne]: Unfortunately, I don't have a wife anymore. I'm a widower. Her name was Julia.
[Vyxxyne] whispers: Oh no, I'm so sorry.
To [Vyxxyne]: Thanks. It's been three years now, and I'm finally starting to get some peace again.
[Vyxxyne] whispers: If you don't mind my asking, what happened?
To [Vyxxyne]: I don't mind. It's not raw like it used to be. She had cancer.
[Vyxxyne] whispers: Oh, no... That must have been horrible.
To [Vyxxyne]: It's not something I recommend, no.

He eased into his story, well rehearsed and deployed so often he almost felt he'd really lived it.

To [Vyxxyne]: By the time they caught it, it was too late.
[Vyxxyne] whispers: Didn't she have any symptoms?
To [Vyxxyne]: She did, but she was the type of person who wouldn't go to the doctor right away. She used to say that the doctor would just tell you to come back in a few weeks if you still had the same symptoms, so you might as well wait a few weeks before going. She had some pain in her abdomen, but she waited to see if it would go away, about a month before going to have it checked out.
[Vyxxyne] whispers: And it was already too late that fast? That's so scary.

To [Vyxxyne]: Maybe it was too late already, I can't say for certain. The doctor didn't test for it at first, because she was on the young side for it, she was only 30. He tried a few other things first, and by the time he ruled them out, it had metastasized.

[Vyxxyne] whispers: Shit, that's really horrible. I'm so, so sorry. You must miss her terribly.

To [Vyxxyne]: I do. And I feel a bit like I was cheated; we were only married a year when she was diagnosed. She's been gone longer now than I knew her. I know she would want me to move on, but it's been harder than I ever imagined to do that.

[Vyxxyne] whispers: No, that can't be easy. :(

To [Vyxxyne]: Still, life goes on, right? Bad things happen every day, and I just tell myself that there must be some reason to it, even if I don't see it. Hopefully I'll see her someday again, and in the meantime, I know she'd kick my butt if I kept wallowing in it.

[Vyxxyne] whispers: Wow, that's a really great way to look at it. I hope you find someone you can love again someday.

To [Vyxxyne]: I hope so, too. :)

[Vyxxyne] whispers: Did you two have children?

To [Vyxxyne]: No. We didn't have time. But I'm glad we didn't. I wouldn't have wanted them to go their whole lives without their mother.

[Vyxxyne] whispers: That makes sense, I guess.

Time to change the subject back to her.

To [Vyxxyne]: Do you have any children?

[Vyxxyne] whispers: Yes, two.

To [Vyxxyne]: D'awww…that's nice. :) Boys? Girls?

[Vyxxyne] whispers: One of each. My girl is 12, my boy is 10.
To [Vyxxyne]: Those are nice ages. Right before all the drama starts, lol.
[Vyxxyne] whispers: You'd think so, wouldn't you, but Susannah came into the world with a chip on her shoulder. More like a boulder. I'm afraid of what she's going to be like once the hormones hit, lol!
To [Vyxxyne]: LMAO!
[Vyxxyne] whispers: Anyway, I hate to do this because I'm enjoying talking to you so much, but it's getting late. I have to log.
To [Vyxxyne]: Noooooo!!
[Vyxxyne] whispers: ROFL! Yesssssss!!
To [Vyxxyne]: *sigh* It was nice chatting with you. It's not every day you meet someone worth talking to in this game. Add me to your friends list, maybe we can quest or queue up together sometime.
[Vyxxyne] whispers: Isn't that the truth! Okay, I will. I should be on tomorrow, maybe I'll see you then. :)
To [Vyxxyne]: I should be on tomorrow. That would be fun.
[Vyxxyne] whispers: Ttyl! :)
To [Vyxxyne]: Bye for now. *waves*
Vyxxyne has gone offline.

Martin scrolled up and studied the conversation with Vyxxyne. He nodded to himself; it had played out well. He'd been sympathetic in the right places, had divulged enough about "himself" to make her feel safe. And placed a few seeds that would take root quickly in the soil of her discontented life.

*

Emily smiled as she logged out. Porrthos was right, it wasn't every day you met someone in-game that you could have a real conversation with. Lots of teens and twenty-somethings she didn't have much in common with, and of the rest, lots of people who were very intense about the game and didn't want to chitchat much. And something about the anonymity of it made some people unimaginably nasty—but that was anywhere on the internet, really. Porrthos, though. He was nice, kind even, and intelligent to boot. That didn't come along often.

She pulled out her lesson-plan materials and clicked open a file on her computer. Her eyes flicked down to the clock, and she sighed. Already 11:00 p.m. Too much time on WoW, first to avoid thinking about work, and then because she was enjoying the time with Porrthos. And now she only had a half hour to pull things together for tomorrow. She needed to get to it.

But the smile stayed perched on her face, and her mind kept returning to Porrthos.

CHAPTER FIFTEEN

"Lab results for the Hammond case are in. You said you wanted to join us with Marzillo?" Arnett said.

Jo closed her eyes against the piles of folders and papers on her desk, which had multiplied like virulent amoebae onto the bookshelves and cabinets that lined her cramped office. She was lieutenant now, yes, but space was at a premium, and her status was marked by the very fact that she had her own office, unlike the detectives who shared an open-space floor plan cordoned by semi-strategic portable partitions. She even had a window, albeit one that looked out over an ancient cracked-cement courtyard. She sighed. She really did need to bring in something to hang on the walls, to brighten it up a little.

"On my way." She dug out her notes and wove through the corridors to Janet Marzillo's lab. Arnett and Lopez were already waiting, both studying folders, Lopez's legs pulled up in lotus position on her chair. She dropped them back to the floor as Jo entered.

"Chris, how's your mother doing?" Jo grabbed an empty chair by a bank of computer monitors.

Lopez's welcoming smile disappeared, replaced by a cautiously blank face. "They moved her to a rehabilitation center to recover from her hip surgery, but her memory still isn't right."

"I didn't realize she had a memory issue," Jo said.

Lopez shot a look at Arnett.

"Trust me. Tell her." He gave a sharp nod.

Lopez hesitated, then took a deep breath and answered. "She was disoriented when I found her, didn't know where she was, what year it is, nothing. Apparently, she was drunk when she fell and laid there for nearly a day before I found her." She glanced down as she revealed the information, then met Jo's eyes directly. "I found a stash of gin bottles in the kitchen, several empty."

Jo winced—drinkers were devious about hiding their habit when they wanted to be, and it sounded like Lopez had been caught unaware. Jo reached out to put her hand on Lopez's shoulder, but stopped. She didn't know Lopez well enough to judge how she'd respond, and as her supervisor, she didn't want to step over any boundaries. "I'm so sorry. What's the prognosis?"

"She may never get back to normal, they aren't sure. At least for now she can't get at any alcohol."

"Let me know if you need any time off—"

Janet swept in carrying a stack of folders, her black curls skewered into a bun with a pen. She nodded to everyone. "Jo, Bob, Chris—oh my god, you're not on your phone. What, no new levels in *Candy Crush*?"

Lopez's vulnerability slammed shut, and she made a show of rolling her eyes. "Please. Like I'd waste my time on *Candy Crush*. And soon enough everything in these files will be digitized, and I'll never have to be off my phone."

Arnett pointed to Janet's three-inch cork platform heels with a grin. "Big accusations from someone wearing shoes like that. What happens if you get called out to process a scene?"

Janet winked at him. "I keep Nikes in my locker and the trunk of my car, Sherlock."

Arnett laughed and made a dismissive gesture. "Then why not just wear them?"

Janet exaggerated a headshake and a sigh. "Newsflash—male-dominated fields can be dismissive of professional women. Even more so when you're five-five. These bring me up to average height for a woman, and they're more comfortable than they look. So, now that you've had your fashion lesson for the day, shall I get started?"

Jo tried, and failed, to keep the smile off her face. "Please."

"First, the swabs from under her nails found no foreign DNA. But that doesn't surprise me—based on the bruises on her arms and side, she was restrained and couldn't reach anything. We also swabbed the neck, just in case, but didn't get any DNA other than hers. Also not surprising, since that would require transfer from the ligature that in turn had transfer from the perpetrator. Not impossible, but many shades of unlikely." She paused and checked everyone's faces.

"With you," Jo said.

"Given the aforementioned bruise placement, we looked for contact DNA on her dress in the areas he would have had to touch. Let me be clear, this was a long shot. Luminol didn't reveal any bodily fluids, no sub-visual drops of blood from a small cut that opened, nothing like that. So it's very good news that we did manage to isolate a profile that wasn't hers. But"—she raised the palm of her hand to short-circuit the signs of excitement—"it's not at all complete. Certainly not enough to run through CODIS."

"So we can't use it anyway." Lopez's eyes narrowed.

"Not yet," Jo said.

Janet pointed at Jo. "Exactly, don't give up all hope yet. If you give the lab a sample of a suspect's DNA, they may be able to do a comparison. But there are two important caveats about that. One, since the profile is incomplete, the best they'll be able to do is say there is a *possibility* your suspect matches it. They'll either be able to exclude your suspect as a match, or be unable to exclude them, and that's a big difference from a match." She paused again to check their comprehension.

"And the second caveat?" Jo asked.

"Even if your suspect is excluded, it doesn't mean he's not your murderer."

"You lost me," Arnett said, rubbing his chin, a gesture he'd taken up since he'd quit smoking.

"If the sample comes from something like blood or semen, we can be fairly certain of how it got there. But with this sort of transfer DNA, what you're looking at is skin cells. And say she was at a bar right before she returned home. Maybe someone bumped into her, knocked her over, and they grabbed her to help her back up. They could leave skin cells behind, especially if they were sweating."

"So, it could have come from pretty much anybody?" Arnett asked.

Janet's voice sped up as she threw herself into the topic. "That's the problem with touch DNA; since it's so easy to transfer skin cells, it's very difficult to know how your sample got there. You've heard of the Katie Ann Marchant case, right? Little girl kidnapped and murdered? After fifteen-odd years, they reopened the case and tested for touch DNA on the underwear. Since it didn't match anyone in the family, they said they could exonerate the family members, and it splashed all over the press. Only problem is, you can't exonerate on that basis, because that DNA could have been from another type of contact altogether, something not at all relevant to the murder."

"Like what?" Arnett's voice rose an octave.

Janet shrugged. "I just read a paper on this, where the lab tested several objects to see how easy it was to contaminate contact DNA. One tested panties straight out of the package. They found two profiles that didn't belong to anyone in the lab, one from a sub-visual blood smear, most likely from factory workers or inspectors. Now imagine those panties were on your vic and you made the mistake of thinking that DNA came from your perpetrator."

"You'd mistakenly exonerate the real killer when the DNA didn't match," Lopez interjected.

Arnett sank back into his chair. "So why bother testing it?"

Janet nodded. "Frustrating, I know. Most likely the profile we got came from your killer, given the bruising patterns—that gives us reason to believe epithelial cells found in that area would be related. But you need to be aware that even with a match, this evidence won't be enough. A defense attorney will rip it apart."

"So, it can point us in the right direction, it just won't convict." Jo tapped her pen on her knee.

"Correct."

"So, we get what DNA samples we can, and see if we find someone that's compatible with this profile. If not, that doesn't tell us much, but if so, we go after them like the furies of hell."

"Correct." Janet grinned.

"On it." Lopez made a note, the gleam fully back in her eye.

Jo smiled at the sight. "Anything else?"

Janet shuffled through her notes. "We found a few small fibers on her neck most likely from the ligature. They're yellow, some sort of polyester. Not any sort of rope I've ever seen, probably some sort of fabric. But more than that I can't tell you unless I have something to match them against. That's it."

Jo's phone vibrated. She glanced at the ID and let it go to voicemail.

"They don't match fibers from anything in the room?" Lopez asked.

"No. We tested the drape pulls, the towels, everything."

"Well, at least we know to be on the lookout for anything yellow that can be used to strangle someone. It's something." Jo turned to Lopez. "Any leads from the computers and phones to show us where to look?"

Lopez sat a little taller. "We're still recovering deleted e-mails and such, but so far nothing even remotely suspicious."

Jo stood up, and the others followed suit. "Keep me updated. Anything else before I go return a call?"

They all shook their heads. Jo headed back to her office and locked the door behind her, then pulled out her phone and returned the missed call.

"Josie. Thanks for finally calling me back." Eva Richard had been Jo's closest friend since she moved to Oakhurst from New Orleans at age thirteen. There was a joking-but-not-joking edge to her voice.

"Always so dramatic, it's only been a day since you called." Jo laughed and dropped into her chair.

"My guess is you know why I'm calling, since you're dodging me."

"I don't want to go on any of my mother's blind dates right now, Eva. I can't help it if she won't take no for an answer."

"She's freaked out, Josie."

"She freaks out every time one of my relationships end."

"This is different. You didn't tell anybody after it happened, and now you won't even humor her with the blind dates. She actually told me I should mention artificial insemination to you."

Jo choked on the coffee she'd just sipped and narrowly avoided a spill down her chest. "You really have to warn me if you're going to put my mother and *artificial insemination* in the same sentence."

"Then you can imagine how I felt."

"Yeah, I can see how that might not have been a comfortable conversation," she conceded. "I'll call her and talk her down."

"Talk me down, too."

"Come on, I told you what happened. Why is this so different from the hundreds of failures that came before?"

"That right there, that's why it's different. It's like you've given up. You didn't even call him after he left to find out what was happening, and you didn't tell anybody about it until you absolutely had to. Something's going on with you and I've given you enough space to process it on your own. Maybe too much. So out with it."

Jo fingered the edge of Jeanine's case file and sighed. "It didn't feel important enough to get everyone worked up over, I guess."

"Not important because you figured he'd come back, or not important because you didn't want to deal with the fallout?"

"I don't think I ever expected him to come back. And I miss him, but not enough. And no, I didn't want to have to explain it because as horrible as it sounds, I just don't think I care enough. I know my mother won't get it, and I'm not sure you'll even get it. But by thirty-seven, if I haven't made it a priority, there's a reason. I don't want kids, but I'm also not sure I want a relationship. Not if it interferes with other parts of my life, and it always does."

Eva paused for a long moment. "Okay, what can I do to help? Tell your mother to back off? Take you to some male stripper deal and get you drunk? Girls' spa weekend?"

Jo smiled. "I'll talk to my mom, but I'm sure I'll end up going on one of her dates to keep her from sacrificing live chickens in the name of grandchildren. You can keep the strippers, but some friend time would be good. Maybe a hike this weekend?"

"Um, I'm pretty sure we've got snow coming this weekend, and even if we don't, I'll pass on the forty-degree frozen death march. How about some boring old coffee? I'll talk to Tony about watching the kids and get back to you with a time."

"Sounds like a plan." Jo disconnected and pulled open Jeanine's file to update her notes.

CHAPTER SIXTEEN

Having a secret made it all so much easier to bear.

"I'm sorry, Mom, but your lasagna is just not good." From the look on Susannah's face, you would have thought there was flattened possum roadkill on her plate, complete with open sores oozing green pus.

"That's probably true." Emily smiled, picked up her and Eddie's empty plates, and headed for the dishwasher as Eddie beelined for the living room and turned on the TV.

"Maybe you should do something about that." Her sarcasm was viscous.

"Hmm. Since you hate my recipe so much, go online and find one you like. You'll make it for us Saturday night."

"No way!"

"Yes way. I'm sure you'll do a great job, and I'll pick up some tips."

"Not gonna happen."

"If you want your allowance this month, it will."

Susannah threw her fork down and stormed out of the room. Emily listened to her footsteps fade, punctuated by a door slam.

She shook her head, a smile touching the corners of her mouth. "Wade, when you're done, remind your sister it's her turn to do the dishes."

She crossed into her den, powered up her computer. The complaining, the attitudes, the absent husband—none of it rankled the way it had before she began spending time in-game with Porrthos (real name Peter, she'd learned). Simply knowing she'd be talking to him soon formed a force field around her that deflected the negative crap that would normally gnaw to her core.

She'd been playing with him every night for nearly three weeks and couldn't remember the last time she'd had so much fun, in-game or out. He was smart, he made her laugh, he cared about what she had to say. Her company wasn't an imposition, she didn't have to fend off annoyed sighs and loud silences. He *wanted* to talk to her, *wanted* to know her opinions, had endless questions he asked her. He made her feel good about herself. They quested and ran instances, but mostly it was about the chatting. Two lonely people who found comfort in each other.

She'd been wondering more and more what he looked like. Not that it mattered. She'd never see him, and they were just friends. But still. A girl could fantasize, right? No harm in that.

She had no reason to expect he was attractive, but she let herself pretend he was. Not jaw-droppingly handsome, that would be taking it too far. But good-looking in an average sort of way. Maybe even in a slightly geeky way, like extremely nearsighted or with ugly button-up shirts closed to the top button. The kind of man that other women would overlook, but when he took off his glasses and unbuttoned that shirt, your heart would race out of your chest.

She caught herself and shook her head to clear it. Ah well, what did it matter? Every woman fantasized about someone, didn't they? It was harmless, and it made her happy. She deserved a little happy for a change.

CHAPTER SEVENTEEN

Abuse comes in many forms.

Martin's father left when he was eight years old. He'd never been around much anyway, always off traveling for some sales trip or other; he never really understood what his father did. But he did understand that when his father was gone, his mother would go out in the evenings. She left Martin home alone and returned each night with some sleazeball, both usually high out of their gourds.

The end came when his father arrived home early and found her in bed with one of them. Martin woke that night to the sound of his father throwing the bedroom TV through the wall.

He'd bolted from his bed, and stopped short in the hallway when he heard his mother's voice.

"Dammit, Johnny, you didn't have to do that—there's plenty of room in here for three."

His father stormed out of the house with his still-packed suitcase, without even a look back at Martin.

After that, Martin and his mother were alone. He was his mother's "little man" from that day until she died when he was seventeen. She picked out every outfit he ever put on, chose his hairstyle, and kept him always at her side, except when she went out searching for a "date." When she was happy, she'd put on music and make him dance with her until she dropped onto the couch out of breath, insist he continue on by himself to entertain her. If she had a long dry spell with no "dates," she'd even give him his baths and feed him by hand.

If he went along with it, did what he was told, he was her beloved pet. She lavished him with praise and gifts, made the dinners he loved, let him watch his favorite shows.

But if he objected to anything, she beat him until he was a broken bundle of pain. She locked him in closets. She forced him to go without sleep. On rare occasions when she deemed his behavior spectacularly bad, she'd force him to eat or drink concoctions that made him violently sick, often for days. More than once he needed medical treatment. Sometimes she even took him to get it.

And no matter what, she fondled him.

There was never a time when she hadn't done it, and he never questioned it when he was young. She'd do it as he fell asleep at night, or when they were curled up on the couch watching TV, her hand slipped into his pajamas. To him, her hand fondling him was no different than if she'd been stroking his back or his forehead.

But then his body changed. One night while watching *The Cosby Show*, the sensations were different, better than they were before, in a new way. He felt a tension build up in waves, then burst out of him. He looked down to see his mother's hand jerk out of his pants, quickly wiping itself on her skirt. She shrieked like she'd been burned with acid, and held it out and away like her flesh was being eaten off. With her other hand she picked up the remote and beat him with it while she screamed at him.

"You perverted little fuck! How dare you! I'm your mother! You're just as fucked in the head as your father!"

She kept on for several minutes, beating him until the remote fell into pieces. Then she fled to the bathroom, leaving him stunned, covered with contusions and blood running down his face while she continued to weave her tapestry of profanity.

While she scrubbed her hands, he escaped into his room and curled into a protective fetal position on his bed. Shame burned through him as he tried to make sense of what had happened. He hadn't meant to do it! Why had his body reacted that way?

Whatever it was, it wasn't normal. It was wrong and dirty, and he was a foul, disgusting boy.

She threw open the door of his room. In an icy voice, she commanded him to sit up and look at her.

"If you ever do that again, I'll beat you within an inch of your life, so hard you'll wish you were dead. Only a sick, demented person does that because of his mother, only an evil, twisted freak. Do you understand me?"

He nodded.

He lay in bed crying that night. How could he prevent it if he didn't know why it happened? He didn't know the answer, only knew that he was defective and must never, ever let it show again.

*

Martin decided it was time to take the next step.

He'd been flirting with Emily for about three weeks. They spent time together every night, chatting and playing the game while he built up the cache he needed to turn himself into everything her husband wasn't.

He quoted poetry to her, talked about books with her, even suggested they read the same book so they could discuss it. If only men realized how many women they could bed if they'd pick up a book once in a while.

She mentioned in one conversation that her husband never gave her gifts, so he waxed on about how many men squander their opportunities, and how he'd give anything to see the look of joy on Julia's face again when he gave her a bracelet or a CD. The next day he made sure there was a present waiting for her in her in-game mail when she logged on, a rose wrapped up with a bow.

In another conversation, she complained that she'd kill for a day off of cooking once in a while, so he told her he loved to cook, and some of his favorite memories were cooking for Julia. Based on her gushing response, she nearly swooned into the computer over that one. Hadn't Julia been just the luckiest woman in the world?

He'd been lacing their conversation with hints about his developing feelings for her—an inappropriate pet name here, a hastily unfinished sentence there. In each case she responded perfectly, didn't shut down or push him away, been pleased and gently encouraging. She was ready.

Martin logged in and puttered around with his fishing dailies so that he could monitor exactly when she logged on. Mere seconds later, the game announced her arrival:

Vyxxyne has come online.

Martin smirked. She logged on earlier and earlier these days and stayed on later than she should. He had no idea how she was keeping up with her work, and he didn't care. Although, of course, he made every show of concern.

To [Vyxxyne]: Hello my dear. :)
[Vyxxyne] whispers: Hello! How are you?
To [Vyxxyne]: I'm good. :) What about you? Did you have a good day today?
[Vyxxyne] whispers: Ugh, not great. I'm glad it's over. I've been looking forward to getting some questing done with you tonight. :) How was yours?
To [Vyxxyne]: Good. Average I guess… I've been nervous about something all day, though.
[Vyxxyne] whispers: Oh no! What's that?
To [Vyxxyne]: I have something I need to talk to you about, but I'm extremely afraid to do it.
[Vyxxyne] whispers: What do you mean?
To [Vyxxyne]: The thing is, it's really not…appropriate, and I know that.

[Vyxxyne] whispers: You can tell me anything.

To [Vyxxyne]: It's just I've enjoyed getting to know you more than I expected, and I don't want to jeopardize that friendship. But I think I have to be honest with you.

[Vyxxyne] whispers: Okay, now you're worrying me. Out with it! :P

To [Vyxxyne]: Promise me you won't get mad.

[Vyxxyne] whispers: I promise.

To [Vyxxyne]: I really enjoy the times we spend together, we have a lot of fun. I haven't laughed so much in such a long time.

[Vyxxyne] whispers: I feel the same way.

To [Vyxxyne]: And when we're not playing, I find myself really looking forward to seeing you in the evenings.

[Vyxxyne] whispers: I know what you mean… I've been missing you, too. When the day gets bad, I just think about logging on and hanging out with you. :)

To [Vyxxyne]: The thing is…I'm starting to feel more than just friendship, but I know that's wrong because you're married.

[Vyxxyne] whispers: Oh, Peter, I'm so glad you said it first, I don't think I could have. I've been feeling the same way, but I've been trying to ignore it!

To [Vyxxyne]: I can't tell you how nice that is to hear… but I'm not sure how to deal with it.

[Vyxxyne] whispers: I know what you mean.

To [Vyxxyne]: I don't want to stop spending time with you, but I know if I keep it up, I'm probably going to fall for you. I'm on that path already.

[Vyxxyne] whispers: I don't want to stop spending time with you, either.

To [Vyxxyne]: So what do we do?

[Vyxxyne] whispers: Well, I mean, when I think about it, it's not like we're doing anything wrong.

Excellent. Let the self-justification begin.

To [Vyxxyne]: No, that's true. We're just talking.
[Vyxxyne] whispers: It's not really like cheating, is it? It's just being with someone that makes you feel good about yourself.
To [Vyxxyne]: True. It's not like we can even hold hands. At least not our real hands, lol.
[Vyxxyne] whispers: And, you always hear that it's not right to expect your spouse to fulfill all of your needs, right?
To [Vyxxyne]: That's what the experts say. I don't know, but it's hard for one person to be everything, I think.
[Vyxxyne] whispers: So I can't see how it would be wrong to just keep hanging out and enjoying each other's company, when nothing can ever come of it anyway?
To [Vyxxyne]: I guess that's true. And who knows, we'll probably get bored with each other in another day or two anyway. ;-)
[Vyxxyne] whispers: LOL! I could never get bored with you. :)
To [Vyxxyne]: Okay, then, if we're going to keep enjoying each other's company, I have a suggestion... feel free to cruelly reject it.
[Vyxxyne] whispers: Okay... *is curious*
To [Vyxxyne]: It would be so much easier if we talked over Skype so we didn't have to type. I've been meaning to suggest it anyway since we're going to start doing heroic instances together, it would be far easier to voice while we're doing that, so we can concentrate.

[Vyxxyne] whispers: Ack! I look like hell right now. Might not be the best idea.

To [Vyxxyne]: I don't believe that for a second. I just meant voice chat, anyway. But I have my picture up on my profile, so you can see what I look like there if you want to. And if you happen to have one of yourself on yours, I wouldn't complain *nudge, nudge*

[Vyxxyne] whispers: ROFL!! Okay, that sounds like a plan. Let me open it up.

He laughed. *Hook, line, and sinker.*

Once he got them onto Skype, video chat was easy—by that point, their curiosity to see what he looked like was eating at their imaginations. And he didn't disappoint, even if he didn't bowl them over. He was six foot, his dark hair had a tendency to be unruly if he let it grow a fraction too long, and his pale blue eyes were set above a nose too broad for his face. He worked out to keep his upper body and core strong, but in his long-sleeved button-downs, the muscles read as a few extra pounds. Not ugly, but nothing to catch the eye, either. But by then, they didn't care. They were just happy he looked the way he'd described himself, rather than the worst-case scenarios they feared.

While he waited for her to tinker with the settings for her headset, he looked at her profile picture. She had a pleasant enough face—not ugly, but nothing that would get her noticed. Her flat brown hair came just below her chin and curled in toward her face. She had unexceptional blue eyes you'd call "washed-out" rather than "cornflower," and her nose was just a touch too wide and gave her a mannish look. Her best feature was her dimpled smile, warm and welcoming. He couldn't see much of her body, but from what he could, she hadn't lied to him; there was enough cleavage to support her claim of a C-cup, and while she was plump, she wasn't obese. No matter, but still, he had a role to play, and it was easier if he could at least bear to look at her.

He relaxed back into his chair and basked in the warmth of his success. The biggest hurdle was making it acceptable for them to admit they wanted something beyond friendship; he'd never lost one after they'd done that. Emily had taken the first step down a path of self-justification that would snowball quickly, and now it was only a matter of time. Voice chat would help speed it; women found his deep voice sexy—it would feed her fantasies. Before long she'd want to see him, and they'd be on video together, looking into each other's eyes. Pretense would dissolve at that point, and flirting would turn into descriptions of dates they'd go on if they could. Then he'd hint about romantic scenarios for lovemaking. When he saw her fully primed, her face flushed with desire, he'd get her thinking about how they could meet in person.

She typed a message that she was ready to go, and he put through the call.

CHAPTER EIGHTEEN

Jo's eyes flicked between the e-mail insisting she take her built-up vacation time, and the file in front of her.

Jeanine Hammond.

More than five months later, and they weren't an inch closer to knowing who murdered her. They'd followed every lead, looked everywhere for even the tiniest clue, but couldn't put the smallest crack in Jeanine's case. Jo closed the file and shoved it a few inches away from her.

Rockney had been crystal clear that morning. They had neither the time nor the money to keep investigating a case that refused to yield anything new. She was the lieutenant now, and it was her job to make sure the cooling cases made it to the deep freeze so the department's scarce resources could be reallocated. *Responsible prioritization*, he'd called it, heavy emphasis on the *responsible*. Said she couldn't afford to have pet projects, couldn't afford to hold open cases on *instinct alone* when so many others needed attention. She needed to *step up and draw the line*.

But dammit, this was the first and *only* case she'd been able to work in months, the *only* opportunity she'd had to use her training and her experience and her brain for something other than oversight. How could she give up on the *one* chance she'd had? As it was, she saw Jeanine's face when she fell asleep at night, felt guilty she wasn't able to give the case her full attention. If you couldn't catch the bastards, couldn't put things right, what was the damned point?

The cases that went cold kidnapped your peace of mind, sat on your shoulders wherever you went, invalidating your job, your life, the very core of your soul. At least when you were a detective and you were ordered off a case, you could get away with working it harder on the sly, between other responsibilities, or on your own time. But as lieutenant, extra time was a thing of the past, and her late nights were spent catching up on a million administrative tasks. She was impotent.

And to make matters that much worse, Rockney had also vigorously denied her request to reschedule her vacation. She'd been accruing vacation time even before she made lieutenant and, with the thousand new responsibilities hanging over her, had already put off going twice in the hopes of catching up on them. He made clear the department couldn't roll the vacation days over any longer and couldn't afford to convert them to pay. She had to take the vacation, and she had to take it now. End of discussion.

She sighed. She knew it was past time for personal reasons, as well. The already-terse conversations with her father had become progressively more strained in the year since she last visited New Orleans. Communication was not her father's forte, but he had mastered the brusque guilt trip that silently declared his daughter's neglect a foregone conclusion. She needed to halt the compounding resentments.

Jo slid the file back in front of her and stared at it. Then she glanced up at the commendation letters on her wall, the only thing she'd managed to find time to hang up. The time she'd spent on this case had reminded her in a visceral way what she'd been missing out on in the field. She committed herself to Jeanine Hammond, and she wasn't going to turn her back on the case.

She fired off a text to Arnett, and he appeared at her door five minutes later, notes in hand.

He plopped down into the chair closest to the desk. "Okay, boss. One last shot."

"No Lopez?"

"Personal day. She's moving her mother in."

"Ah. Okay, you and me, then." Jo opened the file and pulled up the computer information. "Husband?"

"Rock-solid alibi. Everyone confirmed he was at the group get-together and didn't leave for any period of time. Cell phone pics with the relevant metadata tags hold up. No way he or anyone from their circle of friends could have been at the hotel with her. And the DNA profile didn't match, for what that's worth."

"To rule it out—what about a hired killer?"

"She was comfortable and happy with the guy in the video. Strange for a hit to go down like that." He took a gulp of his coffee and looked down at the folder in his lap. "Also don't see a motive. Life insurance policy won't cover much more than her funeral expenses, no evidence of explosive fights, cheating, anything."

Jo nodded. "It doesn't feel right to me either. And if he's the guy, we have zero evidence against him regardless."

Arnett continued. "If she was diddling a co-worker, she was doing it with superhuman discretion. Nobody saw anything, and there's nothing incriminating at work or home. Every minute of her time away from home was accounted for. The cozy with the guy on camera still bugs me, but I can't see how she managed an affair with anyone, at work or otherwise."

"And the fired employees?"

"Hard to say. Everyone has found good jobs, so there doesn't seem to be serious damage to anyone's life over the loss of employment. Most have alibis, except for Renke, one of the problem children she fired. We couldn't find anything to connect them to her visit here, but we couldn't rule it out, either. Neither would consent to a DNA test, and we don't have enough evidence for a compulsion order."

Jo fingered her necklace. "Too bad the department doesn't have enough funds for us to steal their garbage and test everything in it, like they do on TV."

Arnett eyed her warily. "I know that tone."

She held his eye and sipped her coffee. "Renke still lives in Oakhurst, right?"

He rubbed his eyes. "You seriously want me to do this?"

She waved a hand. "Want you to do it, yes. But you and Lopez are both stealing time to deal with this as is. I don't see how you'd be able to find enough time to stake him out and wait for him to toss a coffee cup. But if you happened to run into him, I wouldn't complain."

Arnett laughed. "Thing is, I know you'd be out there doing it yourself if you had half a chance."

She wiggled her eyebrows and flipped to the interviews and search reports on Jeanine's colleagues. "At the conference, nothing strange in anyone's luggage, nobody even had a hat or a trench-style coat of the right sort, or anything in any shade of yellow. Everyone's movements accounted for?"

"Most of them didn't show up until after the murder, and all of the flights and alibis checked out. Two co-workers were in town already, one with his spouse. They were all sharing a room and had been out that night together."

"Could they be lying?"

"Don't see how. Their waiter identified the party of three, and the owner of their B and B remembers them coming in at eleven. They each vouch that the others weren't in bed until eleven-thirty, not enough time to sneak out after the others were asleep. And again, no motive, no evidence, no nothing."

So, unless some *Murder on the Orient Express* craziness had taken place, her friends and co-workers were in the clear.

Jo turned over her notes. "That leaves the niece. Any updates there?"

"Actually, yes. Her fiancé, Philip Begemack, turned out to be quite a piece of work. I did the background check on him myself, found two restraining orders filed by previous girlfriends. Just heard back from the second one a week ago, finally. Both broke up with him because he was controlling to what they felt was a dangerous degree. After, he kept showing up at their houses and jobs 'trying to win them back.' But as soon as they got the restraining order, he stopped. Both said he never overtly threatened them or any other family member, but they felt a clear danger from him. From what I can see, he skirted the line but kept on the right side of the law."

"Do we have anything final on his movements the night of the murder?"

"Still shaky. Teresa was out visiting her grandmother, and he was home alone, reading. Told us with a little too much pleasure that he'd been reading *Gone Girl*. He did produce a charge receipt for pizza delivery, and we confirmed that a pizza was delivered to him that night. But the guy who did the delivery couldn't pick out his picture. He could have had a friend at the house order it, I suppose. Search turned up nothing, no fedora, no overcoat."

"But," Jo finished for him, "while shady or not, his pattern doesn't seem consistent with flying across the country to murder an aunt who was already out of the picture."

"Doesn't seem like it, no. We also didn't find any calls, texts, or e-mails between them, or between Jeanine and Teresa. And his DNA didn't match up with the sample."

"Okay, then—how about Jeanine's other phone records, credit cards?"

"Hard to say on her phone. She used her personal cell for business too, and there are pages of different numbers that have checked out as business associates, although we can't rule out a relationship that went past business. Her credit card records for the past few months didn't show anything out of the ordinary. Only thing strange, no charges for her dinner or drinks on the night she disappeared."

"So, someone else paid, or she paid cash."

"Husband says she always paid by credit card for anything more expensive than coffee. But her expenses that night wouldn't have been reimbursable, so who knows, we can't rule it out."

"Computers?"

"Nothing out of the ordinary at work, she didn't even check Facebook there. Work contacts check out same as the phone records. Nothing compromising on her laptop: no love letters, no strange e-mails, no questionable contacts. She corresponded with a few longtime friends who lived in other states, but they're all women and they've all checked out." He paused to gulp his coffee. "Same with Skype—same long-distance friends and a few contacts set up for some computer games. They all checked out except two that were deleted and untraceable, but Lopez says it's common for people to put together temporary groups and accounts for an evening."

"And we checked all the restaurants within walking distance of the hotel, nobody recognized her?"

"Every restaurant within two miles. Not even a hesitation."

Jo stood up, poured a refill for Arnett and herself, and then paced the office. "So, what's left? The scenario my mind keeps returning to is, she met a man she found attractive at a restaurant or bar and decided to have a fling. Blood alcohol levels were high enough for impaired judgment, and her life and marriage didn't seem to have much excitement in it."

"True." Arnett sounded hesitant.

"It's human nature, right? She wouldn't be the first to succumb to the thrill of a one-night stand on a business trip. Tale as old as time, middle-aged woman coming to the realization that romance is dead in her marriage. Away from home, on her own, easy prey for the right kind of man. He gives her a few compliments, buys her a few drinks, and she'd feel young and attractive again. She'd think, 'Why not? I may never get this chance again.' But she chose the wrong guy. Or maybe she changed her mind when they got back to the hotel, lost her nerve, and it turned ugly."

"Possible," Arnett agreed without nodding.

Jo sat back down, leaned back in her seat. "Or a random attack? Maybe her 'friend' on the security video had been seeing her home safely because she was intoxicated and got handsy. Maybe they parted ways outside her room, and some random psychopath attacked her minutes later. Maybe she interrupted him trying to rob her. The 'friend' would be too afraid to come forward later and incriminate himself."

Arnett peered at her. "And the wedding ring?"

"Maybe we're overthinking that. Maybe she took the ring off earlier when she first got interested in her new 'friend,' and lost it."

Arnett's eyebrows rose briefly. "Possible. But there are just too many 'ifs' and 'maybes' there for my liking—it doesn't add up. And the timing is too coincidental."

Jo nodded. "No, you're right. None of it feels good." She shuffled the pieces in her mind. She could feel herself forcing them to fit, looking for any scrap of a lead, or at least a theory that would give her closure—anything to get rid of the gaping dread she felt when an investigation was destined for the cold files.

Arnett spoke. "I don't like it either, but the bottom line is, we don't have any evidence. No idea who this mystery man might be. No tips have panned out, no useful forensics. No leads, nothing. We don't even know where she spent her evening. I'm game for any ideas you have, but I can't see what else to do on this one."

Jo's fingers twisted the diamond on her necklace. Arnett was right, there was nothing more they could do. They didn't have enough evidence to know where else to look, let alone prosecute a case. If any new leads came in while she was gone, Arnett would resurrect it and do what needed to be done. That would have to be enough.

CHAPTER NINETEEN

Emily peered past the man next to her, trying to glimpse something other than clouds out of the plane window. Normally, she hated the middle seat, but nothing could steal her joy today. Not the obnoxious woman on her right who took the armrest and pushed well into Emily's space, not even the man in the window seat who removed his shoes and filled the entire cabin with foot musk. All she could think about was seeing New Orleans for the first time, wandering through the French Quarter, listening to music in jazz clubs—all on Peter's arm. Her mind swirled it all into swaths of excitement and nervous self-doubt.

She closed her eyes and leaned her head back as best she could. She'd felt vital again for the last few months. Alive. Like maybe her life wasn't over after all.

Peter easily slipped into the hole in her life, like he was meant to be there all along. He made her laugh. He made her feel interesting, always wanted to hear what she had to say, always had some comment in response. He made her feel valued and protected. He took her side when things went wrong, encouraged her to stand up for herself rather than be pushed to the back of everyone else's life. She wasn't bothered anymore when Eddie didn't listen to her, mostly because she didn't spend much time talking to him these days, and as far as she could see, he didn't even notice. Neither did the children.

And Peter made her feel sexy, something so foreign she barely recognized it. She had to be careful at home, couldn't risk that someone would overhear or try to come into the den, no matter how unlikely it was. But she'd arranged several very intimate conversations over Skype, on her cell phone after school let out. Twice, hidden in the farthest corner of her office, they had phone sex. He told her what to do and where to do it, and she brought herself to orgasm while he listened. She felt lush and sensual and naughty, with a delicious secret to hold close to her heart.

Of course she had to meet him. She'd fallen in love with him, was even considering leaving Eddie to be with him, but she wasn't stupid. She had to see how compatible they were when in the same room, and the same bed. He jumped at the suggestion, as she knew he would—he'd already said he was in love with her and had dropped hints that he wanted her to leave Eddie and marry him.

Getting away had been tricky. She'd racked her brain trying to find a solution until he made the brilliant suggestion that she look for training workshops and programs to attend. She was skeptical at first, but when she looked, she found quite a fair few. Most were too expensive, but she found two that offered fellowships to teachers who came from struggling districts. She applied and was accepted almost immediately to one; the low performance statistics for her district and the teaching awards she'd won early in her career worked together in her favor. Her department chair and principal were thrilled. The award would reflect well on the school and help them attract other opportunities, with no cost to them. They also seemed to see her initiative as pouring oil on troubled waters, and were happy to provide a substitute teacher for her.

From there, everything was easy. Eddie would rather die than go to something related to her work, and of course the kids couldn't be taken out of school.

"Something to drink?" The flight attendant barely made eye contact.

"Diet Coke, please, and can I keep the can?" She'd lost almost ten pounds since meeting Peter but was insecure about the extra ten she still carried. And no way she'd be saving any calories on the cuisine in New Orleans: jambalaya, gumbo, remoulade, étouffée, fried catfish. *Then again, I'll be burning a lot of calories, too.* She giggled, and a delicious shiver ran through her. The woman on her right shot her an odd look.

Five days with Peter. For three of them she'd lose eight hours during the teaching workshop, but Sunday and Thursday were theirs to savor, along with the evenings. She sipped her soda, then closed her eyes again to imagine strolling hand in hand with Peter through Jackson Square. And how they'd spend those nights back in the hotel room.

CHAPTER TWENTY

The touching changed for his mother with that first ejaculation. More frequent, and more pointed. He tried to make sure he didn't have another accident, and his fear helped at first. But after a few days, he slipped again. As promised, she beat him, so bad that his left eye swelled nearly shut. After that, there was no doubt she was purposefully testing him. She'd change the way she moved, and monitor his response. When he slipped, she beat him within an inch of his life. Luckily, it took only a few more mistakes for his mind to shut down when she touched him. He stopped getting erections.

And when anything else stimulated him, he'd have panic attacks. His heart would pound like rifle fire. He'd have trouble breathing, feel like he was outside of himself, watching. His doctor put him on anxiety medication, which helped. He still felt a type of stress when it happened, but it was more like anxious anger. But over time, the feeling of anger intensified and he was suspended twice for fits of rage directed at other students. The school counselor talked to him about his temper and gave him strategies for channeling it. Running helped metabolize it, and he distracted himself through reading and computer programming.

Martin's mother touched him for the final time when he was seventeen, while watching some pedestrian made-for-TV movie. But this time, his brain didn't shut down the way it normally did. He never did figure out why; there was no difference he could see from the thousands of times that came before. All he knew was this time the rage took over, a fountain overflowing its basin, and rushed out of him.

He flew off the couch, causing the remote on his lap to flip unnoticed to the floor, and turned to face her. "Don't ever touch me that way again!"

For a moment she shrank back and her mouth dropped, but she recovered quickly. She jumped up, her face screwed into a twisted moue. "Finally! Finally, you've decided not to be a disgusting pervert anymore!"

What the hell? He shook his head, confused, felt like his mind had left his body and was hovering over it. What the hell was she talking about? She was the one touching him, he had never asked for it. Or had he? Had he done something when he was younger, was he still doing something he didn't realize?

His hands flew up to cover his ears. "Shut up! Shut up! Stay the fuck away from me!"

"Don't you dare talk to me that way! This is *my* house, you perverted bastard!"

He shook his head, tried to block the words out, but they ping-ponged off the sides of his skull. *Pervert. Perverted bastard.* He tried to breathe, closed his eyes against the intensifying dizziness. When he opened them again, a smug smile covered his mother's face, and something inside of him snapped.

When he thought back on what happened next, it played in his mind like a scene on TV, like he was watching it happen to two other people in slow motion. He saw himself pick up the fire iron, then lunge toward his mother. He watched realization dawn on her face, saw her jerk around to get away. Her foot landed on the remote control, and it slipped out from under her, pulling her foot with it. She fell, and her head struck the corner of the table with a crunch like a car hitting a tree, before bouncing off onto the floor. Then time sped up as thick blood rushed from her head, covering the aging carpet.

He watched the crimson stain grow, fascinated. Watched her outstretched hand twitch and stared into her wide-open blue eyes. He scanned her body and watched something change, almost imperceptibly, as the muscles lost their tension and her skin turned pale and waxy.

He waited another moment, then took her pulse, confirmed she was dead. Then he walked with awkward difficulty over to the phone and punched in 911.

Because for the first time in years, he had an erection.

CHAPTER TWENTY-ONE

Emily's flight arrived early and the hotel shuttle made excellent time. After checking in, exploring the room, and freshening up, it was only 4:05 p.m. She wasn't due to meet Peter until seven.

She pushed open the heavy hotel drapes and gazed out the window at the bright, clear sky. She had far too much excited pent-up energy to hang around inside on such a gorgeous day, and she couldn't bear to waste any of the precious hours she had in New Orleans. Three hours was plenty of time for a stroll through the French Quarter, she decided. But was it a good idea to go out alone? She'd been warned the city could be dangerous. But no, it was broad daylight and her hotel was on Canal Street, only a stone's throw from the Quarter. And by the time the sun went down, she'd be with Peter, and he'd keep her safe. She slipped on her black flats and grabbed her purse. Should she take her heels along just in case? No, they'd just be extra weight to carry, and she'd have plenty of time to come back before meeting him.

One push through the revolving door, and she was strolling down Canal. When the first block ended, she was tempted to turn into the Quarter, but decided to hold off until she got to Bourbon Street—she wanted her official introduction to be along that most famous of NOLA streets. What was that song she'd loved when she was a little girl, the one by Sting? "Moon over Bourbon Street," that was it. The melody floated through her mind and she tried to remember the lyrics. Something about an innocent girl wandering around New Orleans...

When she reached the corner and turned, she had to laugh—the first thing she saw was a sex shop. Yep, this was the Bourbon Street she'd heard about. She grabbed her cell and snapped a picture; it was too perfect not to record for posterity, even if she did look like the silliest sort of tourist. She took a selfie in front of it, too, and started along again.

Her head swiveled back and forth, taking in the shop displays and the signs and all the wrought-iron balconies that lined the narrow street. In the distance, the older buildings pulled her in with avocado greens, muted oranges, periwinkles, and pinks, and gave the streets a foreign feel, not quite American, but not fully European, either.

As she closed in on the corner of Bienville, a double-balconied hotel dominated her view, the second and third stories wrapped with ornate art deco iron balconies. She stared up, mesmerized, and nearly fell as she tripped on the uneven sidewalk. Everywhere she looked, down each street and around every corner, the myriad buildings and colors blended into a unique harmony that recalled another era but placed it in a parallel universe. Like it should be filled with horse-drawn carriages and ladies in brightly colored hoop-skirted gowns nodding genteelly at the vampire from the song lurking in the shadows.

She continued on to St. Peter Street and turned right. She almost passed Preservation Hall without realizing, it was so inconspicuously decorated compared to its surroundings. She stopped again to take a picture, humming.

She turned another corner and crossed around to the front of St. Louis Cathedral. She plopped onto a bench to rest while she absorbed the facade of the church and the square in front of it, amid the sounds of street artists hawking their paintings. She checked her phone—5:30 already, she'd taken longer than she realized. No way she'd have time to go back to the hotel before dinner unless she took a taxi there and back. She considered. She was enjoying herself too much to rush, and she was wearing the dress she'd picked for dinner tonight anyway, even if her sexy shoes were back in the room. Ah well, the flats looked fine with the dress, and there'd be plenty of time for sexy heels later.

As she made her decision, a full band appeared around the far corner of the church, playing and dancing their way across the promenade.

You have to be kidding me. This kind of thing only happens in movies!

Her shoulders bobbed with the beat of the music, and as the band passed by, the entirety of the moment flooded her—the exotic beauty of the city, the roaming musicians that embodied its romance and freedom, the excitement of the impending rendezvous with her knight in shining armor. The allure of the present and promise for the future swirled together and filled her with happiness so intense it brought tears to her eyes.

Magic. New Orleans is magic.

CHAPTER TWENTY-TWO

As Emily swayed to the beat of a zydeco band in front of St. Louis Cathedral, Martin stepped out of the café across from her hotel.

He'd been in New Orleans for several hours, had double-checked the hotel's security and parked to avoid the one sad camera. Then he ordered a latte and settled into the café's cozy interior to monitor the hotel. He watched as her shuttle arrived and she awkwardly maneuvered her rolling bag down to the sidewalk, evaluated her height and weight for the first time in three full dimensions. She looked shorter than her claimed five foot six and was slightly thinner than she seemed on Skype. But neither was a large enough discrepancy to make a difference for his purposes.

He sipped and watched the exits. Sure enough, she came out again barely twenty minutes later. From the front window, he monitored her progress until she entered the French Quarter via Bourbon Street. He laughed at her choice. Always acting the quintessential tourist, these women—you'd think at their age they'd be past that. He settled in with another latte and checked the time. He'd surveil for another hour, ensure there was no unexpected return before he needed to put on his persona and slip into the French Quarter after her.

They were meeting at a Cajun restaurant he'd found on Yelp. There was no point in driving through the nightmarish morass of one-way streets, and she'd mentioned that she wanted to explore the Quarter after dinner anyway. To experience the nightlife. They'd spend a pleasant evening wandering until they found a jazz club to take in, or at least, that's what she'd think the plan was. He didn't care for chance, so he'd picked out a club in advance, and he'd finesse their wanderings in that direction. He needed one where people went to dance. He wanted to feel her body following his lead, moving when and where he wanted it to go. Combined with the walk, the excitement, and the drinks he'd be sure to keep flowing, the dancing would tire her out. By the time they got back to the hotel, she'd have enough fight to make it exciting for him, but no more.

He'd been to New Orleans several times before and never could understand the appeal of it, especially the oh-so-famous French Quarter with its nefarious Bourbon Street. People found it quirky and charming. Eclectic and intriguing. Romantic and mysterious. A bastion of American "culture," filled with food, music, history, and booze. He found it lurid. People drinking themselves sick, vomiting and urinating on the street. Sex everywhere: strippers, hookers, couples in not-so-hidden enclaves, girls flashing their breasts for little pieces of plastic. Electric lights and garish colors. People seeking out anything "voodoo," trying to make the supernatural real. That made him laugh—the irony of the need to invent vampires and spells when there were very real monsters already walking among them. He laughed again. *No amount of gris-gris can save them from the likes of me-me.* The Quarter summed up the worst side of human nature, made clear mankind was just as much base animals as every other species. Most of them, at least. On every bell curve there were exceptional individuals that rose above the rest.

When he left, he ambled along at a medium pace, careful to be sure nobody would remember a man hurrying toward the heart of the Quarter wearing a fedora and carrying a dark overcoat. He forced himself to enter via Bourbon Street—he certainly wouldn't draw much notice among the sensational sights there. He placed a pleasant, interested expression on his face and glanced around casually, just another happy visitor taking in the (in)famous destination.

He arrived at the restaurant half an hour early to ensure everything was as it should be, and so he'd be waiting when she arrived. As promised, the restaurant was "romantic" and "intimate" (translation: low lighting and unobtrusive waitstaff) while still being "popular" (meaning, with enough business that the staff wouldn't remember every couple they saw on a Saturday night). He confirmed they'd have an out-of-the-way table, which would keep them somewhat hidden in the back. The decor was intended to give the feel of a hidden courtyard, with arches in the red-and-cream walls, viney plants hung from the ceiling, and paintings of fountains and flowers next to each table. Satisfied, he ordered a coffee at the bar and settled in to wait.

A few minutes before seven, he spotted her. She looked nervous, and checked her face and hair in the glass reflection before pushing through the door. He took in the blueish-purple swirled pattern of her wrap dress, which washed out her pale features and made her look like a walking bruise. Her makeup echoed the same shades, probably an attempt for a sexy, vampy look, but gave her eye sockets a sunken, sleep-deprived look.

She paused, eyes adjusting to the light, and he savored the jolt of electricity that coursed through his body. He took a deep breath in anticipation, relishing the knowledge that the final act was about to begin. First, he'd make her eat what he liked, feed her from his fork, a farmer fattening his lamb. Then he'd take her to music and make her dance, a puppeteer masterfully plucking the strings of his marionette. He'd touch her when and how he liked—her face, her hair, her neck, her breasts. Then he'd raise her emotions to a frenzied peak, make her body ache, make her willing to do whatever he asked. And once he controlled her completely, he'd complete his victory by wringing the life force from her and using it to feed his own.

*

The police ruled the scene of his mother's death an accident almost immediately. Martin told them the truth, that she slipped on the remote and fell onto the corner of the table. No lies to keep straight, only the omission of what happened just before, and so the scene matched the story perfectly. The police, overburdened and jaded, were happy to have an open-and-shut death on their hands, and when the medical examiner's report came back, everything tied up all the ends into a nice tight bundle. They turned her body over to the mortuary closest to his house and returned her personal effects to him: a bag of clothes and the wedding ring she'd always worn on her right hand. He'd fought back a wry smile at the irony—the same hand she'd used to fondle him for so many years.

Fortune had favored him, he had no doubt about that. Because even though he hadn't technically killed her, he had no doubt he would have if the fall hadn't done it for him. His only regret was he didn't get to deliver the deathblow, didn't get to feel her skull caving in under the poker. He knew he'd caused her death and was energized by the rush of that knowledge, the fierce sense of power. He relived the scene in his mind every night for nearly two weeks, adding in what he imagined the crunch of bone would have felt like, and allowed the surge of omnipotence and his orgasm to lull him to sleep, her ring clasped in his hand.

A continuous, joyful celebration, because now he was free. Free to figure out who he was, out from under her thumb.

Almost.

He was six months shy of his eighteenth birthday, too young to be on his own. Nobody knew where his father was. And if his mother had any family, he'd never heard her mention them, and nobody showed up when she died. So, by default, he became a ward of the state and the court placed him with a foster family.

Bile still rose in his throat when he thought of that "family." Five other boys, the six of them sharing two rooms. His foster "parents," Larry and Rhonda Lloyd, were the lowest form of white-trash parasites, living off the misfortune of others. They met their official obligations but did nothing more, feeding and caring for the children as cheaply as possible while the rest of the money went for drugs. The day he moved in, they made him unpack while they watched, under the guise of checking for anything that was against the rules.

"Lemme see that watch," Larry had said.

Martin handed it to him. "Why?"

"You can't expect us to blow our own money feeding you so you can keep expensive toys." He looked it over.

Martin's blood froze at the thought of his laptop and his mother's ring buried at the bottom of the duffel bag.

Larry slid the watch into the pocket of his greasy jeans with a snide smile. "We all have to contribute where we can." His eyes flicked to the bag.

There was no way for Martin to sneak the laptop out unnoticed, and there was no point in delaying. He dumped out the bag and brushed a shirt over the ring as he picked up the computer.

"The rest is all clothes, except this." As he spoke, he locked the computer under his arm.

"Give it here."

Martin shifted his weight to his forward foot and looked toward Rhonda. He turned a cold, hard smile on her and tilted his head to the side.

"You remind me so much of my real mother. Not in looks, you're much prettier. But something else. Did they tell you how she died? About the *accident*?"

She blanched as he emphasized the word. The blood drained from her face and seemed to fill up Larry's.

"I said give it here." But Larry sounded less sure.

Martin didn't break his eye contact with Rhonda. "She told me I should sell my laptop, too. Funny how everyone seems to want me to get rid of it."

Rhonda's hand reached over and impotently pulled at Larry's arm. Larry jerked away, but said nothing. Martin kept his eyes on Rhonda, and she took a step backward.

For a moment, nobody moved.

"Huh. With all them stickers and scrapes on it, prob'ly not worth much anyway. Keep it." Larry turned around and stalked out. Rhonda followed, watching Martin over her shoulder as she went.

He overheard them later that night whispering in their bedroom.

"I don't feel safe with him here. That look in his eyes—it gave me the shivers."

"You're just being overdramatic. He got his computer, that's all he cares about. He'll only be here for a few months, and we need the money. Just leave him be."

"I don't like it, Larry, I'm telling you."

"I heard you fine. Now shut up, my show's about to start."

That was mostly fine by Martin. As long as they left him alone, he'd be happy to leave them alone. But a tiny part of him, way back in a corner of his mind, was disappointed, wanted them to make trouble. Wanted a reason to kill his new "mom." But fortunately for her, the larger, smarter part of his mind just wanted to be gone.

That night he started taking small coding jobs through an online freelancing site. The money he earned was paid through the site; his employers paid the company, then the company took a percentage and kept the money in his account until he requested it. He let it sit so nobody could legally get their hands on it. He was good at what he did, so even by his eighteenth birthday, he had a nice amount waiting to be paid out. He went off to school that morning carrying his duffel bag and never came back—go figure, the Lloyds didn't look for him. He stayed with a friend for three weeks until graduation, then caught a bus out of town, to

San Diego. He'd been accepted to several universities earlier in the year, with full scholarships thanks to his outstanding GPA, and had chosen UCSD because of its strong computer science program.

But as luck would have it, the last few months had provided him a much more compelling reason to move there.

*

San Diego was close to Mexico, and Mexico was a safe place to kill. Relatively safe, anyway.

The moment he watched the life drain out of his mother, the hunger was born inside him. It took its first baby steps during the confrontation with Larry and Rhonda, and since then clamored to be fed, sending out powerful pangs of need. A few weeks before he left the foster home, Martin passed a woman waiting for the bus on a deserted street, alone and vulnerable in the dark, and nearly succumbed to an overwhelming desire to cave her skull in. When a teenage girl strode past his window late at night a few days later, the need was so strong he rammed his knee into the wall hoping the pain would drown it out. There was no point lying to himself about it—he would kill again, and he needed to find a way to do it safely.

So, he set about devising as foolproof a method of killing as possible, one that would never lead back to him. He'd heard men laugh and joke knowingly about how you could get away with almost anything in Tijuana, things you'd go to jail for in the States. He'd never been brave enough to ask what those were, but there were always overtones of sexual deviance, drugs, crime, and an ineffective police force. If Tijuana was what they said it was, his considerable intelligence would find a way.

He freelanced at night to pay for his education, spent his days majoring in computer science, with a minor in psychology. He hoped the psychology classes would give him some insight into his need to kill, but even the abnormal-psych texts were of limited help regarding serial killers. He did his own research, read everything he could find about them and studied the mistakes that got them caught. And when he saved up enough for a car to get him away for the weekend, he visited Tijuana.

He explored the streets, did what the other American men were doing, and scoured everything for options. Shows, strippers, clubs, hookers. Foul women who polluted the world—he'd be surprised if anyone even noticed they went missing. He canvassed systematically and gradually narrowed his prospects to several sex workers on the Calle Coahuila.

On his next trip, he set out with several possibilities in mind, intending to let fate decide which he'd pursue. He sauntered along the Calle, impersonating a man choosing what brand of good time he wanted for the night. Eventually, he saw one of his potential marks leave after her shift, and followed at a discrete distance. Two blocks down she went into a club called Allegra, and he slipped in after her.

He bought a drink and kept his distance. She made a beeline for a group of working girls in short skirts and ridiculous heels he vaguely remembered seeing around La Zona Norte. Allegra must have been where she and her friends hung out after hours. Now that he knew that, it would be far less suspicious to return another night and wait for her to leave the club than linger around her place of business. The next time, he waited until she left for the evening, and watched where she turned off the street. On his following trip, he watched the spot where she had disappeared from sight, and noted her next turn. In that way, over several weeks, he mapped out her path after leaving the club.

The next week, he slipped through the district to one of the side streets he knew she would use, and hid in the open space he'd identified behind an abandoned building. Safely out of sight, he settled in to wait.

Within minutes he heard footsteps approach, but they weren't right. There were two sets, and they were heavy. Not the dainty clicks of high heels, but the solid pound of large men. He shrank back into the darkness and waited for the sound to pass.

Two men in black suits appeared around the side of the building. Before he could react, the bigger of the two swung back and sank his fist into Martin's abdomen. The air exploded from his lungs and he doubled over in pain.

The second man grabbed his head and lifted it up, then spoke to him in perfect English. "My friend and I see you spending a lot of time around La Zona. Funny that you're always alone, and you never do very much. We think it's time for you to find another place to hang out, before you get yourself in trouble." He lifted his shirt, and the FN Five-seven in his shoulder holster caught the light.

There was no point objecting. Martin nodded.

The big one hit him in the stomach again, and then a third time. Martin fell onto one knee. The man with the gun gave him a moment to recover, and then gestured *after you.*

Martin rose slowly and hobbled out from the hidden space. The men followed and watched as he limped down the street and around the corner. Once out of sight, he broke into a jog, as fast as he could manage after the beating. He didn't stop until he reached the parking lot and locked himself safely inside his car.

Looking back, they'd done him a favor. It was a wake-up call, one that probably saved his life. If he'd been so inept that two thugs could spot he was up to no good, he wasn't close to ready. He had to be far smarter, meticulously consider every angle, even how he went about his scouting. A beating was nothing, far preferable to jail or death, or both.

So he waited and researched, searched for a solution, his psyche split between the hunger that demanded to be fed and the fear that he'd be caught and killed.

CHAPTER TWENTY-THREE

Martin stood up from the table, planted an excited smile on his face, and stepped toward Emily. The movement caught her eye, and she turned, her anxious expression replaced by relief as she recognized him, and her doubts and fears melted away.

He embraced her and kissed her cheek, then pulled away and smiled warmly down at her. "You look so beautiful. I'm glad you made it, I was worried you'd change your mind."

She beamed up at him. "Never. I was nervous, though. I've never even been on a blind date before, let alone something like this."

He signaled the hostess that his dinner companion had arrived. She picked up two menus and led them to the farthest corner in the back. Once they were settled in, she took their drink order and left.

Once she was out of earshot, he reached over and covered Emily's hand on the table. "This is so strange, isn't it? I feel like I've known you for so long, but it feels odd to be sitting across from you in the flesh. Familiar but unfamiliar."

"I know what you mean." She giggled and he cringed internally—he'd come to despise that horrendous titter. "It's like I'm meeting someone I knew in another life or something. I can't get over the fact that I can reach out and touch you anytime I want." She lifted her other hand to run across his.

He watched her fingers trace a path on his skin. He called up a goofy grin, gently shook his head as if at the wonder of it all. "I just want to sit here and look at you all night." He paused for a moment, gazing into her eyes. "But I have a feeling they'd prefer it if we order some food and at least pretend to eat."

They both laughed, and she picked up her menu. "Did your friend give you any recommendations on what was good here?"

"He did. I thought I'd order for us, and we can share everything."

"Mmm, I love doing that. You get to try so much more that way." She giggled again.

Their waitress arrived with their drinks and a lagniappe to welcome them, a small dish divided into two sections with fried okra and calamari. Martin ordered for them, then turned his attention back to Emily. He dipped a plump piece of okra into the creamy red sauce and held the fork out to her mouth. She smiled and blushed. She took the bite but poked herself with a fork tine in the process, and her blush deepened.

"I'm always so clumsy," she mumbled, hand covering her full mouth.

He asked her how her trip had been. She answered in excruciating detail, from the incompetent gate agent to the "snotty" flight attendant who wouldn't give her a full can of soda, to the fat woman and smelly man that sandwiched her on the plane. She could turn the most banal day into a never-ending stream of complaint—how on earth did her husband manage to tune her out? But he, her attentive lover, must listen and empathize with every endless word, ask the right questions, commiserate, and make her feel important and interesting. He suppressed a yawn. Only a few more hours.

The gumbo they'd ordered was a vague memory and they were halfway through the jambalaya and crawfish étouffée before she made it to her discovery of Bourbon Street. Her tone shifted, but was no less trying. She was ridiculously charmed and fascinated by everything in the city, like a child at Disneyland for the first time. He assuaged his contempt with biting mental rejoinders:

"The streetcars run right up the middle of Canal Street!"

Yes, that's what streetcars do. Hence the name.

"The wrought-iron balconies are so intricate!"

What an original observation, my love. I don't think anyone has ever noticed those before.

"I saw romantic horse-drawn carriages all round the cathedral square!"

Waiting for silly girls like you to pretend you're a princess in some fairy-tale kingdom.

"The names of the streets are all so French, it's like being in a miniature Paris!"

Such an odd coincidence in a place named after a French city, in a state named after a French king, settled in large measure by people of French ancestry.

With deliberate discipline, he continued his game of transforming each sarcastic retort into a thoughtful comment or question. And in the meantime, he kept topping off her wineglass, a little here, a little more there.

By the time they'd finished their dinner two hours later, he'd had less than a glass of wine, and she'd had close to three. During their Skype sessions together, he'd paid close attention to how much she drank, and knew he'd have to watch her carefully from this point on. She liked her alcohol a little too much and if she got sloppy drunk, killing her would be no challenge. She might even pass out before he was able to. He did a quick calculation factoring in the large dinner and the half hour of "wandering" they'd do before they got to the jazz club. She'd most likely want another drink when she got there, and that would be cutting things too close.

"Darling, would you like to take a ride in one of those horse-drawn carriages you mentioned?"

Her eyes lit up, and she squeezed his hand. "That would be so perfect! I'd love that!"

He motioned to the waitress for the check and smiled back at Emily. "Anything to make my sweet angel happy."

The waitress handed him the check and he glanced at the total. He took a money clip from the breast pocket of his suit and peeled off ten twenty-dollar bills. He placed them on the table and stood up, holding his hand out to Emily. As they left the restaurant, she picked up one of the restaurant's business cards from the podium and put it deep in her purse.

She saw him watching and said, "For my scrapbook," with a laugh.

He put his arm around her, pulled her close, and made a mental note to retrieve it after he strangled her.

CHAPTER TWENTY-FOUR

A news clip had spurred the next phase of Martin's evolution. Women were being murdered almost daily in Juárez, Mexico, and nobody seemed to know or care why. He took in every detail with rapt attention. Nobody had been convicted for killing any of the women, and the police were investigating in name only.

He pulled up everything he could find about the murders and about Juárez itself. The more he read, the more he recognized the universe had handed him a great gift. The men killing the women were most likely Mexican drug lords. Nobody would think twice if a few more went missing at his hand—the police would assume they'd been killed by the same perpetrators, and what were the killers going to do, object to being blamed for the extras? The women would never think to be wary of him, the epitome of the slightly geeky, white-as-can-be American tourist, about as diametrically opposite as anyone could be from a powerful drug lord. The police wouldn't give him a second glance for the same reason. And El Paso was right across the border. If he lived there, he could kill and be home in a different country within minutes. It was almost too good to be true.

He doubled up his course load so he could graduate a year early, then packed his few belongings and moved to El Paso.

He applied the lessons he'd learned in Tijuana to Juárez, that there were always eyes watching, and they knew better than he when something was out of place. The look of a tourist wasn't enough, he needed purpose to give his movements legitimacy.

An authentic Mexican dinner. A night in a club looking for a *hookup*. Something he could act on while he hunted, and it had to be different every time, so he wouldn't become a remembered regular anywhere. And the prostitutes and strippers he'd assumed nobody cared about? He'd overlooked the obvious fact that they were a source of income for someone far more powerful than he.

From the safety of his home, the smartest bet seemed to be one of the popular-but-not-too-popular discos. The whole point of their existence was so men and women could find each other, after all. His behavior would be right in line with everyone else's, an ideal way to blend in and get the lay of the land. Plenty of alcohol to dull the girls' sense and their senses. Loud music to prevent conversation, no need to give details about himself.

But the reality was traumatically unpleasant. A minuscule patch around the bar contained only a handful of tall tables with no chairs, and nobody stayed there for long. The only way to blend in was to move onto the dance floor, a pit of writhing, sweaty bodies with barely room to breathe and no chance to avoid being touched. Pulsing neon lights punctuated the feel of body parts he couldn't identify moving against him from behind and from the side, and women ground their hips into his groin to the beat of the music as he struggled to pass. His breath came in gasps, and a wave of nausea washed over him. He closed his eyes, tried to slow his breathing to short-circuit the panic attack, but someone's hand cupped his ass, and he felt vomit erupt into his mouth. He didn't turn to see who it was, just plowed his shoulder through the crowd toward the exit sign.

Outside, he leaned against the wall, hand over his mouth, trying to keep his dinner down. He took in long breaths through his nose, let the absence of cheap cologne and body odor flood his lungs. How could anyone in their right mind enjoy that?

Once the nausea receded, he set off down the street, trying to keep his pace casual—if he appeared sick for too long, someone might offer help or remember him later. As he worked to keep from stumbling, his mind retraced his earlier steps, looking for a place to get off the street. He remembered a café a few streets down—maybe some sweet, hot tea would help.

The rhythm of his steps helped restore his balance, and the surroundings penetrated his consciousness. Flashes of color on the buildings coalesced into posters, and a set of three identical images together caught his eye. Elegant couples swirled around a spacious dance floor, advertising a club that featured Latin dancing. Words he recognized slashed the posters in bold font: salsa, reggaeton, merengue, bachata.

Ballroom dancing. Why hadn't he thought of that? His mother had taught him all sorts of dances, new and old. He knew what to do there, could maintain control. Because he'd certainly never set foot in another of those nightmarish electric sweat pits.

On his next trip into town, he took a refresher course at one of the clubs and enjoyed it far more than he'd anticipated. When he held the women, spun them around, made their bodies move how and where he wanted them to, he felt an intoxication, a wave of power. He felt something akin to the rush he'd had when he killed his mother—not a replacement, but an appetizer that introduced the main course. From that moment, the dancing became the first act of a delicious opera, populated with his very own little puppet.

He mapped out similar dance clubs in the area. He studied the landmarks nearby and considered everything in relation to the areas where murdered women had been found. He picked the easiest location and came up with a skeletal plan for abducting a woman as invisibly as possible. He planned as much as he could, but would have to finalize the details when he saw the area on the night of the trip.

Then, to his delight, he discovered he didn't have to abduct anyone at all.

As he was eating in a taqueria during his next trip, he scalded his hand opening a steaming packet of tortillas and spilled his water as he jerked away. A woman eating alone at the next table jumped up with a handful of napkins to help him stem the flow.

"Thank you so much, but you don't have to do that," he said, hoping she'd go back to her table.

"It's no problem. You look like you're dressed for a fun night, and wet pants won't look good wherever you're going." Her English was accented, and her smile was shy.

Martin flushed. The woman had noticed him, including what he was wearing, and the incident would imprint him in her mind. Now he'd have to abandon his plan for the evening and come back another night. Desperation flashed through him, so raw it almost brought him to tears. He wasn't sure how much longer he could wait before he lost control.

Unless—unless he could find a way to make *her* his kill.

He glanced around quickly to see if anyone was watching, but if anyone else in the crowded restaurant had noticed, they'd already lost interest. "Then the least I can do is buy you another of whatever you're drinking as a thank-you?" He made a show of peering over to her table, where she'd been sipping a glass of wine.

"You don't have to do that." She stood up and shook her head.

"I insist. A kindness for a kindness." He smiled warmly and went up to the counter for her drink. He set it down in front of her with a flourish.

As he'd hoped, she felt obliged to thank him. A few polite questions followed, and within moments, to his delight, she was laughing and at ease with him, and invited him to join her. He shouldn't have been surprised—girls had been drawn to him in high school and college, had trusted and confided in him, but he always assumed that was only because he never tried to get them into bed the way other guys did. But apparently there was more to his charm, because when he asked her if she'd like to go dancing with him, to his astonishment, she said yes.

They danced and sipped wine for several hours, then he invited her for a romantic stroll with him. And once they were out of sight, he strangled her.

The mistakes of that first kill taught him almost everything else he needed to know. He tried to strangle her face-to-face, which proved to be a mistake. He struggled to get the leverage he needed, and she put up a fierce fight, raking his face and arms with her nails. If he'd chosen a place where someone would actually investigate, he'd have been in deep trouble—the scratches would have been impossible to explain away, and the police would have his DNA besides. As his eyes ran over the lifeless body lying in the dirt, he assessed the problem. He'd need more upper-body strength, for a start. And he'd have to figure out a way to strangle them that made it impossible to fight back the way she had.

With beautiful irony, the solution came from the dancing itself. When he spun his next victim and pulled her into him, her back nestled perfectly against his chest while his arm held her torso in place. He playfully mimicked the twirl during their "romantic stroll," and pinned her arms against her torso as he pulled her into him. His newly weight-trained upper body held her arms and body firmly in place, and he strangled her from behind. She was powerless, apart from backward kicks against his legs that hurt like hell. As he surveyed this one lying dead in front of him, he saw bruises already forming—the pattern on her neck would show his hands too clearly. He'd need something to strangle them with that would leave more generic marks. Something that wouldn't physically match up to him, wouldn't be traceable, and that he could dispose of easily.

With the addition of a common tie from a cheap chain store, the third kill was magnificent perfection. Quick. Effective. And with no evidence that could be traced back to him.

After a fourth kill, he left the women of Juárez alone. Because they'd also taught him something even more important—not just any woman would sate the hunger. The initial thrill of figuring out how to kill dropped off dramatically with the second woman, and he felt almost no pleasure when the third life drained away through his hands.

He pushed and probed at the problem, tested out the thought of killing different women, replayed the evenings of his kills. The only relevant emotion came from the dancing, making them step and spin the way he wanted them to. Wielding control over them, rendering them compliant while they still lived, excited him.

But he'd done that with these women, so why hadn't the kills been satisfying?

He thought back to the day he killed his mother, and the answer flared through him. Justice. That was missing with these innocent, naive single girls who had only been looking for a kind man to date. They'd done nothing wrong. His mother had been a liar, an abuser, a cheater—he'd done the world a favor, and nobody had missed her. He tested that scenario out in his mind—finding another cheating liar and making her pay for her immorality—and he felt himself respond. That was the answer, then: despicable, selfish women that the world was better off without. There were certainly scads more women like that out there, destroying their husbands and their families with their selfish infidelities.

But how could he find women like that, get to know enough about them, without getting caught?

CHAPTER TWENTY-FIVE

The trite, contrived carriage ride was excruciating. Many of the carriages didn't even try to look authentic, with multiple rows of seats to carry as many gullible tourists as possible. What was the point? Why not just take a tourist bus? That was honest, at least.

He directed her to one designed for couples, with a small white fairy-princess canopy. As they wove through the Quarter to the rhythmic clip-clopping, the driver noted points of interest and told them stories, almost certainly made up for effect. Emily snuggled into him and listened to the driver with rapt attention; her silence was a refreshing change, at least, and he was grateful for the respite. When the rehearsed litany was finished, Emily looked at the crescent in the sky, sighed, and hummed softly. He recognized the song—that one by The Police about the moon on Bourbon Street—and distracted himself from the claustrophobic feel of her clamped against him by calling up the lyrics. Then he dug deep and pulled her in closer to whisper into her ear. "The moon is beautiful tonight, but it can't hold a candle to you."

He worried for a moment he'd gone too far. *That was horrendous—even she can't fall for that, half-drunk or not.*

But he'd underestimated the sensibilities of a woman desperate to be swept off her feet by a romantic lover in a romantic city. She responded with a shy smile. "I'm so glad I'm here with you, experiencing this in your arms. It's just how I imagined it."

He tilted her chin up toward his face. He gazed into her bland eyes for a moment with a dreamy expression perfected long ago in his bathroom mirror, and gently kissed her. She sighed and returned the kiss, then laid her head on his shoulder, humming again while she stared off into the night.

As Martin helped her out of the carriage back in Jackson Square, he risked a surreptitious glance at his watch. The ride had taken longer than he planned; she would have metabolized more of the wine than he anticipated.

"Let's take advantage of New Orleans' liberal open container policy and grab a Hurricane to share while we walk."

"Oh, great idea, I wanted to try one anyway. So strange to be able to just walk around with a drink in your hand…" She prattled on about how random liquor laws were, and he struggled to pay full attention. *Steady now, focus on the goal. Her chatter will be finished soon enough.*

The club reenergized him. The music was loud, the people were happy, and Emily's shoulders began to sway before they were five feet into the club. With the seal of the first kiss broken, their flirting became a dance of its own, bordering dangerously on foreplay—a kiss, then he'd twirl her, practice pulling her back into his chest. He'd kiss her neck, then spin her out, then back in again with soft kisses and caresses that deliciously foreshadowed the pending culmination of his effort.

After three dances, both his anticipation and hers had been teased to the edge. It was time. He pulled her in for the last time and kissed her urgently.

"I can't wait much longer, darling. I want you badly. Let's head back to the hotel."

Her cheeks colored, and he swore he felt her pulse quicken at the thought of sex with him. She stood on her toes to whisper in his ear, "Let's hurry."

*

Martin had come almost full circle. "Bad" girls were easy to find, and Juárez would have worked if that were the only issue. But he needed to know them for more than an hour or two, needed to build that connection and trust with them. He'd draw too much attention to himself if he spent enough time in Juárez to establish that even once, especially in a foreign city where he didn't speak the language.

He staved off his frustration for a time by turning the problem into an intellectual challenge to be savored. He redoubled his research on how serial killers slipped up, determined to find the least dangerous way to fill his needs. Other than being recognized, the real danger was the forensic evidence killers either left behind or took with them. Blood was the worst offender; it was messy, hard to control, and traces were easy to miss, so he'd eliminated it from the start. Strangulation turned out to be far superior to watching his mother bleed out anyway. With his hands on them as they died, he could feel the life draining out of them, could speed or slow it like twisting a faucet. And he'd figured out how to strangle with no possibility of defensive wounds, none of his DNA under their fingernails.

The next problem was evidence left behind. A fingerprint on something, a hair from your head or body, some dirt from your shoe or a thread from your clothes. Sure, you could wipe off fingerprints, but what if you missed one? Gloves would interfere with his ability to feel them die, and depending on when and where they were, would look out of place regardless. If this were TV, there was the option of shaving your head and body to keep from leaving hair, but in the real world you simply couldn't live that way.

His eureka moment came during a vile hotel stay on a business trip. He found a large black hair on one of the towels, another on his sheets, and a complete fingerprint on one of the glasses in the bathroom. Filthy beyond words, in a high-class, well-known hotel chain! He'd almost vomited in the moment, but ultimately recognized another gift from the universe. So many people went through those rooms, it would be impossible to build a case around an errant hair or fingerprint found in a hotel room. He couldn't rely on that fully, he'd still need to take every possible precaution, but it was an insurance policy of sorts. Any slip would go undetected—his DNA and prints weren't on file, because his mother's death had never been considered suspicious. And a hotel room was so much better than trying to find a secluded enough place out in public or killing a woman in her own home—no chance of anyone coming around a corner or coming home early to find him.

So, he was one step closer, but was still left with one nearly insurmountable question. How do you build a relationship with someone without ever being seen with them or in the places they go?

He puzzled over that one for well over a year, grew so restless he even considered killing a stripper or prostitute in Juárez. Then, while he and some fellow guild members ground heroics in World of Warcraft, one of the guys kept droning on and on about flying across state to meet some girl in real life that he'd been playing with in-game. They'd been "dating" for several months through the game, spent hours playing together while chatting on Skype, and he'd finally saved up enough money to go visit her. Several other people chimed in about couples they knew who'd met in-game, some who were married now, even. His reaction to it all had been dismissive at first, because, really, the sort of people you'd find looking for love in *World of Warcraft* were either extremely twisted or extremely desperate.

Until it hit him that he was the first, and the women he needed were the second.

He basked in the perfection of it. No physical proximity with his victims while he pulled them into his cyberweb, no need to be anywhere the victims habitually went. And for the murders themselves, he'd get the women to travel somewhere neither he nor they had any tie to as a perfect excuse to use a hotel room. He had enough computer savvy to make it impossible for the police to find him, even if they knew where to look, but why would they?

So he'd tried it. His charm worked all the better in-game, since he had time to shift and adjust as needed. And after his first domestic kill kept him sleepless for nights worrying about his name on flight manifests and rental records, he figured out how to visit a city without a trace—no flights in or out, no hotel reservations, no credit card charges. Even if the police thought to check out all men flying out of the city's airports—and there'd be no reason to think the killer wasn't local—his name would never be on that list. Even if someone thought they saw the victim at a restaurant earlier in the evening, there would be no charge receipt for the police to pull. And even if some cop didn't like the look on his face someday for some reason, none of his personal activities or records would be in proximity to any known pattern of crimes.

He honed the process over three kills by the time Jeanine Hammond was dropped into his lap—a little gifted cherry on top of the *World of Warcraft* sundae. And now he'd perfected it all. Four women met and killed, and nobody even knew he existed. He was unstoppable.

CHAPTER TWENTY-SIX

They hurried, both eager to get back. She hummed the Police song as they walked, and he joined in. He paused occasionally in the middle of the sidewalk to simulate the twirling moves they'd done on the dance floor, and each time, she laughed and fell into his arms.

He kept his head down as they passed the security camera, turned toward her, ever the attentive lover. In the elevator, he buried his face in her neck, in case there was a camera there as well. Once in the hall, he relaxed, and leaned in to kiss her again as she opened the door.

Inside, he pressed her against the wall and feigned urgency. He broke the kiss and mumbled into her lips.

"I don't know where the light switch is, darling."

She flipped it, and a soft light illuminated in one corner of the room. He watched as she threw her purse on the nightstand, calculated the best angle to work from. He reached up to his neck and loosened his tie as he shifted over to the bed.

"Come to me." He held out his hand and let his most lascivious smile slide over his face. "You're so beautiful, and you've been turning me on all night."

She took his hand gently by the fingertips. He twirled her body into his, watched her hips as the garish dress flared out, then nestled her into his chest. He brushed his lips against her neck and she tilted her head up, presented the full length of her throat to him. He kissed along the skin to her ear, lingering to take in the warm feel of it. He savored the gentle press of blood pulsing in her carotid artery, and the musky scent of her neck. So supple. So flushed with life.

Your blood flows because I allow it—soon I will turn you cold and still as stone.

His hands slid down the sides of her body, gently, slowly, taking in the muscles and bone he now controlled. She let out a sigh and relaxed, leaned back against him.

Foul little slut. No more than a slave to your primal desires, and now a slave to mine.

His left hand traveled up her rounded abdomen to her thick breasts, and his finger rubbed back and forth over the nipple that sprung up to meet him. She gasped, her breathing ragged, and the long-awaited flood of power and adrenaline rushed into his mind.

He laughed, then pulled the tie out of his collar, masked the motion by brushing his fingers across her flushed cheek. His heart galloped in his chest—the next move was the crucial one, would crown or destroy all his work. He glanced at her profile, chin raised and mouth slightly open, eyes closed, waiting.

He trailed his fingers along her neck, then brushed her hair to the side. He distracted her with one last pinch of her nipple as he slid his left hand into place over her arm.

He tightened his grasp. She moaned again, surprised delight tingeing her voice.

He laughed again. *She thinks she likes it rough. We'll see.*

But he felt something ping in the back of his awareness. This wasn't quite right.

There was no time to process the thought now, so he brushed it away and reached behind her head for the tie. He draped the ends over his fingers and took a final breath of anticipation, then twisted them together and clamped down.

She moaned, but the sound caught, and she stiffened. She tried to bring her arms up to her neck and he tightened his grip across her, braced for the fight.

But her arms went limp.

What the—? Didn't she understand what was happening? Where was the struggle, the panic, something?

"Don't like it *that* rough, do you?" he blurted without thinking, and winced—it felt wrong, like some tawdry line from a dime novel. Beneath him. Another pang pulled at him.

His tone kicked in her instinct for self-preservation. She jerked a leg out to kick back against him, and he felt the sharp crack as her shin rammed into the bed's frame. She braced the sole of one foot against his leg, tried to push it out from under him, and he felt his erection stir—nobody'd ever tried that before. *Yes. Better.*

She changed tactics, tried a quick swivel of her hips against his arm. When that didn't work, she yanked her head forward, then tried to reverse it into his face. He shifted his head to the side and laughed, then twisted the tie again, harder.

He turned to check her profile, thrumming with pleasure at the terror on her face. Yes, she was starting to panic. Her eye turned to the corner of its socket, searching for him. She tried to speak, tried to wrench her torso around in his arms, but his grip held firm.

And then, she stopped.

What the hell? Was she playing dead so he'd let her go? He wrenched the tie into her skin to let her know he wasn't fooled.

Her body went slack.

Does she think this is a game? She must know her oxygen is running out. Does she think it's some sort of autoerotic asphyxiation kink?

He gave another jerk, prodded for a response. None came. Within moments he felt her falling back against him, felt the ticking shifts that signaled her body was shutting down. Tensed and alert, he waited for some last jolt, some last trick up her sleeve, something.

But it never came. He stayed in position far longer than necessary, waiting.

That wasn't right. This isn't right.

No, it wasn't, but he couldn't deal with that now. He needed to focus his mind on the task at hand.

He closed his eyes, centered his thoughts on the adrenaline surging through his body. He bounced her, let her limbs dance randomly against him, tried reminding himself she was his powerless marionette. He focused on the warmth of her limp figure, imagined the heat leaving her body and entering his. He shifted to the perfume of her hair, then the synthetic texture of the polyester tie constricting his fingers, the soft flesh yielding under his hands. Opened his eyes and memorized her distorted features. Traveled from sensation to sensation, cataloging, filing all of it away to be retrieved later.

The weight of her corpse pulled him forward, distracting him. He flipped her around and lifted her onto his feet, then pulled her hips into his. He stepped forward, then stretched his left leg forward and into a series of samba rolls. So easy to shift her body along with his—why hadn't he tried this before?

But the exhilaration didn't come.

He gave up, disgusted. He stepped her over to the bed and forced himself to focus as he dropped her. If nothing else, he could relish the motion of her body crumpling to the floor, a perfect, supplicant, used rag doll. He bent to adjust her, lifting one hip up and back. He bent one elbow and extended the other arm, then studied the effect. Not perfect, but as close to a samba roll as he was likely to get.

He committed the final scene to a mental snapshot, grabbed his tie and put it back on, then went over his mental inventory. Had he touched the wall when he pinned her to it? No. Had he touched anything else? Nothing. Then he reached down to remove her wedding ring.

It wouldn't budge.

He tamped down the stab of frustration. He knew this would happen eventually, and he always came prepared for it. He reached into his pocket and pulled out the tools, an elastic strap and a small pair of tweezer-like forceps. He wrapped the strap tightly around her finger to compress the flesh, moving up from the knuckle. When he reached the edge of the ring, he used one point of the forceps to push the elastic under it, and out the other side. End in hand, he rotated the elastic under the ring, pulling down toward her fingertip. The ring slowly swiveled down the compressed tissue, then slipped off into his waiting hand. He put the ring and the accoutrements back into his pocket.

He took a last look around the room, satisfied himself that he hadn't dropped anything. Something nagged at the corner of his mind, but he couldn't identify it. He went over his list again, made sure he hadn't forgotten anything. What was different about this kill? She'd died too easily, but that should create *less* disturbance to the crime scene, not *more*. He shook himself mentally. *You're just thrown because she didn't fight and the ring wouldn't come off. It disrupted your pattern. Get on with it.*

He grabbed a tissue and used it to let himself out. As he pulled his fedora down and strode out of the building, lyrics from her song tugged at his mind, reminding him that the killer in the song had hidden *his* face behind the brim of a hat, as well.

He smiled at the irony and slipped out of the hotel.

*

Something was definitely wrong.

As Martin drove out of New Orleans with the song looping through his head, his thoughts didn't settle the way they had after the other hotel kills. No enveloping satisfaction of a job well done, paired with anticipation of a future reward. No Thanksgiving-dinner afterglow, sated from a glorious meal, blissfully aware of the leftovers waiting in the refrigerator. This felt like Juárez.

He became aroused when killing her, but the arousal wasn't as intense, and it faded far more quickly. Fear that it wouldn't return once he was home tugged at him, distracted him from the success at hand. The procedure was practically rote now, this should be the pinnacle of his pleasure—with less to worry about, he should be able to give his mind over to savoring the kill.

Why wasn't that happening?

His mind circled the problem during the long drive and continued on the flight home. Only one answer came to him—it had been too easy. Not just how she died, although that's where the problem crystallized. The whole thing had been too easy from the start. Hell, she'd even mentioned video chatting before he did. There'd been no challenge.

Was he escalating? That's when even the best killers got caught. When they needed more, and then changed something. Got sloppy. No way was he going to risk that.

Besides, he didn't even know for certain there was a problem. Maybe he was too stressed, just having a bad day. Maybe once he was home everything would be fine, and this odd feeling of dissatisfaction would disappear.

CHAPTER TWENTY-SEVEN

Jo sat in the garden courtyard of her father's house, sipping café au lait and avoiding a plate of pain au chocolat and beignets. She glanced at her father, reading the day's paper. He felt her eyes on him and glanced up. "What? You want part of the paper?" Frank asked her.

"I'll take the front section when you're done."

"Why you wanna delve into that when you're on vacation? Your mama's right, you never stop."

Jo sighed. "Gotta keep track of my city, you know. Love watching the comeback."

Frank grunted. "Nothing's gonna kill this city. Never has and never will. But that don't mean it's easy."

Jo always had mixed feelings about visiting, and not just about her father. New Orleans was a complicated city. The ultimate party town earned the motto "let the good times roll," but it was also a cauldron of poverty and crime. She grew up there and loved it without reservation; she came from a large extended Cajun family that threaded through southern Louisiana, and it would always be where her soul called home. But she was under no illusions about how the dark side of humanity manifested here.

"Sho' you right." Jo let the dialect take her over, and her father laughed.

"Same for everything that comes from this place. Including you." Frank's chin jutted out at her, gaze already back on the paper.

She closed her eyes against the words as they echoed in her head. *Including you.*

No, not including her. The ghosts here made sure to remind her of that.

Jo's parents divorced when she was thirteen, and her mother moved them back to her native New England. At that age, Jo couldn't help but put down some roots in Oakhurst. She formed lasting friendships and had eventually fallen deeply in love with Jack, the man she'd hoped to marry. She loved it there, especially the snow, something rare as a hen's tit in New Orleans. But she also never stopped loving her complicated first home.

Katrina intensified the city's complexity, along with her feelings about it. So much had been physically destroyed during the storm, and economically destroyed after it. Why would tourists looking for a good time come to a town in the middle of a crisis? So, there was less money, fewer jobs, and more poverty. Still, the locals were fiercely proud of their city and their unique culture, and were determined to bring it back to health. Returning since Katrina spiked a mix of pride to see her city survive, and sadness to see it in such need.

Her father had refused to leave his historic Garden District house when the storm hit; he was as stubborn an old Cajun as the world had ever seen. But he was also the youngest child of parents raised during the Great Depression and was sharp as an ice pick. He always kept plenty of provisions and cash on hand and knew full well how to deal with the aftermath that hit like a biblical plague. His generator kept him functioning, his extensive stash helped him and his neighbors in need, and he'd ascended to near sainthood in the eyes of many. Jo wouldn't go so far as to say her father had made the right decision to stay—it had been reckless, in her opinion—but she was proud nonetheless. He was certainly made of stern stuff. But was she?

No. She couldn't even solve the one case—*one*—that she had touched in the last half a year. Why had she ever believed she'd have time to do casework? She'd known how overworked the department was. Had she sabotaged herself subconsciously, to get out of doing what was right—once again?

Jo tried to distract her thoughts with a small beignet and a refill of the thick coffee. She closed her eyes as she sipped and kept her moan silent. As addicted as she was to Starbucks and Hill of Beans, they'd never come close to making coffee taste the way her father's did. She took a bite of the beignet, savoring the pillow collapsing as she bit into it.

But it was no use. Try as she might, the unintended implication of her father's words rattled around her head, refusing to leave her be.

She'd returned to visit her father at least once a year since moving to Oakhurst. As a teen she stayed for a large chunk of the summer. The visits kept her in touch with the city and her old friends, but the distance made their gradual changes in appearance and personality appear abrupt and dramatic. From the safety and comfort of New England, she saw the hard knocks her friends took back home, and how they changed in the face of them. That perspective convinced her that who people became had everything to do with their circumstances and opportunities.

Her comfortable distance from those hard knocks was ripped away during a visit when she was sixteen.

"Hey, I need to go meet someone." Marc, her long-distance semi-boyfriend, made this announcement while they were hanging out with a mutual friend, Trevor.

"I was bored here anyway. Where you need to go?" Trevor asked.

"Congo Square." An area in Louis Armstrong Park, just north of the Quarter. They headed out, the boys laughing and kicking rocks they found in the street as Trevor bragged on about girls.

As they neared the park, a crash startled them all, but Marc nearly jumped out of his skin. Trevor let him have it.

"What's wrong with you, looking over your shoulders and squealing like a girl? You smoke too much weed or something? Getting paranoid? They coming to get you?"

"Psh, shut up." But the smile didn't reach Marc's eyes.

Jo had become uneasy as they neared Congo Square. Never a safe place to hang out after dark, something was even more intense since she'd last been there. The few people they passed sized them up with open hostility, then whispered behind their hands. She told herself she'd just been away too long, wasn't used to how things were anymore.

Marc pointed down and told them to stay put, then jogged a few hundred yards away to a group of men hanging on the edge of the square, mostly hidden from the dim lights. Jo peered at them as best she could through the oppressive darkness. Her eyes ran over their clothes as her vision adjusted, and her blood ran cold. These weren't friends. These men were older, in their mid-twenties. They were bangers, and they were pissed.

They watched Marc approach, and when he was a few feet away, one stepped forward. The others fell into place behind him. Raised voices drifted across the humid air to Trevor and Jo; they couldn't make out more than snippets of the conversation, but it wasn't hard to fill in the blanks. Marc had been selling weed for them, and he was short. Very short.

Trevor took a step toward Marc, but Jo grabbed his arm. "He told us to wait."

"They're gonna do something to him. I gotta help."

"How? You know they have guns or at least knives, and there's six of them. What exactly are we gonna do?"

"Not *we*, girl, I said *me*. I can't just stand here."

A stranger approached from the far end of the square, now close enough to see what was happening, and fear choked Jo's throat. He veered over to the group and tried to pull Marc away from them. Two of the men turned toward him, but he wouldn't back down. He took a step toward the leader and yelled, "I'm not afraid of punks like you!"

The leader pulled out a pistol and shot the Samaritan in the head. Then he swung his arm around and shot Marc too.

Jo bolted forward as Marc's body jerked and fell backward, but Trevor restrained her. She tried and failed again, then turned and stared blankly at Trevor's hand gripping her arm. "What you think you gonna do?" he echoed her words back to her. "Come on! We gotta get the fuck out!"

Two of the gang members noticed them staring and started running toward them. She whipped around and almost fell as her leaden feet fought with her. Trevor yanked at her to keep her upright, and after several steps her feet coordinated again. She ran after Trevor without looking back until he stopped, breathless, behind an empty warehouse.

They'd reacted fast enough to get away, but her hesitation cost Trevor his life, regardless.

In that vital moment of flailing delay, the men got a good look at him, and the following week, they killed him in a drive-by. They'd probably seen her clearly, too—she never knew if she was still alive because she wasn't known around town any longer, or because she'd gone back to Oakhurst a few days later. Her network of friends told her the stranger had been a tourist, visiting from Canada. Because of that, the police were pressured to find the killers, and asked anyone who had information to come forward.

Three things still haunted Jo about the events of that day. The first was her discovery that Marc had been selling weed so his family wouldn't be evicted—his father had lost his job, and the dinner she'd eaten at Marc's house that night came from government food-bank groceries. Second was the hypocrisy of an investigation fueled by concern over a tourist, when so many similar killings were abandoned because of manpower and money shortages. But most haunting of all was the knowledge that she'd been helpless to save the boy she loved in that moment, and that she'd been too scared of what would happen to her or her family to go to the police with what she knew.

Neither Marc nor Trevor got justice. And that was because of her cowardice. Her failure.

Frank thrust the front section of the *Times-Picayune* under Jo's nose, breaking her trance. She thanked him and set down the beignet to take the paper from him. Her appetite was gone. She pushed her plate away, leaned back, and spread the paper open.

When she reached page five, her body stiffened.

A woman had been murdered in a large chain hotel, the Sleep-Tight. She'd been strangled, had checked in alone, and her hotel room was nearly untouched. When Jo saw the security camera still that captured the victim and her companion walking into the hotel, she bolted upright.

The man wore a fedora.

CHAPTER TWENTY-EIGHT

"Detective Robinson, this is Josette Fournier, visiting us from the Oakhurst County SPDU in Massachusetts." Lieutenant Benville, a tall, heavy man with dark hair and kind eyes, poured her a cup of coffee while she shook hands with the detective. Jo silently thanked the heavens for southern hospitality or professional courtesy, whichever she was benefiting from. Not every department gave a warm welcome to an out-of-town lieutenant nosing in on a case, and some were downright hostile about it. She dialed up her hometown accent and, after a round of initial civilities, got to the point.

"So, we may have a serial killer on our hands?" Benville asked.

"Unfortunately, I think so. Let me ask you this. Was there a wedding ring missing from the victim's hand?"

Benville and Robinson exchanged glances. "Yes," Benville answered.

"Then I think we do. Same MO, same man in a fedora, same missing wedding ring." She gave a concise overview of the Oakhurst murder. "I'll have my team send over the files to you right now, so you can take a look." She pulled her cell out of her pocket and punched in instructions to have the information sent over.

Benville watched while Robinson passed the current case file over to Jo and summarized what they knew. "Her name is Emily Carson. She lived in Frazer, Tennessee, with her husband, Edward. She was an elementary school teacher here for a three-day workshop, which starts today."

"So, nobody else that she worked with was in town with her?"

"No, ma'am."

"And I'm guessing the husband has an alibi?"

"Not solid, but good enough that it's hard to see how he could have made it here with enough time to kill her. He took the kids out to a movie and they were home about an hour before she was killed."

"Any other leads?"

"None so far, and frankly, we don't have many more balls to throw into the air."

"What's your take on it?" Jo asked.

"I think she was in the wrong place at the wrong time, and things didn't end well. From what you're saying, it sounds like she may have run into the wrong serial killer." Robinson laughed.

Jo fought to keep from wincing. "I think you may be right." This is where she had to tread lightly, make sure all plumage remained in place. She knew what *her* next investigative step would be, but this wasn't her office or her team. Both departments had jurisdiction over their own case, and neither would want to give that up; if they thought she was trying to take over, they'd shut her out. But she couldn't let them roll over her, either.

"From your perspective, what's the best way to handle it from here?" Jo was careful to make eye contact with both Benville and Robinson as she asked.

Benville leaned forward. "I can see why this caught your eye. But I think we need to assess how similar or different they really are, and then we can determine how to proceed. Could be a connection, could be a coincidence."

Jo nodded while watching Benville's blank face—he wasn't sold.

"We need to take a closer look at your case file, and you need to take a closer look at ours. Then we'll know what we're truly looking at here."

"Do you have a desk and a computer I can use to review the files?" Jo reminded herself they hadn't seen the Oakhurst murder yet, that their caution was probably reasonable. In the meantime, this would get her access to their information, and an opening to get their cooperation.

Benville turned to Robinson. "Bring everything to the conference room, we'll set up in there."

Jo looked out the door and asked, "Can you point out the ladies' room on the way?"

Robinson pointed to the left. "Down that hall. The conference room is that black door over there. We'll get started."

*

Jo opened the door to the bathroom and scanned each stall to make sure she was alone. *Too bad I'm not a smoker; then I wouldn't have to have my private conversations next to a toilet.* But since lung cancer probably wasn't worth the added flexibility, this would have to do—at least they kept their bathroom relatively clean. She pulled out her phone and dialed.

Arnett picked up on the third ring. "Aren't you on vacation? Why are we sending the Hammond file to NOPD?"

Jo gave him a quick run-down of the relevant details. Arnett swore.

"I'm trying to convince them that the killings are related. In the meantime, I need you to run whatever searches you can for other stranglings that look like this one in, say, the past five years. Stranglings in hotel rooms, married women, no sexual assault, no burglary. Across all fifty states."

"Want me to search for some black pearls in the ocean while I'm at it?" Arnett replied.

"Funny. I know what I'm asking. But if this is a serial, he's most likely killed before, and if we can find another murder, it'll be easier to convince them there's a connection. So I need you to do it as fast as possible."

"Look, I'm happy to do it, it makes sense regardless. I have a big smile on my face, I'm so happy. What I don't understand is why you care so much about their cooperation. We can investigate just the same without them."

Jo laughed. "Your political savvy is impressive as always, Bob. Yes, it matters. Especially if we want help from the Behavioral Analysis Unit."

Jo heard a noise on the other end that sounded suspiciously like a palm hitting a forehead.

"Oh, boy, the feds. Happy Monday to me."

Jo laughed. "You'll get over it." She hit "end," ignoring the growl that came from the phone.

*

Jo made her way back to the conference room. Robinson pulled three chairs up to a table in the front of the room, next to a large aging whiteboard on the side of the wall. Three files and a laptop waited in the middle of the table where Benville was working his way through his own stack of files.

"I printed out copies of the information your guys sent over, easier to compare that way. I have our files pulled up on the laptop, and what we have on paper is there." He nodded at the table and poured two new cups of coffee.

Jo smiled her thanks for the coffee and sat across from Benville. She pulled the Carson file over and quickly paged through it to get an overview, then began again, perusing the information thoroughly, jotting down notes as she worked. Robinson settled in with the remaining Hammond file. They worked in silence, except when one needed something from another file.

The more she read, the more convinced she became; except for a few small details, you could take out Emily Carson's name from this file and put in Jeanine Hammond's. In both cases, the ladies checked into their hotel the day of their murder and were expected at a work gathering the next day. Both rooms were largely untouched—the ladies hadn't unpacked or used anything other than the bathroom. Both ladies left shortly after their initial check-in, according to the security camera in the front of the lobby. Then, later that night, both had returned with a man in a dark overcoat and a fedora, a man they seemed to be friendly with, giving no signs of duress. The ligature marks on their necks were nearly identical, same with the bruise patterns. Both victims were found close to their beds, which were largely undisturbed. The medical examiner report showed no sexual assault of any sort. The interviews weren't finished in the Carson case, and they didn't have full phone or credit card records back, but they knew from her phone that Emily, just like Jeanine, had only made one phone call that day, back to her husband at home.

Something kept pulling her back to the picture of Emily lying on the hotel carpet. Once she finished her read-through, she returned to it, and stared, her fingers clutched around her necklace. She'd had the same sense of unease when looking at Jeanine Hammond's body at the crime scene, and she couldn't shake it. She pulled over Jeanine's pictures and compared the bird's-eye angle to Emily's. The positions weren't the same, but her initial disappointment was immediately replaced by excitement. In both cases their arms were askew, in a way that looked like—what? She couldn't put her finger on it, but there was an odd dynamism, something that made them look like they'd been freeze-framed in the middle of some action.

She flipped her pen back and forth as she waited for the two men to complete their appraisal. Jeanine's file had more documentation than Emily's, and they weren't hurrying. She needed to get up, to move, *something*. "Is there a vending machine nearby?"

Robinson gave her directions. She took her time grabbing a bag of trail mix and the potato chips Robinson had requested, and as she started back to the conference room, her phone rang. "Fournier."

"I may have found something." Arnett sounded as surprised as Jo felt.

"Give me the quick version." Her heart pounded.

"Another girl strangled, similar circumstances. Aleta Rivera, in Salt Lake City, Utah. She was from Trenton, New Jersey. In Utah for a yearly conference her company held. Strangled the night she checked in, no sexual assault. Wedding ring was missing, that's how I found it."

"Can you get the file sent over from Salt Lake?"

"I'm on it."

"You, my friend, are a rock star."

"Don't I know it."

Jo laughed and disconnected.

Three cases. There had to be something here.

CHAPTER TWENTY-NINE

Martin was exhausted by the time he arrived home the next day. Not so much from the long drive, but rather from the endless second-guessing. Try as he might, his mind refused to settle. He headed directly for the kitchen and made himself a cup of tea; Irish breakfast, with plenty of kick.

He unpacked as the caffeine eased into his system, then began his cleanup. He scrupulously ticked off every step, then went over it all a second time. Finally, when his *WoW* changes were confirmed, he sat back in his chair and felt himself mentally release.

He set up another cup of tea, this one chamomile so he wouldn't be up all night, and considered his options as he watched the red kettle heat on the black stove. It was early for bed still. He could get some coding done. No, he was too tired to jump into that. Watch some TV? No, that didn't appeal, and he'd probably just fall asleep while watching, which would throw everything off. He wanted his reward, and truth be told, he was anxious to be sure all was well. The kettle whistled, and he poured his cup. He'd go to bed early and read for a while, then linger over the evening's pleasures.

He made a detour into his office and pulled open the drawer that held the rings. He picked up Emily's. Hers was the prettiest of the six, with an intricate antique filigree pattern that formed the band. He slipped it onto the tip of his finger and closed his eyes, let the feel of the soft weight take over his senses. This ring was her essence in his hand, and her soul surrounded his finger. He channeled her, pushed himself into the life he'd taken. He felt a familiar stirring. He removed the ring and carried it into the bedroom.

He pulled his Kindle out of the nightstand and pressed the power button. Nothing—the battery was dead. He plugged it in to charge and sighed. It would take at least ten minutes to resurrect. He might as well have a first go while he waited.

Excitement flitted through him, tinged with a thread of anxiety. He lay down in the bed, a single sheet pulled up to his chest. He replaced the ring on the tip of his finger and closed his eyes.

He called up the myriad images, sensations, and thoughts he'd cataloged while killing Emily. The woodsy smell of her hair when he was behind her, poised to take her life. The warmth of her skin, flushed with excitement under his lips. The electric surge of power knowing he would decide precisely when that warmth ceased. The press of her body, soft and compliant, pushing back against him.

He moved to the moment he began the kill, felt the synthetic surface of the tie rub into his hand with the vicious twist. Let his mind sink into the memory of her muscles pulling tight, reacting to that first pain. Heard again the faint rasping noises she made, heard them speed, then fade as she ran out of breath. He let the flood of omnipotence wash over him.

Yes. I am the one who decides. And I decided this one would die.

He stroked his erection as he savored the subtle shift of life draining out of her—the slackening muscles and the shift of her weight to his arms as lack of oxygen shut down her brain. Blood pounded through him as he zoomed in on the pull of that body draped against him, remembered the limbs flapping when he bounced the little rag doll in his arms. The rush of pleasure and absolute power enveloped him, grew and expanded to fill every corner of his mind, tugged at every nerve until his orgasm pulsed through his body.

He lay against his pillow for a long, relieved moment, catching his breath. What was he worried about? All that fuss over nothing.

He laughed. That's what happens when you start anticipating problems you aren't sure exist.

He rolled out of bed to clean himself up and to make another cup of tea. He brought it back to his nightstand and pulled over the Kindle, now charged enough for use. He'd read for a while, give his body a chance to recover, and then revisit the *events* again. His normal routine was to continue on through the night, three or four times the first night after a kill, sometimes more. Then the frequency would taper off until the memories didn't feel as real anymore. The peace would remain for a short while longer after that, and he'd cherish every moment of it until the hunger returned.

He swiped through his books and decided a noir classic would complement the rain pounding on his window. He propped himself up in bed, sipped his tea, and enjoyed the book. A pleasant evening, indeed.

Around eleven, he put the book aside and settled the ring on his finger again. He closed his eyes and called up the memories, initiated the flood of sensations through his mind.

But this time, his body would not respond.

CHAPTER THIRTY

Jo returned to the conference room to find Benville and Robinson gathering up papers into the files. Neither met her eye; they must have taken advantage of her absence to discuss their thoughts on the case. Perhaps they'd been waiting for her to go.

Jo handed Robinson the potato chips.

"I just got a call from the detective on the Hammond case. He found another murder he believes is related." She gave them the brief details about Aleta Rivera.

Benville listened. "Do you know her physical description?"

"She was Latina. Black hair, brown eyes. Forty-five years old. Five foot two, I believe."

"And her job?"

"Sales rep for a direct marketing company called Stampin' Up! Apparently, it's like Tupperware, but with craft supplies. Home parties, like that."

Benville exchanged a look with Robinson and cleared his throat. "I understand why our case caught your eye. There are similarities between the murders and it's never easy to watch something like this go into cold storage. But I have to be honest with you—I'm not convinced we're looking at a serial."

Jo's heart sank. She glanced from one man to the other. Robinson was staring down into the bag, searching for the perfect potato chip. "Let's talk it through. What's your thinking?"

Benville's face relaxed, and he sat back in his chair. "Now, admittedly, we don't have all of our information back yet, and we don't know much about the Rivera murder. But unless something else comes back, as far as I can tell, they aren't as similar as you seem to think. The commonalities are such almost any case might share 'em. I could pull up several women strangled in hotel rooms in Lou'siana alone this year, let alone across the country. And the women are all different. Different types of jobs, different body types, different ages, different hair color. Even dressed in different styles. Serials don't just wander the earth and kill randomly, there's some connection between the victims, some sort of a type."

"The women were all away on business trips, that's a connection."

The corner of Benville's mouth pulled to the side. "More of a circumstance than a connection. Lots of bad things happen to women traveling alone. No cohesive underlying factor there."

"What do you make of the fedora?"

"You see fedoras all over New Orleans, especially on musicians. They've been very popular here for, oh, quite a few years now, there's a word for it. Even women wear 'em. I don't think we can draw any conclusions from that."

"Hipsters," Robinson chimed.

"And look here. The coat's different. Same type, same color, but this one has black buttons and this one has gold." He pointed at the two pictures on the table.

Jo leaned forward. Shit, how had she missed that? "Maybe he has more than one coat."

Benville remained silent.

"What about the similarities in body position?" Jo pushed forward the two photographs.

The men exchanged a glance, and Benville responded. "They're completely different. The hips turned on Carson, not on Hammond... I think you're reaching."

"And the wedding ring?"

"Pretty common around here to have missing jewelry when people are victims of violent crimes." He smiled and drew out the syllables in "violent."

"Sure. But it's usually not the only thing that's been taken."

"We're not sure yet it *was* the only thing taken."

Jo started to object, but Benville held up his hand. "But let's say it was. I'm still not sure I'd find that convincing. Maybe this was a burglary gone wrong, interrupted before he finished. *Ve-ry* common."

"And the ligature marks? They're so similar."

"They are. It might be worth doing an analysis on that. But from what I see, not close enough to rule out different killers."

Jo inhaled and forced down her frustration, then shook her head. "Any one similarity in a case can be explained away. But when you start getting two, three, more, isn't that time to sit up and pay attention?"

"Of course. But that's where I think you're jumping the gun. There are plenty of differences here too, important ones, like the buttons, and the issue of physical type. And diverse location, diverse occupations. There's nothing to connect these women in any way, and that's big trouble for your theory."

Jo knew they were arguing in circles now, but couldn't stop herself. "How so?"

Benville leaned forward in his seat and spread his hands out. "Look. I'm not saying that we don't have a serial here. I'm saying I'm not convinced that we do. Those are two different things."

Jo remembered herself and nodded. "I do understand your point. I'm just not sure they're two different things from my point of view."

"Sure they are, and here's why. What I'm telling you is, a big factor in my decision-making process is my lack of resources. I know you know how that is, but I promise you haven't seen what we're fighting here. We have more murders than we can handle, by a factor of ten at least. If I had unlimited manpower, sure, I'd send a fleet of detectives off to investigate your theory. But I don't have manpower to devote to pie in the sky, and that's what this adds up to right now. Doesn't mean my mind is shut to your interests. I'm happy to support you if you want to investigate with your own team. We'll give you access to all our information and will be happy to let your men come talk to whoever they want in New Orleans, investigate however they want. And if you get something more, we surely want to hear about it."

Jo's eyes skimmed the files. That was something, but it wasn't enough. "Would you support a Behavioral Analysis Unit request from the FBI?"

Benville shrugged. "My position on that is the same. I would be open to assisting the FBI, and I won't stand in your way of putting in a request for a BAU. But if they ask me what my honest opinion is, I'll have to tell them I'm not yet convinced. I won't put my department's neck out for it."

Jo put her hometown smile back on. "That's fair enough, I suppose. But can I ask you one more favor? Will you take a look at the Rivera file when we get it, see what you think?"

Benville looked at Robinson, who nodded. "In my opinion, I'd bet you could find twenty, thirty cases nationwide that look just like this but aren't related. Send it over and Robinson will look at it, maybe something will jump out. But unless it does, nothing changes."

Jo nodded and stood up. She extended her hand first to Benville, then to Robinson. "I appreciate your time, and the access to your information. I do know well what it's like to run an effective department with limited funds. I can't blame you for trying to make sure you're making best use of what you've got."

Benville nodded. "Those difficult choices are the hardest part, aren't they?"

"That they are." Jo picked up the case files and took her leave, thinking no, they were not. The hardest part were the cases you failed at, and the ghosts of the victims you couldn't help, who came to you at night when you were trying to sleep.

*

The FBI was no better.

Through local contacts Jo managed to get an appointment the same afternoon with Agent Forest Lancaster. He listened with polite but strained attention until she finished, his effort to ignore the barrage of alerts from his phone palpable.

"My office is swamped, Lieutenant, and I don't see enough of a link here to justify the use of our resources." His voice was dismissive and tired, a combination Jo recognized well. He continued, and her frustration reared as Lancaster made many of the same points that Benville had made, starting with the buttons. The methods were similar, but not distinctive enough to stand out from other killings of the same type. There was nothing linking the women, but serial killers chose for a reason. When Jo objected that three cases surely must be cause for concern, Lancaster surprised her.

"In fact, the Rivera case makes me even more skeptical because of the additional variation it adds. She's different in almost every physical way possible: short, dark, different race. And she worked from home rather than a place of business. Did she even have business attire with her?"

"I'm not sure yet."

"From the outfit at the crime scene, she looks like an empty-nester on a road trip looking to make girlfriends that share her hobby. That's a pretty different type than the two ambitious career women. I'm not sure it makes sense to try to put a profile together, regardless."

Jo's head spun as she left the office. Was she simply seeing what she wanted to see, grasping for any potential lead on a case that otherwise had none? Was her judgment so clouded by her desire to catch Hammond's killer that she was seizing on vague similarities while ignoring large, inconvenient differences? Was she so desperate to be involved in casework again that she'd lost her perspective? Lancaster, Benville, Robinson, they were intelligent, well-meaning men, even if they were overworked and possibly jaded. Agent Lancaster hadn't taken a single note. But, she forced herself to admit, he remembered every detail precisely. These were seasoned professionals who knew what they were doing.

But she wasn't a slouch, either. She was sharp, and her instincts had never yet let her down. Those instincts were telling her there was a connection between these cases. When she looked at the stills from the Carson case, she felt the same dark presence she felt with the Hammond case. Like the same man was watching from a shadowed corner, waiting.

At the end of the day, they were partially right. There was no obvious connection between these women, other than they were traveling alone and were married. Just like thousands of other women who were killed every year. If she were right, if the killings were the work of the same man, there had to be some underlying connection. Some logic to who he chose, when, and where. But if it was there, she was going to have to find it without their help.

She pulled out her phone and told Arnett to set up for a task force of three, immediately.

CHAPTER THIRTY-ONE

Jo drove straight from Hartford Airport to SPDU headquarters. She'd smoothed things over as best she could with her father by taking him out for his favorite dinner, and gave him an overview of the case as they worked their way through a mountain of fried oysters and crawfish. Frank asked questions here and there—they'd always been able to connect best when discussing her job—then, with a wrinkled brow and a lingering air of resentment, told her, "If you're right, you better make sure you get the monster."

Jo's resolve steeled as she approached the redbrick building, so much that for once she didn't shake her head at the contradictory gigantic schoolhouse-esque facade and the industrial-factory back. She swept past the back holding cells and through the general office space, waving absently to the detectives working at their desks. She whipped into one of the small conference rooms ringing the common area and slid her attaché onto the black laminate table carpeted with laptop computers and stacks of manila folders. "Right then, let's get ourselves up to speed."

Lopez looked up from her phone, and Arnett from the file he was reading. "Your father still talking to you?"

Jo grimaced and opened the attaché. "He'll get over it. If not in this lifetime, the next."

Arnett laughed. "And ADA Rockney?"

Jo straightened. She met first Arnett's eyes, then Lopez's. "Is of the opinion that if neither NOPD nor the FBI think this is worth their time, we shouldn't either. So, to put it kindly, I don't have official permission to reopen the case. If either of you have an objection to that, I'll let you off the case with no hard feelings."

"You couldn't pry me off this case with a crowbar," Lopez said, her smile mischievous.

"What she said." Arnett grinned.

Jo dipped her chin in thanks. "Then let's do this."

"What do we have on Carson?" Arnett asked.

"A nearly identical batch of nothing. No leads from the other attendees at her workshop. Nobody missing, most of them hadn't even arrived in New Orleans yet when she was murdered, and the ones that did had a solid alibi. Nobody admits to having known her, and there were no fedoras or overcoats in anyone's luggage. They're checking into any possible connections, and the officers in her hometown are checking out the alibis for everyone close to Emily. Benville said he'd send them over as he got them finished, have any come in?" Jo asked.

"Yeah. Best I can make out, she was the sort of woman that strangers forget about in minutes, or you remember her because she annoyed the shit out of you. And, like Jeanine, everyone they've talked to laughed the idea of an affair out of the park. Worse, her husband barely remembered the details of why she'd gone away, just that it was a 'work thing,'" Arnett answered.

Lopez rolled her eyes above the files she was scouring. "*Such* a devoted husband, I can't imagine *why* she'd look elsewhere."

Arnett flipped the page of notes in front of him. "Nobody could say very much about her life except in broad strokes. A life where everybody looks right through you can eat away at your soul. Ring a bell?"

Jo nodded and popped open her briefcase.

Arnett continued. "One issue, though. Couple months ago, some parent filed a complaint against Carson, and Carson claimed the parent had threatened her." He glanced at the notes. "A Mrs. Nancy Morgen. They're trying to interview her as we speak."

Jo's eyebrows rose. "Stranger things have happened."

"True." Arnett pointed toward the laptop in front of him. "I'm still searching for similar homicides, going back as best I can for the last ten years."

Jo turned to Lopez. "How about Jeanine's devices?" She'd instructed her to get back everything Roger Hammond still had in the way of electronics, and scour every program Jeanine had, as well as everyone she'd been in touch with, no matter how insignificant the reason. She'd asked Benville to do the same thing with Emily Carson's devices in the hopes they'd hit some significant overlap.

"We have the computer. Roger kept it for backup, so it's mostly intact. Her phone is gone, but he still had her Kindle HD. I'm still putting the lists together. It'll take time because I have to squeeze it in around my caseload, but I'll work through the night."

Jo scanned her face. "If you need to go home to be with your mother, I understand."

Lopez pushed her hair behind her left ear, eyes still down. "It'll be fine. She's doing much better, and she gets annoyed if I hover too much anyway. Besides"—she looked up with a wry smile—"my mother's a badass bitch. She'd kick my ass if we didn't catch this guy."

Jo recognized the pain in her eyes. She gave her a kind smile and nodded. "What about Aleta's devices?"

"There's not much left, unfortunately. Her husband sold the house a few months after the funeral because he couldn't stand being there without her. He gave her laptop and her iPod to the youngest daughter, who's a sophomore at Princeton, but both have been wiped. I'll go over them as soon as they arrive to see if I can recover anything, but the daughter knows computers and wanted to maximize space for other applications. The phone is long gone, same with the paper records, so we're trying to recover what we can from the carrier."

Jo's fingers fiddled with her necklace as she glanced between them both. "How are you all feeling about the three cases? Am I reaching?"

"Nothing concrete yet to connect them, but no, I don't think so. When I look at the other cases, I get déjà vu all over again. Too many similarities," Arnett answered.

Lopez flicked her pen up and between her knuckles. "I agree, there's too much to ignore. I think it's worth a shot to assume they're related and see where that takes us. I ran the pictures over to Janet on the way here. She agrees, the way those bodies fell is odd. Not impossible, but *highly improbable*." She air-quoted the words. "I'll feel better once I get the run-down from her computer. There has to be something there."

Jo gave a brisk nod. "Then I think our next step is to sort through what we know about the cases while we wait, see if we can come up with some sort of basic profile on the guy who did this, and how he found these women."

*

While Arnett made a fresh pot of coffee and Lopez ordered dinner delivery, Jo shifted her laptop and stack of files over to the nearest whiteboard. On the flight home she'd compiled the similarities between the cases, and she copied her list onto the board. "Let's start with a timeline. All the women checked into their hotels in the late afternoon to early evening. They all left their rooms again within an hour after arrival, two of them in less than half an hour." She noted the times on the board as she spoke. "They returned within half an hour of midnight with a man in a fedora and an overcoat, then the man left between fifteen and twenty minutes later. Death occurred while he was in the rooms. What else?"

Lopez responded instantly. "For Hammond, the ME estimated that she had dinner around 8:00 p.m., based on stomach contents.

Same approximate time for Rivera, and we're waiting for the ME's report on Carson."

"Excellent." Jo wrote "Similarities" across the top of a second board. "We need to consider every similarity, however small, if we're gonna figure out what connects these three women. All of the basic details are the same, same cause of death, et cetera." She wrote the details on the board. "Which reminds me, we need to have the techs compare the ligature marks as best they can, see if they were made by the same person," Jo said.

Lopez's pen shot up. "I'll request it."

"What else?"

Lopez pulled her legs up under her. "All murdered in hotel rooms. Is that coincidental to them being from out of town, or is there another reason?"

Arnett rubbed his shadowed chin. "He could have killed them in an alley somewhere, or taken them to his house, especially since he didn't have sex with them. Hotel security is risky, why bother?"

Lopez leaned forward. "Maybe that's how he got them alone. Most women these days wouldn't go off to a place they didn't know with a stranger; they'd feel far safer in their own hotel room."

"Good point," Jo said, scribbling furiously.

"They all had alcohol in their system," Arnett said.

"Yet"—Lopez grabbed a sheet and waved it—"none of them had credit card charges for anything they ate or drank that night. They either paid cash or someone else paid for them."

Jo consulted her notes again. "They were all dressed up like they were going out. Nice dresses, makeup, hair done. So, they either met the killer on the town or had an appointment with him to start."

"All killed their first night in town, strange coincidence if he didn't know them beforehand," Arnett said.

Jo's eyebrows lifted. "I'll be damned. You're right. Any alternative explanations for that?"

Lopez bounced her pen against the table. "Maybe he staked out the hotels looking for new arrivals traveling alone, to grab them asap? Easy to do surreptitiously if you work for the hotel."

"Didn't we interview everyone working that night?" Jo asked, flipping through the file.

"He didn't have to be working that night. And he didn't have to have contact with the victims. He could work behind the scenes, but with access to the records. Maybe not even on-site," Lopez answered.

"Good, check into that. Maybe he gets jobs at different hotels, finds the women that way. Check shuttles from the airport, too, plenty of time to chat women up when you're a driver." She nodded to Lopez.

"On it. But that raises a question. Does this wipe our current suspects off our list? Philip Begemack, Jon Renke?"

"I was thinking about this on the flight. I think it gives us a different set of questions we need to ask. When we were looking into Begemack, didn't we find out he travels for work often? We need to dig deep, find out where they've been and when, cross-check not just the flight manifests our victims were on, but other flights in and out around the same time. Look for other names they might be using, all of it."

The edges of Lopez's mouth curled up into a wicked smile, and her eyes narrowed slightly. "I've got some fun little behavioral engineering tricks up my sleeve I can pull out."

Jo shook her head. "You scare me, in the best possible way. Okay, this is what we have to work with for now, then. Several of these are clearly related." She studied the boards and drew arrows from some points to others, reorganizing and erasing as she went.

Traveling alone
Murdered in hotel
Large, well-known hotel
Killed same night as check-in

Dressed up
Significant alcohol in system
No credit card charges

Same timeline for evening
Same approx time of death
Strangled, no sexual violation

Married
Missing wedding ring

"Our assumption is, if something happened in all three killings, there's a reason, and that reason will lead to the killer. Start here." Jo circled the first group with her finger. "All three women were traveling away from home. Makes sense if he works for a hotel, but let's assume he doesn't. Is there any other reason for this MO?"

"Because they're out having a good time, getting trashed, maybe they're an easy opportunity?" Lopez said.

Arnett shook his head. "Women do that in their hometowns too."

"But they're more vulnerable away from home when they don't know anybody, or their way around," Lopez shot back.

"Let's say he goes to places tourists go. Asks questions until he finds someone." Jo pointed to the second grouping. "Not many people pay cash these days, especially when traveling, especially women. Someone else paid for them."

"Maybe they're at a bar. Plenty of creepers look to buy you a drink and chat you up. So, they go to dinner, she drinks enough alcohol to impair her judgment, and they end up back at her hotel room," Lopez said.

"How does the timing end up so similar?" Arnett jutted his chin at the timeline. "They end up dead at the hotels within a few minutes of one another."

"Like he'd turn into a pumpkin if he wasn't outta there by 12:30 a.m." Lopez's eyes narrowed.

"That suggests it was planned out beforehand. Just stumbling on someone at dinnertime feels too risky," Arnett said.

Jo's free hand flew to her necklace. "Okay, follow it through. Maybe they'd met before and this trip was some sort of rendezvous. The women were married, they had to be discreet. A work trip away from their husband's watchful eyes could be an opportunity."

"Then we're talking about a long con. That has to leave some trace," Arnett said.

"Especially since they're all from different places, and were murdered in still *different* places," Lopez said.

Arnett sat up in his chair. "Maybe some sort of vendor or consultant, who has to travel to different sites?"

"Or maybe he met them on the plane?" Lopez said, then shook her head. "Can a man talk a married woman into cheating on her husband in a few hours?"

"Depends on the woman," Arnett said, face blank. "And how many cocktails they'd had."

"Ha!" Lopez laughed, missing the expression on Arnett's face. "Maybe our killer flies a lot for business. I'll compare the list of passengers on each flight, at least Hammond's and Carson's. Not sure I can still get it for Rivera's."

Jo tapped the marker against her leg. "We need to dig deeper into the possibility of a lover, find out as much as we can about these women. Where they grew up, went to college. Any clubs they belonged to, now or in the past. Previous boyfriends—maybe they dated the same guy, and he never got over being dumped."

"I'm already cross-checking all phone numbers and e-mails in their address books, their social media, text, IM, Skype," Lopez said.

"Be sure to check everything, not just personal and business contacts, but companies they did business with. Places they liked to shop. Maybe they all loved shoes and he's a shoe vendor that supplies stores they went to. There has to be something to connect them to him, and each other, and if we do it right, it'll pop out."

Jo's eyes moved over to the last cluster. "So why only married women? The missing wedding rings suggest that has important psychological significance for him."

"Is it possible it's just a trophy? Maybe it doesn't matter it's a wedding ring, per se? Just an easy thing to grab?" Lopez asked.

"The file says he had to force the ring off in Emily's case. Apparently, there's bruising." Jo flipped through the file and held up the photo, then tossed it back down on the table. "Dammit, this is why we need an experienced profiler."

Arnett spoke. "But if he knew them, why go through the charade of date night at all? Why not just meet at the hotel?"

"Maybe they didn't know him very well. Like, if they'd only met once before, the visiting-shoe-rep thing," Lopez said. "But what's bugging me most of all is, why no sexual violation? Sure, not all serials do that. But with the date, the way they walked in together, they were all over each other. Wouldn't sex be a part of that?"

"That's a sticking point for me, too. I'll do some research and see what I can find out about serials that don't assault sexually." Jo turned back to the board. "But this has given us some strong leads to pursue. Any other ideas?"

Lopez spoke. "Personality profiles of each? The key similarity must be there, since they were different physically."

Jo nodded and wrote it down, along with *hobbies, activities, likes/dislikes, NO DETAIL TOO SMALL.* "I think each of us should take a stab at it, see what we come up with. The more ideas the better."

"Son of a bitch," Arnett said, staring at pictures from the files in front of him. "You have to be kidding me."

"What?" Jo stepped over to him.

"Remember I told you Laura wanted to find a way to reconnect when she moved back in? We've been taking ballroom dancing classes." He pointed to Jeanine Hammond. "The women are dancing. The arms and head like this? This is a waltz, I know because we started off with that. We just started the samba a few weeks ago, and I'll be damned if I can figure out how to do a roll." He tapped Emily's picture, then moved to Aleta Rivera, whose left leg was kicked back, and whose arms were down by her hips, wrists bent and palms flat. "I'm not sure, but I'd bet dollars to doughnuts this is a jive."

Lopez was already searching furiously on her laptop. They watched videos of each dance in turn, as Arnett pointed to the relevant moves. "Holy shit, you're right." Lopez's hand shot up for a round of high fives.

"So, our guy's a dancer." Jo wrote it on the board, flushing with adrenaline. "Bob, we need to have the local PDs send out officers to canvas any dancing establishments near the crime scenes. Chris, when you do your searches, pay close attention to anything remotely connected with dancing."

"Will do," Lopez said, and Arnett nodded.

"One last issue. I know you have to fit this in where you can. But nine months elapsed between Aleta and Jeanine. Five between Jeanine and Emily." Jo paused to let the realization set in.

Arnett's face turned grim. "Less time between kills."

"If we're lucky, we have a few months before his next kill. And if we're unlucky, there are other kills in between we don't know about yet, and we're talking weeks instead of months. Maybe even days. He could be setting up the next kill as we speak. We need to move, *now*."

PART III

Diana Montauk

April–June 2013

CHAPTER THIRTY-TWO

Martin logged onto *WoW* with his rogue, name changed to Otthello. He threw up his bark and settled in. He'd come up with a theory and a plan, but he was still anxious.

[2. Trade][Otthello]: Chastity belt getting you down? I have an app for that. Otthello's Lockpicking: making love possible since the days of vanilla. Tips happily accepted.

He picked some locks. He got some hits from women, including a couple he normally would have responded to, but who didn't constitute viable options any longer.

He'd analyzed it all with trademark precision. Risking all his hard work by escalating into dangerous behaviors was simply not acceptable. He had worked so hard to perfect it all, had it down to a science. But he'd isolated the problem and couldn't get away from it—the sad, average women he'd been baiting before now felt like shooting fish in a barrel. He needed something more. A big prize, like the old legendary bass that stymied all the fishermen on the lake. Which only meant a different type of *fish*, not a different type of *fishing*. That shouldn't add to the danger of getting caught, would keep his methods the same. All the reward, none of the risk.

But a smart, challenging woman was hard to find. He had one prospect, real name Janni, player name Rimetra, who wasn't in-game tonight. She was bright, and didn't fall over herself to respond to his attention—that gave him hoops to jump through and was a clear improvement over Emily's banality. But, still not quite the sharp challenge he needed, either—when he thought about her, he felt like he did after killing Emily. A little more exciting, true, but still like it was coming a bit too easily.

He jumped down off the roof and sorted his bank slots. He completed the fishing daily. He ran around Orgrimmar gathering what he needed to finish the cooking daily. Still nothing, and he was getting bored.

He yawned and looked over at the clock. 2 a.m. Late, even by *WoW* standards. He considered going to bed, and decided to see if stretching his legs helped.

He went to the bathroom for a bio break, then boiled water for tea. The motion woke him somewhat, and he decided to give it one last try before heading to bed. He grabbed a bag of chamomile for his hot water and headed back into his office, then hit his macro one more time.

Thirty seconds went by with nothing. Just as he reached over to log off, a response popped up:

[Serylda] whispers: Clever. It's rare to find someone that crosses Shakespearean sensibilities and pop culture memes with such jaunty witticism.

He felt a tingle at the back of his neck and leaned into the computer. Oh, yes. This—this truly had potential. Intelligent without a doubt—that alone would create more of a challenge. And she was hinting she'd be up for conversation with someone who was a cut above. She was proud of her own intelligence and had a weak spot for men who shared it. That's how he'd get her.

To [Serylda]: And rare to find someone with enough intelligence to appreciate it.

[Serylda] whispers: Do tell—which of us did you just compliment?

Martin's eyebrows shot up. This one wasn't a pistol, she was an assault rifle. He sent up a prayer, to whom he wasn't sure. *Please let her be female, and please let her be married.* He added her to his friends list.

To [Serylda]: You caught that, did you?
[Serylda] whispers: I did, yes. I pride myself on having at least half a brain.
To [Serylda]: An important quality for a woman. And in this game, second only to not having a penis.
[Serylda] whispers: Yes, I imagine that can be quite a hazard in Azeroth.

Shit. She hadn't denied his assumption that she was a woman, but she hadn't confirmed it, either. Should he push the issue? Or just talk around it? There was a feminine feel to her words, but that was often misleading in a game populated by role-players. He paused for a moment to think.

No, he decided. It wasn't likely that a man would leave the error uncorrected, so it wasn't worth the risk of pushing the issue right now. This one wouldn't like strong-arming. He could make a joke about it later to get confirmation, if things kept going well.

To [Serylda]: What are you up to this late at night? Grinding?
[Serylda] whispers: I've been leveling my Warlock, and came into town to level up the cooking on my main. Heading to bed when I finish.
To [Serylda]: Early morning tomorrow?

[Serylda] whispers: I work from home, I can come and go as I please, for the most part. But yes, I have a lot of work coming in tomorrow.

To [Serylda]: What do you do, if I might ask?

[Serylda] whispers: I'm a grant-funding specialist for a non-profit medical facility. You?

To [Serylda]: I'm a software engineer.

[Serylda] whispers: What sorts of programs do you design?

To [Serylda]: My main account is a system designed to facilitate and track data collection for a research and development company.

[Serylda] whispers: What do they research?

To [Serylda]: The division I'm working with tests toys.

[Serylda] whispers: Oh, interesting. What age range?

What is this, the Spanish Inquisition? He was the one that asked the questions.

To [Serylda]: Hold on a sec, a guildie needs help. Brb.

[Serylda] whispers: K.

He flew up and out to Durotar, toward the orc starting area, in case she was watching him or looked up his location. He flew around the desolate fields and killed some beasts to pass a few minutes.

To [Serylda]: Back now. Sorry about that.

[Serylda] whispers: No problem. I think I've done enough cooking for tonight, I'm going to head to bed. Nice talking to you.

Shit. Had he overplayed it?

To [Serylda]: Can't you stay on a little longer? I'm enjoying our conversation.
[Serylda] whispers: Afraid not. I have to at least pretend to be a responsible adult. :)

A smiley face. Okay, probably not too angry, in that case.

To [Serylda]: Sadly, very true. Will you be on tomorrow?
[Serylda] whispers: I'm not sure, depends on how my work goes. Anyway, I'm off. Enjoy your night.
To [Serylda]: Sleep well.
Serylda has gone offline.

Martin stood and paced around the room.
Well, well, well. That was interesting.

He stopped moving and closed his eyes. His mind flitted over her comments, turned them into witty banter over a dinner with her in a strange city. He imagined how it would feel to take that intelligence she was so proud of and bend it to his will, imagined her efforts to entertain and intrigue him, pictured her eyes as she searched his face for approval. The comparison was so clear, he couldn't imagine why he hadn't realized it long ago—so much more exciting to break someone of substance, a true victory, unlike some silly puppy sniffing after him. Oh yes, it would be much more work—he was under no illusions about that—but, oh, the reward.

He felt his body respond.

CHAPTER THIRTY-THREE

Diana Montauk logged Serylda off and quickly logged on as Dauphyne, her mage. She added Otthello to Dauphyne's friends list and checked to see where he was. He showed up as present in Orgrimmar, and when she looked, he was up on top of the bank, right where he'd been. Just as she picked him out of the crowd, however, she got the alert that he had logged off, and his toon disappeared. She waited a few minutes to see if he came back on, but he didn't.

She logged off and smiled as she replayed their conversation in her head. Witty. Glib. She contemplated the two-ended compliment he'd sent. She might have believed he was saying it with humble irony, except he'd responded with "you caught that, did you?," as if he wasn't used to people being smart enough to keep up with him. He was fond of himself. Arrogant. And almost certainly self-centered.

She grabbed her coffee cup and padded across the parquet floors into the living room. She sank down into the corner of her red leather sofa, pulled her long dark hair into a knot, and tossed a tan chenille throw over her legs. She flipped on the television and surfed several news channels until she found one covering live news rather than a pre-taped segment. Not easy so late at night.

The guildie incident was interesting. Most likely there really was a guild friend that had needed help. This guy didn't know her yet, there was no reason he should prioritize talking to her while he helped his friend. But it had a strange feel to her. Even if the dungeon instance had been Otthello's level, he still should have been able to talk, at least here and there, while he helped his friend. So, she'd waited to see what would happen, had pulled the stacks she needed out of the bank to work on her cooking, and bought a few new recipes as they became available. Kept an eye on the general and trade channels for anyone else that might be worth talking to. She'd nearly written him off and truly had been about to log when he sent his tell.

She drank her coffee. Cleopatra, her sphynx, jumped up onto the blanket. She stroked the cat as it settled in. "Don't worry, it's decaf. I'm hoping to get some sleep tonight, I need it." The cat blinked her response.

She smiled as she remembered his pause when she refused to answer his implied question about her gender. He wanted confirmation she was female and hadn't been sure how to handle her response. Definitely looking to hook up on some level.

The question was, was she interested in him? She had to find a man who had no moral compunction about pursuing an affair with a married woman, a man who would scratch her itch, and, crucially, she needed discretion. Unfortunately, self-centered and arrogant were part and parcel of the type who stepped into other men's territory. But ultimately those negative traits didn't matter—they'd make it that much easier for her to end it when the time came.

She'd have to do a little more digging. And, crucially, determine what his motives were. If he just wanted a little ERP rather than an in-person assignation, or if he wanted a real relationship, she'd have to look elsewhere. But even if he was looking for a fling, he'd damn well need to work harder than his half-hearted effort tonight to make any progress with her. She needed to be pursued.

She yawned. The protective warmth of her covers was calling her. She finished her decaf, jabbed the remote to turn the TV off, then carried Cleopatra into the bedroom.

Yes, Otthello was intriguing, and she had a feeling he'd be fun. She mentally crossed her fingers. *Here's hoping he's into married women.*

CHAPTER THIRTY-FOUR

Martin logged out of *WoW*, then dealt with his erection, right at the desk. He sat after for a moment with his eyes closed, letting the implications settle in. Never once had he been aroused *before* a kill, at the mere thought of a potential kill. *Impressive.* She bruised his ego, made him feel small. Just small enough to inflame his anger and jab at the hunger. Remembering made his face flush and his heart pound.

He cleaned himself in the bathroom, then brought his empty mug into the kitchen. He ran the conversation in his mind repeatedly as the water heated, and, still distracted, he reached for the surface of the kettle rather than the handle when it whistled.

"Dammit!" He wrenched the tap on and thrust the burn under the cold stream. *Clumsy. Stupid. Pull yourself together.*

Easier said than done. The ramifications of the conversation wouldn't leave his head, nor would the possibilities. Serylda was smart, and not instantly charmed by him the way other women were. She had fired questions at him, had thrown him for a loop. She wasn't going to be easily distracted, and if he tried another clumsy parry like the one he used tonight, he'd lose her. He had to step up his usual woman-whisperer ways.

But how amazing it would be to best such a woman. So much better than felling a tree anyone can snap.

He retracted his hand and examined the burn. Nothing serious; it would hurt for a day or two but would be fine, no lasting welt or scar. He pulled several ice cubes from the dispenser, wrapped them in a clean tea towel, and secured it around the burn.

He was going to have to prepare. Have strategies at the ready to deal with any possible snag, starting with a parry to change the subject if she started with too many questions again. And he couldn't afford to slip up; she'd pick up on even the smallest mistake. Maybe he should take notes to track what they talked about and what she responded to? He instantly rejected the idea. Too dangerous to have lying around, too tempting to look at while he talked to her. He'd just stick closer to the truth with her than he normally did, minimize the potential mistakes. Memorize her facts, rehearse them at night, have them at his fingertips. One lazy comment would be fatal.

A game of interpersonal chess. The thought sent a shiver of anticipation through him.

He poured his tea and carried it to the bedroom, then changed into pajama bottoms and pulled the sheet up to mid-chest. He gave himself an experimental stroke, and felt a burst of adrenaline thrill through him when his body responded again.

*

For four days in a row, Martin logged on *WoW* early and stayed on late, growing increasingly restless. Serylda didn't show.

He caught himself going over and over the conversation with her, trying to find something that could have put her off. He told himself to pull it together, to stop making assumptions and panting desperately like a dog in heat.

He'd just met her. There was no reason for her to log on for him yet. And isn't this what he wanted? More of a challenge? Who knew, maybe she had a horrendous influx of work, or something had gone wrong in her personal life. Nothing to worry about yet.

On the fifth day, he had to concede that she might not be coming back anytime soon, or at all. The hunger was creeping in, oppressive and demanding, starting to put him on edge, so he'd have to pursue his other opportunities. He begrudgingly made a date with Janni/Rimetra to help her clear out a backlog of difficult quests. She didn't have the impact on him that Serylda did, but after an evening questing with her, he'd know if she was worth his time.

He sighed and logged on. Janni was waiting for him in Hellfire Peninsula, where she needed the most help. He concentrated on flirting and flattering, leading her over the line into the relationship she couldn't admit she wanted. If it went well, tomorrow he'd ask her to join him on Skype.

He relaxed into the quests, which made things easier. The conversation focused on mobs and spotting materials he could gather, so he didn't have to concentrate quite so hard. They joked. They purposefully picked fights with mobs she'd never be able to kill by herself, and he enjoyed blasting Felguards that had killed him with a single stomp thirty levels ago. He was witty, and she came back with engaging responses, enough so as the evening progressed he felt the draw toward her he was looking for, though only a ghost of what he'd felt for Serylda.

When the group quests were cleared, he suggested they run some dungeon instances to get her some easy experience and loot. Underbog in Zangarmarsh—it was one of his favorite zones in the game, with an ethereal sci-fi feel that soothed him after the arid, monotonous desert landscapes and abrasive mobs in Hellfire. She already had the flightpath to Zangarmarsh, that would save him protecting her the entire way while she ran by foot.

They'd been in the instance for about ten minutes when Serylda logged on.

Adrenaline jolted through him. *Damn it*—of course she'd go and log on after he'd given up and was focusing on someone else. He waited a moment, then whispered to her.

To [Serylda]: Hey you.
[Serylda] whispers: Hey. How are you?
To [Serylda]: I'm good, thanks. How are you doing?
[Serylda] whispers: I'm also good.

She wasn't saying much, but she was being friendly.

To [Serylda]: Haven't seen you on for a while. Busy week?
[Serylda] whispers: Yeah, lots of work. Excellent for my
bank account, not so great for my leveling.
To [Serylda]: LOL. Been there. So you're leveling tonight?
[Serylda] whispers: Yes, at least for a little while. What
about you?
To [Serylda]: I'm running a guildie through an instance
right now, but that shouldn't take long. I'd love to come
quest with you if you'd like company.
[Serylda] whispers: You're so considerate to your guildies.
Yes, that would be nice.
To [Serylda]: Okay, be with you in a few minutes. :)

He shifted back to killing otherworldly marsh monsters, now
with less leisure and more focus. Janni had picked up the flirting,
repeatedly blowing him kisses, and was now holding his hand. He
responded in kind while he did some quick calculations. Janni was
a sure thing, making no bones about being interested in him. She
was exactly the sort of woman he normally looked for—married,
lonely, and now poised to go to that next level with him. He'd have
her booked into a hotel within a month, two at the most. He didn't
even know if Serylda was married, let alone interested. And based
on how often she'd been on this past week, it could take months
to get anywhere near a kill with her. He couldn't stomach the
thought of dumping a sure thing for a long shot.

But his hunger had lurched the moment he saw Serylda's name. An overwhelming desire to break a cocky, high-maintenance bitch filled his every cell. With Serylda, the hunt itself was already more pleasurable than his previous kills had been. He couldn't pass up the chance to reel her in.

The smart thing to do was keep both options open—he'd done it before, toyed with two women at the same time to find out which was more viable. He'd work on Serylda while keeping the door open with Janni until he knew for sure what was what.

Too caught up in his thoughts, he didn't notice an elite monster turn the corner behind Janni, who had been hanging too far back. The elite killed her with a single swipe, and her body crumpled into a pile. Now her ghost would have to run all the way back from the graveyard to reanimate her, and that would take time—it was one of the longest corpse runs in the game. He joked about it, and she laughed, said she'd been trying to pick one of the rare orchids and had been a little too careless. She made her way back, and they started up again, only to have her make the same mistake a few minutes later. And then a third time.

He looked at the time and shifted in his chair.

CHAPTER THIRTY-FIVE

Diana had purposefully kept Serylda out of the game for a few days. If there was something odd going on, her absence would give Otthello something to think about. If he had been legitimately called away, no harm done. Men didn't like women who made things too easy, anyway.

Now, as soon as she logged Serylda on, he claimed to be with a guildie again. *Mmm-hmmm.* She kept tabs on his location while she leveled. Fifteen minutes, then thirty went by, and her impatience mounted. At forty-five minutes, clarity set in. How many men, when given an opportunity to engage with a woman they're interested in, chose to spend forty-five minutes with a guildie? She did another location check; he was still in Underbog. At his level it should have taken him about ten minutes to clear it.

Guildie, my ass. He's gotta be with a woman. So let's see what brand of Lothario he is.

Half an hour later her bags were full, and she considered how much she was willing to put up with. He was appealing and the right type, but there was no shortage of men in this game and she could be talking to someone else if this was just a big waste of her time. She headed to Silvermoon City to empty her bags and to watch the chat channels as she worked on her jewelcrafting. She had an abundance of materials from leveling that she needed to clear out now anyway.

She ran back and forth around the city, smelting and crafting, slowly raising her jewelcrafting skill level. Necklaces, rings, and other armor-enhancing objects filled her pack. She put the ones that would sell up in the auction house, and broke the rest down into materials for enchanting. Then back to the jewelcrafting trainer to learn objects that would raise her skill level, and the cycle started again. She laughed to herself. The people who made these games were masters of psychology, they knew how to use up your time with just enough reward to keep you playing for hours. Often, like this, just puttering around, while whole evenings of your life passed by.

And this evening was certainly passing by. She checked the time on the monitor again and yawned. She hadn't been sleeping well this week, and it was catching up with her.

Now at the two-hour mark, her impatience had morphed into a silent, glowing anger. She checked his location again—still in Underbog. It wouldn't take him this long to finish the instance even if he'd been running it at the *appropriate level*. And if he'd had a kitchen fire or seizure in real life, the system would have logged him off.

This was new to her—men rarely jerked her around. While technically twenty pounds overweight, she carried it in a way men liked, with large breasts and an hourglass figure. She had great legs, and loved showing them off. Her dark hair contrasted with the ivory skin she accented with vampy burgundy lipstick, and when she smiled at men, they fell over themselves to get to her. And while guys couldn't see her at first in-game, her successes with men translated to a confidence even in IM. She never had difficulty attracting and keeping men's attention there, or anywhere.

She chastised herself—that was ego and anger talking. Some bone-headed behavior along the way was inevitable when you were looking for this type of guy, and she'd known right away this one was a handful, packed with arrogance that danced on the border of narcissism. You had to take the good with the bad. And the smart thing was to use it to her advantage.

Almost another hour had gone by when his whisper finally came.

> [Otthello] whispers: Shit, I can't believe how long that took. I'm so sorry.
> To [Otthello]: Wow, nearly three hours to do Underbog. I think you set a new record for most ineffective instance run of all time.
> [Otthello] whispers: I know, it was ridiculous. He was trying to get enough of some flower to buy a sporeling pet. I thought it was going to be one or two quick trips through, but it turned out he needed a huge number of them. I wouldn't have agreed if I had known.

Diana laughed at the "he." If Otthello had been with a man, she'd light her own house on fire.

> To [Otthello]: It sounds like he owes you quite a debt of gratitude. I hope you intend to collect at some point.
> [Otthello] whispers: Oh, I do, believe you me. So, you up for some questing?
> To [Otthello]: No, I don't think so. I'm on to something else now.

There was a pause before he answered her. *Good. Let him stew in it.*

> [Otthello] whispers: I'm so sorry. I really didn't mean for it to take that long.
> To [Otthello]: No problem, these things happen. You have to help your guildies when they need you. And it's not like you owe me anything.

Civility with a side of iceberg. Ball's in your court.

[Otthello] whispers: I know I don't, but I feel bad. I very much wanted to get to know you, and then this happens. I feel like I've somehow managed to be a jerk.

To [Otthello]: Look, it's really not a big deal. I'm sure we'll both be on sometime looking for something to do, and we'll be able to quest then. No harm, no foul.

[Otthello] whispers: Okay, then, what are you up to now? Can we do that together?

To [Otthello]: I'm just working on my jewelcrafting, nothing exciting.

[Otthello] whispers: Lol. I'll come join you. Are you in Dalaran?

To [Otthello]: Nope, Silvermoon.

Another pause.

[Otthello] whispers: Silvermoon! Does anyone actually go to Silvermoon anymore? It's hell and gone from everything!

To [Otthello]: I love Silvermoon, it's a beautiful city. That's one of the reasons Serylda's a blood elf, so I could play the starting zones here.

[Otthello] whispers: Ugh, it's such a pain in the ass to get to. Dalaran's a nice city, too…

To [Otthello]: It is, one of my favorites. But I'm happy here. And there's no reason you have to come here. You can whisper just fine from anywhere.

She could practically hear his brain whizzing and clunking, trying to decide whether he really needed to come all the way to Silvermoon to make it up to her, or if he could find some way out of it.

[Otthello] whispers: Don't be ridiculous. I can't emote at you all the way from here. ;-) OMW.
To [Otthello]: Your choice.

A pause.

[Otthello] whispers: And you're truly not mad?
To [Otthello]: Why would I be? Life happens.
[Otthello] whispers: Okay, if you're not mad, then tell me what your real name is. :-P

She laughed.

To [Otthello]: You're bold, I'll give you that. I'm Diana. And you are?
[Otthello] whispers: I'm Peter.
To [Otthello]: Nice to "meet" you. Do you go by "Pete"?
[Otthello] whispers: Ugh, no. That sounds like animal feces in a bog.
To [Otthello]: You mean peat?
[Otthello] whispers: That's the one. Excellent vocabulary.
To [Otthello]: Ha! Then Peter it is.
[Otthello] whispers: So, Diana, where do you hail from?
To [Otthello]: Tampa. You?
[Otthello] whispers: Omaha.
To [Otthello]: Ooo, do you have a cute Midwestern accent?
[Otthello] whispers: No, ma'am.
To [Otthello]: Oh, such a shame.
[Otthello] whispers: Sorry to disappoint. I lost my accent when I went away to university.
To [Otthello]: Where did you go to school?
[Otthello] whispers: San Diego.

She continued on with her jewelcrafting as she chatted with him. She monitored his position as he made his way to her, took endless delight in watching him waste time. Finally, he found her.

[Otthello] whispers: Look behind you.

She turned her toon around, and there he was.

Otthello waves.
Serylda waves.
Otthello blows a kiss.
Serylda blushes.
[Otthello] whispers: See, now isn't that much more fun?
To [Otthello]: It is but...
[Otthello] whispers: But what?
To [Otthello]: But I have to log now. Well past my bedtime.
[Otthello] whispers: Noooooo!!! You can't make me come all the way over here and then log!
To [Otthello]: Not my fault. You're the one that took forever!
[Otthello] whispers: Lol! Touché. Will you be on tomorrow?
To [Otthello]: I'm not sure, but I should be, and we can quest if so. It's going to be a crazy day, though.
[Otthello] whispers: Well, I'll be on, and I hope to see you. I enjoy talking to you.
To [Otthello]: I enjoy talking to you, too. Goodbye for now.
[Otthello] whispers: Night. Sleep well.

She logged off and strummed her nails one by one on the keyboard while she scanned back through their chat. There was something odd here that she couldn't quite put her finger on. And why ignore her for three hours and then come all the way out to

Silvermoon? Maybe he really was just a nice guy who took his loyalty to his fellow guild members very seriously? Too nice, in that case. But there was a strange vibe to the way he talked that didn't fit that scenario.

Maybe she'd tell him next time that she was married, so he could clear out if he was looking for a real relationship. But no, it was still too early for that sort of admission; it would make her look desperate. That would spook even the smoothest operator looking for a no-strings-attached fling.

She tapped each nail down with a final click and smiled to herself.

There was a better way.

CHAPTER THIRTY-SIX

"Did you hear what I said?"

Jo's eyes flicked Brent's face into focus. No, she hadn't heard him. She'd agreed to go out with him, her mother's friend's son's friend, to keep her mother off her back. Objectively, he had every reason to expect her full attention. He was a sexy, dark-haired research analyst with an easy, wide smile, warm brown eyes, and an intelligent sense of humor. Their initial blind date over coffee had gone surprisingly well, and during their follow-up a week later she felt a decided spark, a spark that ended with them in bed. But bed was all it was, and while he asked her out for a third date right away, she'd rescheduled several times, in light of her enforced vacation and the hotel killer case. And so, he wouldn't get ahead of himself. But she was here now, soft music and subdued lighting setting a perfect frame for romance, and the least she could do was pay attention to him.

"No, I'm sorry, I didn't hear you. I have a lot on my mind, but that's no excuse."

His face relaxed, but not completely. "Anything you'd like to share?"

She glanced down at her nearly untouched steak au poivre and considered. She'd been chasing the case around inside her head. Today they'd received final confirmation that Nancy Morgen, the parent who'd threatened Emily Carson, had a solid alibi, and the personal records they'd been able to recover for Aleta Rivera were just as unhelpful as Jeanine's and Emily's had been. They'd had one close call—a customer service rep for the SleepTight, who had also worked the customer service line for Aleta's hotel at the time of her death. All a coincidence, it turned out—he'd been locked up in police custody for a DUI the night Emily died. The additional details on the Rivera and Carson murders had ruled out both Jon Renke and Ronald Craig—each had an unbreakable alibi for one of those murders. They were still cross-checking details about the victims, but it was slow going without official permission to investigate. So, they were left trying to catch a serial killer by his shadow, and her brain was overflowing with attempts to create an effective profile. She'd been trying her best not to talk about it all—in the past she'd found it wasn't a good idea to talk much about work on dates. Even if they claimed to find police work fascinating, when faced with the reality of her world they shrank away. Both physically *and* emotionally, either disgusted, threatened, or a combination of the two.

On the other hand, she'd been inexcusably rude, and judging by the look on his face, he wasn't going to accept any refusal to explain. "You sure you want to hear about this? It's not something I'd normally talk about over dinner."

"Oh, now you *have* to tell me. You can't just throw that out there and let it hang." He ran a hand through his black hair and grinned.

She gave him a brief recap of the case, kept as sterile as she could manage. "So, I've read everything I can get my hands on over the past few weeks about serial killers and profiling, even FBI manuals, until I have terms like *organized vs. disorganized serial killers* seeping out of my ears, and I keep trying to match it up with what we know about this guy. Trying to find some rhyme or reason to guide me because, frankly, I don't know what the hell I'm doing and I don't like that feeling. And I'm fighting down resentment that I have to steal time for the case outside my official responsibilities, which are almost completely administrative, and I can't help feeling it was a mistake to accept the lieutenant job."

He drew in a deep breath and sat back. "No, I can see how that would be difficult."

She reached out and put her hand on top of his. "So, I do apologize. But with every day that passes, I feel myself getting more desperate."

"And you haven't learned anything that helps?"

"Nothing so far. This guy is either very smart or very lucky. Probably both. We're working on leads as fast as we can, but we're slogging through a pile of tar, just trying to grasp whatever we can see floating in it."

"Data mining."

"Data mining?" She reached for her wine.

"Sorry. That's when you run every test on every data point you can, just throw variables together to see if something sticks."

"Exactly." She smiled.

"But I was actually asking if you'd learned anything from your reading."

Her smile faded. "I don't know. Probably, when the dust settles. But for now I feel like I'm cramming for a test and making things worse."

"How so?"

"Well, there are aspects of the killings that seem strange, and when I started I hoped they'd help me get a handle on who this guy is and why he's picking the women he's picking. One example is, he doesn't rape the women, no sexual violation of any sort, doesn't even ejaculate on or near the corpse. We figured that would tell us something important about his psychology, but it turns out, it doesn't really differentiate much at all. At least not the way I'd hoped." She looked up from the fingerling potato she'd stabbed to find Brent's lips tight and his eyes wide.

"I apologize. Bad example, especially over dinner."

He cleared his throat. "No, that's fine. I asked."

She put the potato in her mouth, chewed, then swallowed. "So, at this point I'm reading just to read, hoping the next article or book will give me some clue or lead me somewhere new while we're waiting for something to pan out."

"Well"—his brows lifted—"the good thing about data mining in this case is, type one error isn't really a problem for you, so why not?"

"No idea what that means." She waved her fork across the air in front of him.

He laughed, but didn't smile. "My turn to apologize. Data mining with statistical tests can lead to false positives, tell you something is meaningful when in reality it isn't. That's called a 'type one' error. But in your case, any lead is a good lead."

She cut into her steak. "True. But I can't shake the feeling that I'm missing something, and I just need to look harder."

He gave her a strange look. "Yes. I have a feeling you're right about that."

CHAPTER THIRTY-SEVEN

Diana stayed out of the game the next day. The following night, she logged on as Dauphyne, one of her toons Peter didn't know about yet.

She checked his status. Otthello was online, in Orgrimmar. She leaned back in her chair and watched the chat channels, waiting for an opportunity to throw out the bait. An all-too-common argument in trade about Bush vs. Obama scrolled past, but Otthello wasn't contributing to that. She didn't blame him, the same argument had played out so many times she could predict the next inane step in the conversation. She sipped her coffee and scanned, doing her best to ignore the dissertations on who ruined the economy.

After a few minutes, she spotted his lockpicking bark, followed by exactly what she was looking for.

[2. Trade][Otthello]: Chastity belt getting you down? I have an app for that. Otthello's Lockpicking: making love possible since the days of vanilla. Tips happily accepted.

Two losers responded in trade, sharing their juvenile observations on how to make do with a woman's breasts. She jumped in.

[2. Trade][Dauphyne]: Classy. Neither of you would know what to do with a woman if she gave you step-by-step instructions.

There was a pause, then a torrent of profane rejoinders. One of them insulted her masculinity.

[2. Trade][Dauphyne]: Hmmm, I bet that would have really hurt my feelings if I were a man.
[2. Trade][Ronnjerremmy]: Ya right. UR not a woman. Pics or I call bullshit.
[2. Trade][Dauphyne]: Oh no, are you gonna double-dog dare me to send you a picture? 'Cause I'm just stupid enough to fall for that. Sorry Ronn, real women are very different from sheep.

More predictable profanity, plus two whispers.

[Riyanna] whispers: ROFLMAO!
[Otthello] whispers: Nice one, lol. I love it when someone other than me takes these morons down.

Why, hello there, Peter.

To [Otthello]: They make it so easy, how could I resist?
[Otthello] whispers: I would say "you go, girl," but I don't think I can pull it off, lol.
To [Otthello]: Not in touch with your inner diva?
[Otthello] whispers: Sadly, no. My inner football player keeps beating her up.
To [Otthello]: Okay, +1 for humor.
[Otthello] whispers: Why thank you, my dear. I'm at your service. *bows*
To [Otthello]: How gallant. Such a gentleman!
[Otthello] whispers: My mother trained me well.
To [Otthello]: If only all men had such excellent mothers.

[Otthello] whispers: I couldn't agree more. Basic politeness seems to be dead these days, let alone chivalry.

To [Otthello]: So true. And it's so much nicer to spend time around people who are a little more on the bright, civilized side, don't you think?

[Otthello] whispers: I do. I see you're level 30… Would you like me to run you through an instance or something? I could do with a little stimulating conversation.

To [Otthello]: That sounds like fun. I have to go for now, but tomorrow I'll log on to my main, and we can quest together.

[Otthello] whispers: Excellent. What's your main's name? I'll add her to my friends list.

To [Otthello]: No need. You already have her on it. We've met before; I most often go by the name Serylda. Bye now!

She waited a few seconds to initiate her log-off, just long enough to see his response:

[Otthello] whispers: Wtf??!!

She laughed. Oh yes, he was definitely looking for a hookup wherever he could find it. And she was very interested to see what he'd do next.

CHAPTER THIRTY-EIGHT

Martin stared at his screen, trying to process what just happened. *Fucking bitch.*

He pushed his chair back and strode over to the window, then back, trying to focus despite the adrenaline racing through him.

What did it mean? *How dare she pull something like that! How dare she play games with me, try to pull something over on me? Who the hell does she think she is?!* He slammed his fist into the desk.

But the fact was, she had pulled something over on him. Bested him mentally—but only the battle, not the war. No *way* was he going to let her get away with it, she'd regret ever even thinking of it. He'd taunt her with it as he wrung the life out of her body.

He rubbed his face, tried to calm down and clear his head. He was smarter than she was, but only if he remained calm. She'd pretended to be someone else, had an entire conversation with him that way. Maybe she just forgot she was playing a different toon? He grabbed his chair and scrolled up to their chat.

No. She'd been pleased with herself when she'd revealed who she was. She knew *exactly* what she was doing.

Was it a test? If so, he had failed. Spectacularly. He had come on to her, strong and clear. If she wanted to gauge his sincerity, this wasn't going to play well, and he was done.

Except she said she'd be on to quest with him tomorrow.

What. The. Hell.

Maybe she was lying about questing tomorrow? Just her way of building it up for maximum impact when she revealed who she was?

Or maybe he was overreacting, maybe she hadn't been testing him. Maybe she'd just come on, saw the offensive crap those guys were saying and responded to them before she had a chance to say hi to him. Then, pow, before she knew it, he was hitting on her. *Idiot!* He scrolled farther up to before the beginning of the conversation. No. She had time to identify herself if she'd wanted to.

So WHY?

He slammed his fist on the desk again, and his mug toppled to the floor and shattered. He paled as he stared down at the mess of shards. *Get a fucking grip.*

He ran his hands through his hair, paced the room again. He needed to move, needed to metabolize the adrenaline. He strode out into the hallway and grabbed his coat from the closet, and his keys from the bowl on the table. He let himself out into the brisk night air and headed toward the high school track.

Their conversation ended well the last time they'd talked, and he'd gone all the way out to Silvermoon for the privilege of holding hands with her. Besides, they'd only had two conversations! They weren't going steady, he hadn't given her his letter jacket or asked her to the prom. There was no reason he couldn't talk to someone else in-game.

Except girls didn't think like that. Even if you'd never exchanged a word, they didn't want you giving attention to someone else. No way was she going to see it as fair play. And she wouldn't remember the trip to Silvermoon, she'd focus on how he'd left her waiting for so long the other day.

Was that it? Was this her payback for making her wait? He *knew* it, *knew* she'd been annoyed, *knew* she seemed to let go of it too quickly. And now that he thought about it, she entrapped him, hadn't played fair. Came at him saying things she knew he'd respond to, dangled bait in front of him she knew he'd take. He barely knew her, *of course* he was going to respond to someone else like that. So, is that what this was, just her way of letting him know she wasn't going to take his shit? Of rubbing his nose in it and putting them back on an even footing?

His pace slowed. That made sense. Fit with her claim that she'd meet him tomorrow—if she really intended to show up.

So he needed to focus on a plan of action, based on the two possibilities. She'd either show up tomorrow, or she wouldn't. If she didn't, no way was he going to let her go without a fight, not now. But how to play it?

He could wait until he saw her online again, and then try to charm her. Try to play it off like he'd known all along?

No, she wouldn't believe that, especially if she'd seen his last whisper. Showing his hand like that had been an amateurish mistake. *Damn, damn, stupid, stupid, idiot!* He was better than that. But she'd caught him by surprise and he hadn't stopped to think.

He forced himself to focus again. Too late for regrets, there was no point in that. He had to move forward.

His breath found a more even rhythm, in time with his power-walk stride. Maybe he could send her a gift in-game with an apology? Maybe tell her it was a tribute to her charm that she'd caught his eye twice, and he should have known it was her all along because there could never be two such amazing women on one server? Something like that. Maybe a little more toned-down. She was too smart to fall for something too obviously over the top. But it was the sort of humble apology that could work. Okay, so far so good.

And if she did show up, what then? He'd have to own it. Throw out the assumption she'd been paying him back for making her wait, say now they could call it even and start fresh? Let her think she had the win, smooth her ruffled feathers. And if she gave him a hard time about hitting on other women, he'd turn it around, ask if that meant she wanted his exclusive attention, tell her he was only too happy to give it, all she had to do was say the word.

Yes. Brilliant.

That would leave her wrong-footed. If she was hurt about the other woman, this would tell her he only wanted her all along. It was faster than he normally worked, but if that's what she wanted, faster was better anyway.

He smiled. Both problems solved. In fact, if she didn't show up tomorrow, that's what he'd put in his message to her with the rose. Because, really, this all just meant she was interested in him, right? Otherwise, why bother?

But—it was crucial that he focus on her and only her from now on. Too risky to keep other options open. He'd have to get rid of Janni. He could put Janni off for a few days until he found out if Serylda was interested and married, but not much more. Or maybe it was worth taking the risk on this one even if she was single? He was itching to wrap his hands around her little bitch neck, maybe even force this one to beg for her life.

He shook his head. No, that would be stupid, exactly the sort of major change that would get him caught. All it took was one girlfriend back home to know where she was going and why, spewing information to the police and the media. No. He did it this way for a reason.

He reached the track and worked through his stretches. He was feeling better now that he'd thought things through, but he was still angry with himself—there was no excuse for a mistake like this. He'd run out the anger before heading home.

As he ran, he played out each scenario several ways in his head, predicting her responses and tweaking them until he'd dealt with all possible reactions. By the time he'd run five laps, calm had settled over him, and his confidence was back. He'd pull her back into the web. Not a problem.

He lay in bed that night, imagining himself to sleep. He imagined how much more delicious the kill would be for having gone through this. He imagined stretching out her death, killing her more slowly than he'd ever done before—maybe he'd bring her to the edge of consciousness several times before killing her, build up her fear until he could smell it oozing from her pores. And he'd tell this one why she was dying. That she'd brought it on herself when she tried to humiliate him, tried to outthink him.

And when her hemorrhaging eyes begged for mercy, he'd ask her: Who did she want him to spare, Serylda or Dauphyne?

*

Martin logged on early. He needed to be waiting, eager and repentant, couldn't risk her feeling slighted yet again. He opened lockboxes while he waited, but reined in the flirting in case she tested him with yet a third alt. He organized his bank, thanked people for tips, and remained otherwise silent.

She logged on half an hour later than the previous night. Was she feigning laissez-faire?

> To [Serylda]: Hey you.
> [Serylda] whispers: Hey.
> To [Serylda]: Cute trick last night, you got me good. I'm sorry again that I kept you waiting.
> [Serylda] whispers: What can I say, I hate to be predictable.

No confirmation his conclusion was right, but no objection, either.

> To [Serylda]: You definitely had my head spinning. Now that we're even, shall we start again?

> [Serylda] whispers: I'm not sure what you mean by "even."
> But yes, let's run some instances. Do you want to queue up?
> To [Serylda]: Your wish is my command.
> [Serylda] whispers: Excellent.

Passive-aggressive undercurrent, but she was talking. He'd ride it out.

> To [Serylda]: So how is work going for you? I know you said you had a lot going on.
> [Serylda] whispers: Work, work, work. I know you know how that is.
> To [Serylda]: I do. But all work and no play…you know how that is.
> [Serylda] whispers: I do. I think I'll craft while we wait.

As he suspected. She wasn't going to let this be quite so easy. Time for a distraction.

> To [Serylda]: I had an idea, actually… I'd love to show you my favorite place in the game.
> [Serylda] whispers: Sure, why not? Who knows how long we'll have to wait for a group.
> To [Serylda]: Okay, meet me in Shat. :)
> [Serylda] whispers: Let me dump this stuff in the bank, then I'm OMW.

They met up in Shattrath City, a stone fortress with a circular format. She followed him as he took the lead, flew her over Terrokar Forest, and then to Nagrand, a lush grassland filled with exotic variations of elephants and savanna beasts. Along the way, they fell into a pleasant rhythm discussing the zones they loved and which they hated; he monitored each emotional nuance. Finally he swerved up onto the Elemental Plateau and landed strategically to optimize the view.

Several large rocks floated in the sky above them, islands in place of clouds. On the one closest, three waterfalls cascaded over the sides onto the land in front of them, like columns of water overflowing the edges of a cupped hand. The crystal-blue water formed a U-shaped lake where it hit the ground; the left side tapered down, and the water slipped over the cliff and out of sight. Amazing that pixels on a screen could capture the soothing flow of the real thing, and the view always relaxed him.

To [Serylda]: Have you been here before?

[Serylda] whispers: I have, but it's been a long time.

To [Serylda]: I think it's a very romantic spot…and I've also been thinking that there might be a connection between us, and I'd like to investigate that.

[Serylda] whispers: I'll admit, I'm drawn to you. You make me laugh, and you're witty. But…

To [Serylda]: But?

[Serylda] whispers: Well, first off, I'm not sure about your motives.

To [Serylda]: And second?

[Serylda] whispers: Second is, I'm married.

A jolt ran through him. Of course, so obvious! How had he not thought about it that way before? Of course she'd be willing to give him another chance; she wasn't in any position to call any moral shots, and she knew it.

To [Serylda]: As in, you have a husband who will show up and kick my ass if I flirt with you in-game?

[Serylda] whispers: As in, I'm not a single girl looking for a relationship. I'm complicated.

To [Serylda]: You love your husband, and just want to be
friends, with a little flirting?
[Serylda] whispers: Something like that.

He relaxed. The standard lie they all told themselves to start,
although this one seemed to have a little more self-awareness about
it. Maybe she'd done this before. So much the better.

To [Serylda]: Well, I can't say I'm not disappointed, but
the fact is, I enjoy talking to you, and you can never have
enough friends, right?
[Serylda] whispers: I couldn't agree more, and I'm relieved
to hear you say that.
To [Serylda]: Like we've said before, it isn't every day you
find someone in this game that can provide intelligent
conversation. Or in the world, for that matter.
[Serylda] whispers: LOL! Too true. And now that that's
settled, it's your turn to see my favorite place in WoW.
To [Serylda]: Lead the way. :)

They flew off, with her in the lead this time.

CHAPTER THIRTY-NINE

They chatted for another half hour before she logged out. She sat for a moment, stroking Cleopatra, relief and anticipation lapping at her. The hard part was over. A fair number of men, more than she'd initially expected, said thanks-but-no-thanks when she told them she was married. But Peter was still on board, and, ironically, everything was well underway.

Ironically, because she wasn't actually married.

Diana didn't believe in relationships. Or rather, she didn't believe in the purported romantic love that underlay them. Sure, she had biological carnal needs like anyone, but a long-term relationship wasn't necessary to fulfill them. In her experience, relationships, particularly marriage, led people to unreasonable, damaging expectations. Men made promises that they had no intention of keeping so they could get what they wanted—sex. And in the case of marriage, someone to cook and clean for them. Men were not monogamous by nature (ask any evolutionary psychologist and they'd tell you), and women were the ones who ended up getting hurt in the deal.

And for what? For the privilege of chasing after snotty-faced children and mopping floors while the men watched football and screwed whoever they wanted on the side? The facts were right there in the scientific research: married men lived longer than single men, but *single* women lived longer than those who married. Men got what they needed from the deal; women didn't. Sure, maybe it made sense back in the old days when women had no way to support themselves and had to find a man to take care of them, but not anymore.

She knew other women didn't think the way she did, and that was fine. But Diana had seen early on the consequences that came from *their* way of thinking. She remembered far too well the conversations where her mother laid out, in agonizing detail, how miserable and lonely she was in her marriage. Lucia Montauk complained every day that Diana's father was emotionally unavailable. About how he only wanted to fuck, didn't want to "make love." Diana also remembered all the paranoid questions. Had Diana seen her father do anything odd? Get any strange phone calls? Did he leave the house when he wasn't supposed to? So exhausting, all of it, even just thinking back on it.

When Diana was eight, Lucia decided an affair would cure her misery. She fell hard for her lover, but predictably (to everyone but Lucia), Sammy hadn't ever wanted a real relationship, he just wanted a roll in the hay. Of course, he didn't *tell* Lucia that until he was done with her—why let her insignificant feelings ruin his fun? He told Lucia what she wanted to hear, let her leave Diana's father for him and take Diana with her. Let Diana's father, inconsolable about losing his wife and daughter, throw himself over a cliff to his death in the icy, rocky waters of the ocean.

Then Sammy got tired of Lucia and shifted his attention to Diana. On a near-daily basis for several months. Until that bored him, too, and he left.

Diana had trudged along, fighting her way through the detritus left behind in the maelstrom of his destruction, her father dead, her mother depressed and suicidal. Saw how sex had destroyed everything. Or rather, the confusion between sex and relationships. Nobody wanted to admit that sex drove people. Primal urges were impossible to ignore, and everyone had them, but to admit that was unseemly and animalistic. So, people, especially women, dressed it up. Tried to give it meaning, make it respectable somehow, convinced themselves that lust was actually love. Which was fine by men. They didn't have any qualms about putting lipstick on that particular pig if it got them what they wanted.

She gazed at Cleopatra, eyes closed and purring on her lap. "You're the only love in my life, honey. Pure. And so much simpler." Cleopatra met Diana's hazel eyes and intensified her purring.

She'd gone through a phase where she tried to ignore her own primal needs. She wore a wedding ring to keep men away and was disgusted to find that it made them hit on her all the more—without any qualms about breaking up a marriage so they could get laid, regardless of the fallout. But eventually she realized those were precisely the sort of men who could fill her needs. She had no use for the nice guys who drank the relationship Kool-Aid, who wanted something monogamous and long-term, who would try to build something permanent with her. And once she had that epiphany, everything became so much easier.

But while men who hit on married women were looking for wham-bam-thank-you-ma'am, or at least something with an end-by date, she learned quickly they didn't like being called out on that. It ruined the game for them somehow. So, she played along. If a little romance was what it took, fine, she'd be romantic right along with them. Let them put on whatever facade they liked. Let them puff up their egos and think they were fooling her.

Why not, when it was perfect for *her* needs, too?

CHAPTER FORTY

Jo shifted her weight between her feet, then stopped, afraid to look like a child who needed to use the bathroom.

Which, now that she'd entertained the thought, she did.

Press conferences were only exciting if you were the one holding them. The dance was like a game of Ping-Pong—they lobbed shots at you, trying to get more information than you were supposed to give, and you volleyed back with answers that sounded important but gave nothing away. But ADA Rockney was holding this one, so Jo's job was to stand on the sidelines and look appropriately somber.

Her mind kept wandering. They'd watched nearly every lead dry up on Jeanine Hammond's case, despite discovering an additional murder in Detroit that was potentially related—the crime scene was nearly identical, missing wedding ring and all, but there was no security footage to make a strong connection. The forensic analysis on the bruises and neck abrasions indicated they could have been committed by the same person, but there was enough variation in the pressure point and depth of the abrasions that they couldn't determine that conclusively. They'd found no overlapping names on Jeanine's and Emily's flights, even after extensive background checks for alternate identities, and no overlapping employees with access to the victims' hotel records. They were down to their last desperate shot, the personality profiles and histories they'd been assembling from the device searches and follow-up interviews with family and friends. Arnett and Lopez were waiting for her, so they could do a final synthesis and analysis.

Jo caught herself clenching her hands in frustration and forced herself to release them.

Her cell phone buzzed. She slipped it out of her pocket, and the caller ID brought her to instant alert: Lieutenant Benville, NOPD. She whispered to the officer next to her, then stepped out of the room to take the call.

"Lieutenant. Good to hear from you," she said.

"I'm glad to say I have some news for you, although it's a little embarrassing on our end."

"I'm sure there's no reason for that. What do you have?"

"We released Emily Carson's personal effects to her husband and he found something we missed. Her wallet has one of those hidden sections, and inside of it, she had a card from a New Orleans restaurant called Roulez. We went down there and interviewed everyone who worked front of the house the night she was murdered. One waitress and the hostess remembered her, and the man she met."

"Hold on just one second, I need to grab a pen." She stepped over to the nearest desk and reached across for a pad and pen. "Got it. Go ahead."

"The hostess said the reservation was for 7:00 p.m., under the name 'Smith.' He arrived first, and had a cup of coffee while he waited. She remembered them because when Carson came in, she looked nervous and acted like it was a first date, but then at the same time they seemed head-over-heels in love. She couldn't get a read on them, said there was a strange romance to it, like something you'd see in a fifties movie. The waitress said something similar, that they seemed so in love they were on another 'plane of existence.'"

"Don't they see that sort of thing in the restaurant business every day?"

"Apparently not. They both kept saying there was something different about this, odd, like they were watching a television show."

"Do they know when the reservation was made?"

"They don't keep that information. They don't book very far out in advance, regardless."

"Any way we can send a man out to see if they recognize any of our suspects?"

"We already did it. They couldn't give a positive ID, but they couldn't rule any of them out, either. It'd just been too long."

"Did they give a description of him?"

"Not a good one. They both said he was white, mid-to-late thirties, taller than she was, and they both identified brown hair. Neither of them noticed any distinguishing features or regional accent. He was wearing a dark suit and carrying a dark overcoat. She remembered a hat, but wasn't sure what kind."

"Anything else?"

"Not anything that I think matters, but I'll run it all down for you. He ordered for the both of them, and they shared everything. He fed her from his fork—both women rolled their eyes over that. He paid with cash and left a hefty tip. Oh, there was one other interesting thing—the waitress said that he was 'anal' about keeping Carson's wine filled. She noticed because that's her job, and she didn't get much chance to do it. And she noticed that only *her* glass seemed to go down at all."

"And he paid with cash at the bar, too? Did the bartender notice anything?"

"Nope, he didn't notice anything, probably because a cup of coffee wouldn't warrant a decent tip."

"Well, I thank you for getting this information to me. It's a help."

"Not a problem, but I don't see how. Nothing we can follow up on. Anything new up there?"

"I've been trying my hand at profiling, at least to draw some conclusions about who this guy is and how he meets these women. This confirms some things I've been trying to get a handle on.

Any chance you can spare a man to canvas the area around the restaurant?"

"Already done. Unfortunately, nobody else recognized either one of them anywhere in that area. Saturday night's busy in the Quarter, and it's been long enough now that I'm surprised even the staff at the restaurant remembered her, truth be told."

"Very true. Private security cams?"

"All long cycled out by now."

"Right, of course. Is there a write-up of the interviews yet?"

She heard Benville hitting keys on a keyboard. "I just sent it to your e-mail. I wanted to call you directly about it since we screwed the pooch on finding that card. I'll let you know if we come up with anything else."

"Thank you much. I'll keep you updated, too."

She hit "end" on her phone and looked down at the notepad in front of her, heart pumping—Emily had known her killer before arriving at the restaurant. And she'd known him well. Given Emily's arrival time and when she left the hotel, it would have been nearly impossible to meet someone for the first time and arrange to meet up with them such a short time later for dinner regardless, let alone to establish that sort of intense romantic relationship. And it'd have to be one hell of a whirlwind even if they'd met on the plane. No, she had known him before she set foot in New Orleans. And that meant there was some trace they were overlooking.

She went into her e-mail and pulled up the interviews. As Benville indicated, despite being interviewed separately, both the hostess and the waitress mentioned, several times, the strong feeling the romance had been "strange," "out of a movie," "like on TV." Hyperbole? Not likely from both of them, and with such an atypical description. Maybe they'd talked about it together, built it up in their heads, but even so, something had been off. And it had been from the start, not something that just went wrong at the end of the night. The observation about the wine, the cash payment, and the pseudonym all pointed to premeditation—he'd made sure she was drunk, and he'd covered his tracks.

She glanced back toward the press conference, then walked down the hall away from it. The picture was coming into focus, a careful killer who found these women and built a relationship with them long before he killed them.

And she would damned well tear through every fact they'd found about the victims until she found out how.

CHAPTER FORTY-ONE

Martin proceeded with delicious caution, every step a tightrope walk between skyscrapers. He calculated and recalculated every move, every question, lingered over the agony of getting it right. There were no more gaffes, no bumps in the road. His laser focus paid off—she was interested in him, and that interest grew. Getting her to talk on Skype was effortless; her husband worked the graveyard shift, so he was never home at night when they played and talked.

The need for uber-vigilance left him with a vague feeling he was never fully controlling their interactions the way he wanted to, and that kept the adrenaline constantly coursing. Part of the feeling was due to her freedom—his previous victims had to be careful about what they said, and he used that to his advantage. He'd tease them, say things they couldn't respond to, keep them off-balance and make them want more. He had to work much harder to plant the same seeds with her and watch them grow.

She was extremely inquisitive, and frighteningly quick—always thinking, always asking, always threatening to push him off the rope. He found himself answering questions he didn't know the right answers to; it forced him to take risks he didn't like and give answers that might not please her. When she asked him what sort of date he'd plan if they were ever able to meet, he tried to turn it around on her, get her to reveal her fantasy so he could use it in the future, but she held his feet to the fire. On other occasions, she asked if he liked women who were sexually bold or preferred to make the advances, asked how he liked his women to dress, asked what he found romantic. He found himself in a continual struggle to wrestle power back, the sword of Damocles hanging over him at every step, his metamorphosis into her perfect man a precarious dance against time.

There were missteps, but he diffused them well enough. One he'd found deeply amusing:

"So how do you dress when you take a woman out on a date?" she'd asked.

"I think you can never go wrong with a suit."

"Oh, darling, too stuffy. A blazer, fine. But we need to break you out of that suit, ties are so uncomfortable!"

From then on, he made a point of wearing a tie whenever they were on video together, turned it into a running joke between them. She'd damn sure better be ready for that tie when they met.

He told her he was a widower and was trying to get back into dating but wasn't sure if he was ready to get serious again yet. Close to his usual story, but with an adjustment to explain why he'd been skirt chasing. Overcompensating, he claimed. And the alteration still left that all-important obstacle in place—women loved to be the first one that *mattered to him* after his dearly departed wife, wanted to be the ones able to get him to love and trust again.

But her reaction was odd. She was sympathetic, listened to the story, made all the standard consolations. But she didn't engage with the "wounded boy" aspect as the other women had. So, he adjusted. Played that up less, focused more on how his wife would have wanted him to move on, to live and enjoy his life.

The biggest difficulty was she didn't spend much time complaining about her husband. Didn't like talking about him at all, really. Nice to not have to listen to an endless stream of complaint, but it took away his most effective strategy, gave him no straw man to bash and no information on what *not* to be. He probed a few times, but she'd only say they barely saw each other and didn't share any interests, regardless. So he worked with that, expressed outrage at men who neglected their wives, dropped snide comments here and there to keep it fresh in her mind. And he asked what her interests were, so he could stress his deep love for them—for reading, it turned out, and art exhibits, and the ocean. Since he did love to read, he suggested they read books together, and he threw the ocean into any fantasy scenario that came up. The art was harder, but he did his research and waxed poetic about how wonderful it would be to stroll through the Musée d'Orsay with her, or the New York MoMA, or the Uffizi Gallery.

No, not easy, but most definitely exhilarating and arousing. And in a few short days, all his hard work would pay off.

CHAPTER FORTY-TWO

Jo swept into the conference room where Arnett and Lopez had set up corkboards and whiteboards with crime scene photos and other information while they waited for her to finish the press conference. She poured a cup of coffee as she briefly recapped what she'd learned from Benville, while forwarding the information Benville e-mailed her.

"Confirms he knew her before the trip," Arnett said.

Jo nodded. "Seems that way. I guess it's technically possible they could have met on the plane, but the more I think about it, the more unlikely I think that is."

Lopez stuck her pen behind her ear and leaned back in her chair. "And it couldn't have happened anyway. I just finished the background checks for everyone on the manifests, and there aren't any overlaps. I haven't been able to search any additional flights yet, though. And none of our three suspects were personally connected with the other vics in any way."

Jo nodded. "So, here's what I think we're looking at. He finds these women and builds a relationship with them. Maybe he happened to know Jeanine personally beforehand, maybe she inadvertently drew the attention of a serial killer—but it looks like he found the other women some other way. However he meets them, he then gets them to agree to an out-of-town tryst. He meets them for dinner and drinks, then they go back to the hotel to cap off the evening, and he kills them. Am I missing anything that doesn't fit, or any other options?" Jo asked.

They shook their heads.

"So, we have a tighter set of questions. First, why not just kill them where they live? Why get them to take a trip? It can't be easy to talk a woman into flying out to meet you."

Lopez spoke up. "It's way easier to cheat away from home. Your husband won't walk in on you, and there's nobody to run into when you're walking out of a restaurant or into a hotel together."

"But if they know him, why waste time taking them out to an expensive dinner, why not just head straight to the hotel and kill them?" Jo asked.

Lopez flipped the edge of a file through her fingers. "Didn't the hostess say it looked like they were meeting for the first time even though they knew each other? If I were meeting someone for the first time, I'd want to it to be somewhere public. Like when you meet a guy from a dating site."

Arnett and Jo stared at her for a moment, then Jo pointed in her direction. "Say that again."

"You know, like Match.com or Zoosk, those sites. You talk to them for a while before you decide you want to meet them. And you'd never meet them at your house the first time; you go somewhere public and you have a contingency plan."

"Like what?"

"Whenever my baby sister does it, she texts me when she leaves and when she gets back. Sometimes has a friend go to the same café or restaurant incognito and watch." She shrugged. "But there are no dating sites on the women's computers or devices, I checked that first thing. And nothing in their history suggesting chat room or forum use, either."

"And don't forget, they're all married. You don't find that on a dating site," Arnett said.

"Well..." Lopez laughed.

"You're kidding me," Arnett said.

"'Fraid not. Some exist for that very purpose."

Arnett paled.

Jo tapped the board next to the word "married." "That's still an excellent point. He's doing it this way for a reason. He builds a relationship, gets them out to a location where neither he nor they are known. He spends an evening with them, then kills them. So how does he choose his victims? What do they have in common?"

Arnett looked down at his notes. "History: All three have lived in their respective states of residence for their entire lives, including college—no overlap on that front. If he met them in person, he's the mobile one. Closest extracurriculars are that Hammond and Rivera were both Girl Scouts. But Carson wasn't. Hobbies: all three women loved to read, loved computer games, and loved shoes. Personalities: all the women were considered intelligent and fun to be around. Rivera was an all-around extrovert, Hammond was more reserved until she got to know you. Carson was in the middle. They enjoyed interacting with friends, but Carson and Hammond were homebodies. Rivera was a social butterfly."

"Nothing related to dancing?" Jo asked.

Arnett and Lopez shook their heads.

"Dammit. But that's okay, dancing must be his kink, then, and that tells us something. What did we find across the computers and devices?" Jo asked.

Lopez took over. "No common contacts in their e-mail addresses or phones. E-mail accounts, browser histories, and credit card records showed that the women shopped at different places for their groceries, clothes, and their shoes. No patterns the techs or I could determine. All three belonged to online book clubs through Facebook, but there's no overlap between clubs and members, at least not anymore. They all bought books through Amazon, but even that's complicated because Aleta was old-school and didn't have a reading device. So, Jeanine and Emily bought digital books, while Aleta bought hard copies."

"So we could be looking at someone who works for Amazon, maybe a customer service rep who happened to come into contact with them? Someone who had access to their reading history? Can we check that out? And is there any way to check former members of those Facebook groups?" Jo asked.

"Already doing it," Lopez continued. "The only other commonality is they were all gamers—Oh. My. God."

Jo's head shot up. "What?"

"That's exactly what we were just talking about, a way to meet online."

"How so?"

"Okay, let me back up and look at this again." She scrolled something on her laptop. "All three women were members of Steam, an online gaming site where gamers can buy games and meet other people who play those games. But none of the women had any friends in common, or grouped together through Steam, and only Aleta even posted on her profile." Her finger ran over the information as she summarized. "In Steam, all three played *The Elder Scrolls* games, but those are single-person games, so they couldn't have met anyone that way, and they didn't post to forums. Aleta and Emily played *Diablo*, which is a possibility, and all three played *World of Warcaft*, a game that almost requires you to interact with people you meet online."

Jo's jaw clenched. "Explain, please—my last video game was *Super Mario Bros.*"

"*World of Warcraft* is an MMORPG, a massively multiplayer online role-playing game. Basically, you're playing in a virtual world populated by other players, in addition to non-player characters. People meet up and form all sorts of relationships. For some players, it's their whole social world."

"What do you mean, virtual world?"

"There are different types in different games. Some sci-fi, some fantasy."

"You mean like *Dungeons and Dragons?*"

"You can think of it that way. Some would argue *WoW* is an evolution of *D&D*, while others get Incredible Hulk angry about that comparison."

"*WoW?*"

"*World of Warcraft*, the one they all played."

"How do people form relationships?"

"The same way you would in any chat room. Except in a game, there's built-in activity, as well. It gives the illusion of a shared time and space."

"It's that real?"

"It looks different, but yes, it can become fairly real, with most of the spatial and physical laws found in the real world. Gravity, solidity, things like that. There was even a case recently of some kid jumping to his death out of a real window the way he would in the video game he played. The lines get blurry." She shrugged.

Arnett chimed in. "When we followed up about the hobbies, Roger Hammond said Jeanine started playing so she could spend time with the niece when she was away in college. He said it allowed them to connect even though they were so far away from each other."

"But you can also interact with people you don't know?" Jo asked, her mind racing.

"All the time. In fact, the game is set up so that you can only get certain kinds of rewards if you play with other people. Even if you play with friends, you have to join in with other people to run dungeon instances, to raid, to play in the battlegrounds. There's a limit to what you can do unless you at least join a guild."

"A guild, like medieval craftsmen?"

Lopez scrunched her brow. "Same basic concept, yes. It's a group of people who affiliate together and help one another through game content."

"So how do people meet one another?"

"All sorts of ways. There are a number of public chat channels in-game for different purposes. You can join queues to be put in random groups. People advertise their guilds and their skills. You can see someone in the same areas where you're playing and start a conversation. There are even zones on certain servers where people go to ERP."

"ERP?"

"Erotic role-play."

"You go into these games to have sex?"

"Not me, not everybody, but yes, some people do. Like phone sex. There are servers known for it." Lopez's brown eyes twinkled.

Jo felt old and out of touch—she wasn't a prude, but she wasn't going to pretend the idea of people having sex in a game didn't seem bizarre.

Arnett leaned forward. "Anyone can go to any server? You're not assigned to one?"

"Nope. Different servers have different uses, are in different time zones, are even set up for different parts of the world. You can go anywhere you want."

Arnett's eyes scanned the whiteboards. "Could explain a lot. Why the women are from different states, how he built a relationship with them without anyone in their lives seeing even a hint of it. He goes months between kills, plenty of time to get to know them well, and that would explain the strange dynamic in the restaurant."

"And the married women? Surely you'd be waiting a long time to find someone open to infidelity," Jo asked.

Arnett's face went blank. "Current infidelity rate among married people is around fifty percent. For women too. Not so far-fetched."

Lopez leaned forward, voice excited. "Actually, it makes *a lot* of sense. People do cra-azy things, dick pics fly through cyberspace with the greatest of ease. I remember one of my guildies showed everyone a pic someone sent him of a dyed vagi—um, never mind." She turned from Arnett's stare. "And people who cheat don't want to get caught. They keep quiet about it. So that's less risky for our killer."

Jo considered. "Is there a way to track who the women played with? Who they talked to during the game?"

Lopez's face tensed with concentration, and she pulled her laptop forward. "The company that runs the games, Blizzard, keeps some records, but I'm not sure which or for how long. It's always changing. Aleta and Jeanine's information may be long gone. We should be able to at least get a list of Emily's friends, maybe some chat logs if we're lucky." She paused and looked back up. "We'll need a warrant, though, that's for sure. Gamers are *beyond* intense about privacy issues. Plenty believe there's a huge government conspiracy in place to track their activities, especially now with the whole Edward Snowden deal and that sting with undercover agents looking for terrorists in the game. Some even refuse to use the Real ID system that lets players keep in contact with friends over all their characters and games, for exactly this reason. The companies that run the games care about their reputations, so they're really careful about who they give information to."

"I'll start the process," Jo said.

Lopez continued as her fingers flew over her keyboard. "While we're at it, we might as well get a warrant for the Skype records too. Lots of gamers use it for grouping, and I didn't see any of the other alternatives like Vent on their computers. All three women had Skype, and that would explain why we didn't find any phone calls or e-mails."

Jo kept writing. "Figure out who we have to contact and I'll get it done. Sounds like you play these games."

"I used to. Not recently."

Jo studied her face for a brief flash, hoping this had nothing to do with their late nights, or her alcoholic mother. Lopez's face remained unchanged. "But enough to know what's what with them, right?"

"Sure."

"Then I want you with me when I talk to these people. You may see things Bob and I won't notice."

"Sure thing," she said, red creeping up her neck.

"Is there anything else we haven't covered, or any other ideas you all have about where else we need to look?" Jo asked.

They shook their heads, but their expressions were hopeful for the first time in weeks. "Great work. Let's hope this brings back something we can use."

CHAPTER FORTY-THREE

Lopez helped Jo assemble the paperwork with the information pulled from Jeanine's and Emily's computers, along with the identifying information they had for Aleta Rivera. Lopez and Arnett went to deal with another investigation while they waited, but within the hour, Jo received a call back.

"Hello, Lieutenant. Miles Horace, Blizzard Entertainment."

"Thanks for getting back to us so quickly."

"I try my best. We have some news for you."

"Shoot."

"The news is mixed. In the case of Aleta Rivera, we don't have anything for you, other than confirmation that she did have an account. When she died, her husband canceled the account completely. All her records are long gone now."

"And the other two?"

"Better news there. We still have Jeanine Hammond's account information, and because nobody has logged into her account since she last played, we were able to access a full list of all the players she had friended at the time of her death. She had twenty-three in total, two of whom no longer exist. However, because we only keep chat logs for three months at the current time, we don't have any records of that kind for you."

Jo swore.

"Sorry. But, that means good news for Emily Carson's account, because our current time frame overlaps with the period before her death. We have her friends list, seventeen in total, with only one deleted, and the chat logs for that week."

Jo couldn't keep the excitement out of her voice. "Very good news."

"I e-mailed all of the information to you right before I placed the call, so it should be in your inbox. I think you might want me to stay on hold while you take a look at the records."

"Why's that?"

"It's the end of the workday and I'll be leaving after this call. If there's anything you wanted to follow up on, I wouldn't be here to discuss it with you until tomorrow."

"There's something you think I'll want?"

"Have a look at them. If there is something you need, I can let you know if we're able to get that information for you, and what you need to do to get it. I know time is of the essence for you."

Jo opened up the file and paged past the friends lists; they contained avatar names that meant nothing to her. She got to the chat logs and scrolled through what looked like a bunch of gibberish, with sentences attached, and swore again—she needed Lopez to help her understand all of this. She forced herself to focus on the names. There weren't many, and the ones that were there didn't say much. But the name "Porrthos" recurred, and she scanned the chat between them. Porrthos had been very friendly with Emily's character "Vyxxyne," calling her "darling" several times throughout the transcript. She clicked back to the list of avatar names and found "Porrthos" listed as one of them, and as the one friend whose account had been deleted.

She tilted her head toward the phone. "Can you tell us who 'Porrthos' is? And can you see if it's the same account as any of the friends on Jeanine Hammond's list, either existing or deleted?"

"Because that's information on another person's account, you'd need a separate warrant and a separate written request. Of course, it would be against protocol for me to pull it up tonight just because I thought you might be requesting it, but I can be sure to check for the warrant first thing in the morning, when I arrive at five a.m. That's a full hour before we update our system. After six a.m., if that person has made changes to his account in the meantime, information may be lost."

"Is there any reason to think he would cancel his account?"

"I don't even know if it's a 'he,' Lieutenant."

"I see. I'll get the warrant tonight. Thank you for your help."

"Just doing what the law requires."

"I know exactly what you're doing, and I appreciate it." She hung up.

*

She had Lopez wait in the station when they submitted the second warrant to Blizzard, and this time they received a call back almost immediately.

"What's the news, Mr. Horace?" Jo put her cell on speaker so Lopez could hear, and opened her e-mail in anticipation of the file.

"We found Porrthos. The account still exists, he just transferred his avatars to another server and changed the names. I've sent you all his chat logs as far back as we go. I've also sent you the information he registered to the account. Take a look at it, but from the name, I'm going to go out on a limb and guess it's all fake."

"Why's that?"

"Has the file come through yet?"

Jo checked. "Yep." Lopez watched over her shoulder.

"Take a look," Horace said.

Jo opened the file and read it over.

Name: Aypea Skipson

Address: 3210 Oak Street, San Diego CA 92105

Lopez laughed. "Niiice."

"Okay, what am I missing?" Jo said.

Horace answered. "Oh, sorry. I'm used to picking up on phonetic alternatives for strange names, we have to be good at that. Say the name out loud and pronounce the p-e-a as the vegetable."

"Ay-pee Skipson...IP, as in IP address?"

"That's my guess."

"Ah, I see. Very funny. Our man thinks he has a sense of humor." Jo twisted the diamond at her neck.

"It would appear so. I could be wrong, maybe that's his real name, that'd turn anyone into a killer. Doubt it, though. Especially because we don't get a consistent IP address from him."

"Subscribers can log in from any IP address?"

"Yup. As long as they have an authenticator. They put in a code from the authenticator after they enter their account name and password. They can use any computer from anywhere in the world. My guess is with a name like that, you're not going to find a clear path to his door. But you never know."

"What about a credit card? How did he pay for his subscription?"

"I included the information in the file. He used prepaid game cards. You can buy them anywhere, over the internet, in game stores, even on eBay. We traced the codes from the cards he has redeemed, and they seem to come from all over the country, all purchased at different stores, no pattern that I can see, but maybe it'll mean something to you. No way to trace them further than that."

"Damn."

"Indeed."

"So the account is still active?"

"Yup."

"We need to look through the chat logs. Is there anything else we should talk about?"

"You know the drill now. If there's another person you want information on, we need a separate warrant and written request."

"Will do. Thanks again."

"Yup." Horace hung up the phone.

Jo shifted her chair so Lopez could scoot in front of the computer. She pushed a hank of hair that had escaped her ponytail behind her ear and leaned in, pulling up the friends list.

Jo turned her attention to the list. "Only six friends, all but one female, judging by these strange names."

"Don't be too sure." Lopez laughed.

Jo glanced at her, then back at the computer, and pointed. "This is the name of his guild, right? We should get a list of the people who belong to it, see if there's any overlap."

Lopez looked skeptical. "We can try. But don't expect much. I can't see him involving guild members in this, that's basically shitting where you eat."

Jo watched as Lopez scrolled through the chat logs. Her eyes were becoming accustomed to the strange format, but it still slowed her reading.

"Look at this." Lopez pointed to the screen.

Portthos, now named Otthello, had been talking to a player named Serylda, and from the look of it, they'd become intimate despite the revelation that she was married. They scanned the text and watched him flirt heavily, until several days later when he suggested they talk over Skype. After that, their in-game conversations nearly stopped, showing only sterile communications while in groups with other players.

"From that point on they must have been either voice or video chatting. Most serious players use Skype anyway when they group, or Ventrilo or TeamSpeak," Lopez said.

"I'm assuming no evidence of those on any of the computers?"

Lopez shook her head and continued scrolling, then went back to the beginning. "Look here. Early on, he was also flirting with another player, Rimetra. But"—she scrolled down quickly—"their conversation seems to stop shortly after he started talking with Serylda."

"We'll need warrants for their information, too, and fast." Jo picked up her phone and tried the number listed on Portthos' account information.

"San Marcos Pizzeria. Delivery or pickup?"

She hung up. "As we suspected."

Lopez laughed again. "I'm thinking we need to see what we can find out about these Hotmail and Skype accounts too. I'll get another set of warrants started for Rimetra and Serylda, and for the guild information."

"What about the IP information they gave us? There has to be something there we can trace."

"I'll take it to the techs, but I don't think you should get your hopes up. There are ways to hide your real IP information, and this"—she motioned toward the computer—"suggests he knows how. We'll see."

"Does it say when his last log-in was?"

Lopez paged up. "Yep. Last night, seven p.m."

"Can we set it up with Blizzard to notify us when he logs on again, let us know who he's talking to?"

"We should be able to, if we get the right warrant."

Jo nodded. "Find out what we have to do. Also, have Arnett get in touch with San Diego PD to check out that address."

"On it." Lopez pulled the chair back around the desk as she left.

Jo tapped her pen rapid-fire as she scrolled back up through the file. If the IP and account information were dead ends, the other players were the only viable option left. She needed to talk to Rimetra and Serylda, as quickly as possible—no telling how long before one of them would be coming face-to-face with a cold-blooded killer.

CHAPTER FORTY-FOUR

Martin congratulated himself while waiting to board the first leg of his trip to San Francisco via Phoenix and Sacramento. All his hard work had paid off, and Diana had jumped at the chance to meet him. He kept half his mind focused on the boarding announcements while the other half savored the highlights of their conversations, and the persistent genius that had overcome the missteps.

She'd been reserved but receptive when he felt her out about meeting in person. Every step of the way with her had been nerve-wracking, and even this turned out to be unusually complex. She had a business trip coming up to San Francisco that might work—she had to check in with a Bay Area research group she worked with. She'd been there once several years before and thought the city had a romantic charm, perfect for a lovers' tryst.

Her previous trip had worried him. "You've been there before? You know people there?" He couldn't have her show up to dinner with a friend.

"Only one person that I've actually met before, and he's gone the week I'm visiting. That's the main reason I have to go. I did an initial setup with them several years ago, but the entire team is different and they're in a new location. I need to go meet the new people and see the new facilities. I'm supposed to be there for two days, maybe three, but could go for an extra day or two. I'd like to spend some time enjoying the area anyway."

He relaxed. "Your husband won't mind an extended trip?"

She rolled her eyes and laughed. "Are you kidding? He'll book the flights himself."

"I can help with the costs, or do they pay for expenses?"

"Generally speaking, yes. Hotel, flight. Basic food. Possibly a rental car, depending. Not for the extra nights I stay, of course."

"Do they pick the hotel for you, then?"

"Not exactly, but there are standards to choose from. Mostly chain hotels oriented to business travelers. Nothing five star, no roach motels, no bed-and-breakfasts." She laughed again.

"Oh, thank god. I detest bed-and-breakfasts."

"Really? I've stayed in some that I've enjoyed quite a lot."

Annoyance flashed through him. He'd read her wrong yet again—the way she said *bed-and-breakfasts*, he could have sworn she hated them. But he was committed, so he played it through, lascivious smile in place. "Yes, well. I personally think that ordering room service in between bouts of energetic lovemaking is the epitome of romance."

"An excellent point."

He'd mulled the situation over at length. He could always say the timing didn't work for him and suggest an alternate trip, but who knew when she'd have another opportunity to go away again? She'd most likely want to stick with the cover of a legitimate business trip, and since San Francisco was her main contract now, on a future trip she'd have met everyone on the team.

What were the true risks of going now? He always made sure to meet them at least a day or two before they were due to show up at work; she wouldn't have time to meet any of the new team or have reason to invite them back to the hotel. And if for some reason she did anyway, he could always develop a nasty stomach flu and leave the city, then disappear.

Yes, it was the least risky option. About a week later, he mentioned it again.

"I talked to Tyrone, he wants me to come out as soon as I can arrange it." Her smile took over her face, with a wanton gleam in her eyes.

He slid a matching warm grin onto his face. "That's good news. When were you thinking?"

"We talked about the week after next. I know it's short notice, and I completely understand if it doesn't work for you."

"Hmm. I'm not sure if I can manage it, let me make a few phone calls. Is the exact date already set?"

"It is, but I'm sure I can move it around a little if you need me to."

He didn't need her to, but he would ask her to move it forward two days, just to be sure. He needed to dictate the day of the kill—the more control he had, the less likely something would go wrong. He told her he needed to make some calls, waited half an hour, then Skyped her again.

"I have to be back for a meeting on Friday. I'd have to come for Wednesday and Thursday if that works? I'll pay for the extra nights at the hotel."

"That would be perfect—I'd love a reason to get there a little early, anyway. But I insist on paying for the hotel."

"I'll pay for our meals, then." He smiled. "I have a meeting that Wednesday morning, but let me take a look at flights. I should be able to make it there by dinner." He opened a browser window and pulled up flights into the airports nearby. San Jose was too close, as was Oakland. The Sacramento airport was about two hours away, far enough for his purposes. He checked to see which airlines would work.

"Yep, it looks like I can be in the city itself by about six-thirty or seven, depending on traffic. Would that work?"

"I'll have to check flights as well, I'm not sure I can be there early enough to pick you up at the airport," she said.

"No, don't worry about that. I should get a rental car anyway, so you don't have to drop me back when you need to be working."

"That probably makes the most sense."

"You know, there isn't much food on the planes these days, I'm gonna be starving when I get there. Given the time, can we meet at a restaurant?"

"That'll be perfect. Gives me time to unpack, and then meet up."

"And that way if you're repelled by me in person, you can run and hide." He gave her a wink, and she laughed.

But then she made things difficult.

"I'll do a little digging and find a nice, romantic place for us to eat," he said.

"Oh, don't worry about that. I know a couple of great places I'd like to go back to. I'll set up the reservation."

Shit. He should have expected that, since she'd been to San Francisco before. He tried to think, but his brain came up blank.

He made a motion like he was reaching for something, and "accidentally" knocked his cup of tea off the desk.

"Dammit! Hold on, I have to get something to clean this up." He sprinted out of the room, grabbed a tea towel, and went back to mop up the spill. As he cleaned, he racked his brain for an out.

He took the mug and the dirty towel into the kitchen, then returned. "Sorry about that. What were we talking about?"

"Oh, I just said I'd pick out a restaurant for us."

"No, no, no. Chivalry is not yet dead, at least not in my universe. Let me pick out a romantic spot where I can wine and dine you."

Annoyance flashed across her face. "That's a sweet thought, but there's—"

He struggled to keep a pleasant expression. "My love, you have to let me create some surprises for you!"

She paused and then laughed. "Of course, why not. No shortage of great food in that city, and we can go to one of the others the next night."

"A perfect compromise—the secret to a happy life."

He navigated the remaining details with exquisite care. And he learned an important lesson, to never again go with a victim to a city they'd visited before. She had too many opinions about how they should spend their evening, and he had to call up every bit of his cunning to defuse them without coming across as a bully or losing his temper.

The final boarding call interrupted his thoughts, and he made his way to the gate with his carry-on.

No matter. In about twelve hours, he'd be sitting across from her, reveling in his victory. Every frustration, every bit of anger, would be paid in full. No malleable toy, this—he'd earned every moment.

CHAPTER FORTY-FIVE

Arnett and Lopez appeared at Jo's door with a file and a white paper bag with "Sal's" printed on the side.

Arnett waved the bag in the air. "Haven't seen you leave this office for hours, so we thought you could use some food. Garcia picked up an extra meatball sub when he grabbed lunch for his team."

"He knows the way to my eternal loyalty. Any news?" She waved them in, and they pulled chairs up to the desk.

"That's the main reason we came by. I heard back from SDPD. The address was real, a duplex in a not-bad-not-great part of town, occupied by a single mother and her toddler. She cooperated fully, even gave them access to her computer. She said she'd been living there for two years, and that was confirmed by the property management company. So, she wasn't living there yet when Otthello's account was set up. There wasn't any evidence on her computer that she ever played *World of Warcraft* or was a gamer at all, and she claimed she wasn't dating anybody. We got the name of the two previous tenants and are following up there."

"What about the online leads?"

Lopez jumped in. "The e-mail account is valid, but the name and address on it are the same as on the *WoW* account. No information back from Skype yet. The IP addresses are basically useless. The techs say it's all just end-node information from several different high-anonymity proxies. He could be logging onto them from anywhere, from a different country halfway around the world. There's no way of knowing."

"They must have something. Can we locate the proxies and get a warrant, force them to give us what they have, make them log their traffic in the future?"

"Nope. Our guy is savvy, and he did his research. He knew enough to use proxies that don't log their traffic, so they can't give us an original ISP or IP address even if they wanted to, which they certainly don't. Most likely they don't originate from the U.S. anyway. Their whole reason for existing is to provide people with anonymity, and they do it well. But even so, it's pointless. He seems to use one proxy for a while and then switches to another, which he uses for a few days or weeks. We could go years without ever hitting the right one. Decades."

Jo's eyes flashed. "Can we get Blizzard to report each IP address to us when he logs in, see if we can get them to cooperate fast enough, if they're in the U.S.? Lives are on the line here."

"I mean, if all the ducks lined up just right, it's theoretically possible, but we don't have the capability to track this kind of thing. We'd need the FBI or someone to help us, and even then, I'm not sure it can be done."

Jo tapped her pen on the file. "I'll contact them again. Maybe they'll be willing to help us if we have a highly specific request."

"Can't hurt." Lopez's expression was guarded.

Arnett shifted in his chair. "Any reply from Blizzard on the other avatars?"

"Not yet."

CHAPTER FORTY-SIX

Martin arrived at the restaurant half an hour early, looking forward to a warm cup of coffee. The quote erroneously attributed to Mark Twain was nonetheless right about San Francisco—he was bone-chilled just walking from the car. He pushed open the door and stepped through, scanned the exposed brick walls and the rectangular red paper lanterns that gave off a warm, dim light. He found the bar off to the right side and headed toward it.

Diana sat waiting with a glass in her hand. She was looking in his direction and must have seen him approach, but didn't move to get up. Annoyance rippled through him—he wouldn't have time to ease into the evening or savor the look of anxious hope on her face as she arrived. *How the hell early did she get here, anyway?*

He smiled at her and raised his hand. She smiled back, still seated. He crossed to her, and finally she stood to embrace him. She threaded her arms around his back and he matched the embrace. They hugged for a long moment, then she drew back to look at him. He took in the sleek black dress accented with a red belt and gray heels, the red lipstick that set off her white skin and dark brown hair, the fringe of mascara around her eyes. He'd never seen her dressed up, and a thrill ran through him—his lovely, dressed-up businesswoman doll.

"Well, hello, beautiful."

"Hello to you too, handsome." She looked at her phone. "Oh, it's still early, I don't think our reservation will be ready. Sit, let's have a drink," she said.

He bristled at the instruction, but kept his composure.

"I'm glad I got here early. I hate to think of you sitting here all alone. I've heard nightmares about driving in this city, with the maze of one-way streets, so I left myself extra time to get here. Have you been waiting long?" He motioned to the bartender.

"Not too long. I just couldn't bear to sit in the hotel with only the TV for company. This is much more relaxing."

The bartender reached them. "What can I get you, sir?"

Was she already drinking alcohol, or not? He glanced at her glass, but couldn't tell if it was plain Coke or had something added.

"I'll have what the lady's having."

She held up her glass. "Oh, you won't like it, it's diet."

"Thanks for warning me. Make mine regular Coke." He smiled back and put a twenty on the bar.

He realized too late his order had been ambiguous. Had the bartender understood that if she had alcohol in hers, he wanted it, too, or would he think from the last comment that he only wanted soda? Annoyance surged through him again.

The bartender filled the soda in front of them, then went to make change. Martin met Diana's eyes, reoriented himself. "I'm glad you're here. I was worried you'd change your mind."

She smiled. "Don't be ridiculous. I've been looking forward to this for so long." She took a slow drink from her glass, maintaining eye contact over the rim.

"It's so strange, isn't it? To be sitting across from you, in the flesh," he said.

"It's an odd feeling, I agree. To both know and not know someone. But then, how well do we ever really know anyone else?" Her laugh was low and sultry.

He smiled as his mind searched for a response, considered his next prepared line, but it didn't feel right now.

Fuck.

When in doubt, change the subject. "How was your flight?"

"Not bad at all. Ever since I got my Kindle, I love flying. I just put in my earphones, lie back, and let it read to me. Sometimes I fall asleep, but even if I don't, it keeps me entertained. How was yours?"

He mentally cringed. So, she was well rested for the evening, despite the time change. No matter, booze would compensate for that. "Mine was good, too, nothing too exceptional. I had a talker next to me. I'm never sure how to signal to them I just want to read my book without being rude."

She laughed. "Mm-hmm. That's another benefit of the earbuds and the text-to-speech. Even if you aren't asleep, you can still pretend you are and nobody bothers you."

"I'll have to try that next time." He lifted his drink in the universal gesture for "cheers," and they clinked glasses.

They chatted on about their travels until the hostess called their reservation. She took them to an intimate table in the back corner of the restaurant, in a cozy pocket of the lowest light. Once they settled in, he opened his menu. "I thought I might order several things for us to share. The braciole looks excellent."

She looked over her menu. "I don't think I want anything that heavy. I think I'll get the chicken Caesar salad, nice and light." She closed it and smiled up at him.

The twinge of annoyance shimmied through him and transformed into anger. He stared at the entrées a moment longer before he spoke, struggling to maintain a pleasant expression.

"I'll choose light starters, then."

"Oh, no starter for me. The salad will be enough."

Bitch! She's ruining everything, every step of the way!

He faked a choking fit to cover the expression he knew had crept across his face and took a long sip from his water. He forced himself to calm down. So they wouldn't be sharing plates, so what? He could still feed her. He'd order an appetizer, and he could give her at least a bite or two of the braciole.

You knew this wasn't going to be easy, he reminded himself. *That's the whole point.*

"Are you okay?" She leaned toward him and her eyes scanned the room. Did she have the *nerve* to be embarrassed?

He coughed again. "I'm fine. Not sure what happened there. Anyway. Let's get a bottle of Gewürztraminer then. That should work well with both plates."

Her eyebrows went up and she leaned back. "I didn't realize you knew wine pairings that well. I'm impressed. Too bad we don't have time to go up to Napa or Sonoma."

He dipped his head in a mock bow. "Well, we'll just have to come back another time, won't we?"

She tilted her head and looked up at him. "That sounds lovely."

He smiled and relaxed. *Right back on track.*

After the waitress took their orders, he reached across the table and took Diana's hand. "I've waited so long to be able to do that. To be able to reach over and touch you."

She returned his touch with gentle pressure and leaned over the table toward him. "Mmm. So nice to have you in front of me. Warm. Real." She slipped her foot out of her shoe and ran it up his ankle.

He struggled to suppress the shudder of disgust at her brashness—*that's how whores behave!*—and kept both his leg and the smile on his face where they were. He lifted her hand and kissed it.

"So. Is San Francisco living up to your memory so far?" he asked, hoping the shake in his voice read as excitement.

She nodded. "I didn't drive past much, but the Victorians and the feel of the place are the way I remember. What are your thoughts so far?"

"From what I've seen, it's not like any other city I've ever been in. I like it, it relaxes me." This was true. He was surprised to find he enjoyed what he'd seen so far. A few seedy things, of course, like any major city. But it had *something*. Maybe the hills, or how you never knew which way the next street would go. There was an air of mystery to it, like some strange human maze with secrets around every corner. If he ever had to relocate, San Francisco would make his very short list of places to consider.

The appetizer's arrival broke him out of his reverie. "I apologize, it's not like me to wax poetic about a city." He laughed. "Now, let's see how the food is."

He tried to shift the conversation back to her, but her questions kept coming, each one grating on him. He found himself longing for the abhorrent verbal diarrhea women's nerves normally led them to spew, on topics determined by gentle nudges from him. But this one... Was she nervous at all? Or was she so taken with him, with the lovers' fantasy, that she'd given herself over to it? She didn't give him a moment to relax and savor the buildup; he constantly had to keep the reflexes up, watch what he said. He shifted in his chair and forced himself not to tap his fingers on the table.

He watched her wineglass, waiting to refill it. When the entrées came, the level had barely moved.

"Do you not like the wine? Should I get a different bottle?"

"No, it's lovely. I just don't want to drink too much too fast. With the jet lag and all, I'll fall asleep at the table." She smiled and took a sip.

Maybe her nap on the plane hadn't been restful after all? But what if she kept this up, didn't drink at the club either?

For the first time since Tijuana, he felt twinges of fear.

He took a sip of his own wine and wrestled with his anxiety. Told himself to snap out of it, that he was anticipating problems where they didn't exist. So what if she wasn't drinking much? She was barely eating, and she was tired. She'd feel even one glass of wine, and he'd make sure she had an extra-strong drink at the club.

A shrill voice screamed in his head. *And what if she won't drink it?*

He excused himself to the men's room. He splashed some water on his face, looked at himself in the mirror. Nothing was going right and she was ruining the evening anyway. Maybe he should just call it an early night? Tell her he couldn't wait any longer, get her back to the hotel and kill her now? It would be harder without the help of the wine and the fatigue from an evening's dancing. But it would be safer.

No! No, no, NO!

Petulance bubbled up in him, screamed through his body. He slammed his hand onto the counter.

That ruins the whole thing, the fun! I WANT MY MARIONETTE!

He needed her to dance for him, needed her to melt in his arms, needed to watch the filthy lust build up in her eyes and in her body all night long, snap his fingers and make her come. That's why he'd worked so hard to break her, that was the point of all of it! She was his, dammit, he had worked hard for her, and he deserved his prize. *No. NO.* He *wasn't* going to give that up.

He steadied himself. It would be fine. The whole point of this was the challenge, after all—giving up now would be self-defeating. So what if she was being difficult? He needed to use it, channel it into the kill. Make every bitchy, demanding moment come back to haunt her.

He arranged his face in the mirror, took several deep breaths, and marched back out with a loving grin on his face.

CHAPTER FORTY-SEVEN

"Josette Jacqueline Fournier, you *did not* bring your laptop with you tonight."

"Yes, Ma, I did. And stop it with the middle name, I'm not a child."

Elisabeth Fournier Arpent gave her daughter a withering glare. "Why even bother visiting if you're just going to work?"

"I don't know, for the same reason we have this conversation every time I come for dinner?" Jo met the green eyes that matched her own with a steely gaze.

"One of these days, my words will make it in past that thick skull of yours."

She bit back a retort about the importance of a serial killer strangling women—her mother had enough nightmares about her job as it was, without the graphic details. "You're just going to watch TV, and I have work to do. Would you rather I go home to do it?"

Elisabeth grumbled something beneath her breath and picked up the remote. Jo sighed and shot a surreptitious glance at her mother. The streaks of gray in her black hair were getting wider, as were the branching lines around her eyes. Her mother would turn sixty-seven next month. It wouldn't hurt Jo to be a little more attentive.

"The weather's supposed to be good this weekend. Let's go hiking up by Quabbin."

Her mother smiled. "That'd be nice. I'm free Saturday. I'll pack a lunch. Wear some makeup for a change, you never know what interesting man we might meet out there." She turned back to the television.

Jo clenched her teeth against the insult. She was wearing mascara and a swipe of lipstick the same as she always wore, carefully refreshed before she arrived. But to her mother, anything less than a full face of foundation, concealer, eye shadow, and blush was, and always would be, as good as nude. She shook her head and opened her work e-mail in her browser. She'd used every ounce of willpower during dinner and the requisite game of Scrabble that followed to keep her from obsessively checking her phone for a response from Blizzard, which could still come before morning, thanks to the time difference. Her mother was a patient woman, but short of emergency calls, cell phones while visiting were where she drew the line. But now that Jo's stepfather, Greg, had gone off to bed, official visiting time was over.

An e-mail from Blizzard was waiting, with the information for "Rimetra." Her name was Janni Koskinen, and the file included her contact information. Jo excused herself to the bathroom and placed a call to the number listed in the file.

"Hello."

"Janni Koskinen?"

"That's right. Who is this?"

"I'm Lieutentant Fournier from the Oakhurst County State Police Detective Unit. I'm working on an investigation, and I'd like to ask you a few questions."

She hesitated. "About what?"

Jo put on her most reassuring voice, with just a whiff of motherly warmth. "Nothing about you directly, ma'am. But we're interested in any information you might have about an individual you met while playing *World of Warcraft*."

"Oh my god, a terrorist? I heard the police were on there looking for terrorists in the game. Oh god. I don't know anything."

"No, ma'am, not a terrorist. Just a person we'd like to talk to. His player name is Otthello, and you talked to him a few times just over a month ago. He told you his real name was Peter. Do you remember a player by that name?"

"Oh yes. Complete asshole."

"How so?"

"Hold on a second." Jo heard the sound of footsteps over the line, and then a door closed. The woman's voice dropped, and her mouth sounded closer to the phone.

"We hung out, did some quests together. He was flirting like crazy, totally hot and heavy. We had fun. Then all of a sudden, he gives me the deep freeze. I didn't hear from him even though he was online, and when I whispered him, he ignored me. He was so rude, it was cruel, actually."

"Did you talk to him over Skype or something in addition to chatting in the game?"

"Nope. I thought we were having a great time hanging out, and he was saying things that made me think he felt the same way. Then, suddenly, gone."

"So you only spoke to him in the chat channel?"

"Yep. We talked in the trade channel too, and in group chats. That's it."

"No idea why he stopped talking to you?"

Janni barked an angry laugh. "None at all."

"Did he ever ask you to meet outside of the game, in person?"

"No way. And I wouldn't ever have met anyone from the game in real life, regardless."

Jo wondered how many of the murdered women would have said the same thing. "That's smart of you. I'd like to ask you a favor. I'm going to give you my contact information, and if he talks to you again in-game, or if you even see him log on, will you let me know right away?"

"Oh, I'd be glad to. Let me get a pen."

Jo rattled off the department number and her personal cell. "If he does talk to you, don't respond, don't say anything at all. Just call me immediately, any time of the day or night, okay?"

"You bet I will. Can you tell me what he's done?"

"Right now, all I can tell you is that we'd like to talk to him. And that I very much appreciate your help."

"I always do whatever I can to help the police in any way. I'm a law-abiding citizen, always have been."

Jo smiled. Wasn't everybody? "Thank you very much. Without help from citizens like you, we can't do our job. Remember, anytime, day or night."

"Will do."

Jo hung up the phone. She pulled at the hoop in her ear and stared out the window without seeing. Otthello had been trying to form relationships with women, that was certain. So why cut off contact with Janni Koskinen? He'd been talking to both Rimetra and Serylda at the same time, why abandon one of his options?

Otthello had changed servers and character names after killing Emily. And if he cut ties with his server and character after each kill, there was no point wasting time on other relationships on that server once he had a victim. If that was right, the severed contact with Janni would mean he'd zeroed in on his next kill.

Jo angled the screen of her laptop and pulled up her e-mail. The information on Serylda had come through while she was looking at Rimetra's files. She clicked on it.

Serylda's name was listed as Lucia Peretti. Jo picked up her phone and dialed the listed phone number.

"Hello?" An elderly woman's voice answered.

"Lucia Peretti?"

"What?"

"Is this Lucia Peretti?"

"No. Who's this?" She sounded annoyed.

"This is Lieutenant Josette Fournier from the Oakhurst County State Police Detective Unit. I'm looking for Ms. Lucia Peretti, is she home?"

"I never heard that name before. You got the wrong number."

Jo verified the number she'd dialed.

"Yeah, that's the right number, but there's nobody here by that name."

"Thanks for your time."

"Yup." The woman hung up.

Jo stared at the phone for a moment. Not so strange to have a wrong number; people changed phone contracts all the time. She thought for a moment, then plugged the address into Google. A strange array of hits came up, so she put the address into Google Maps directly: 53700 Robin Hill Way, Atlanta, Georgia 30093.

We could not find 53700 Robin Hill Way, Atlanta Georgia 30093.

Make sure your search is spelled correctly.

Try adding a city, state, or zip code.

She tried the street name alone. There wasn't even a Robin Hill Way in Georgia at all.

What the hell was going on?

CHAPTER FORTY-EIGHT

As the waitress cleared away the dessert dishes, Martin looked at his watch.

"Hey, it's still early. You know what I'd love? Let's go dancing. Someplace with big-band-style music. Very romantic." He squeezed her hand and pulled out his cell.

"Oooh, you know what would be really romantic? The last time I was here, I found a little trail that runs behind the Legion of Honor, down to the Sutro Baths, along the ocean. Strolling along, smelling the crisp sea air and listening to the crash of the waves—it was so relaxing. The moon's nearly full, how romantic would that be?" Her eyes lit up.

No no no no NO NO! I want you to dance!

He pushed down the voice in his head, squashed the flames of anger. He masked his expression by morphing it to look like he was thinking, tried to buy a few seconds to come up with an answer.

"The sun's just set; I don't think the twilight will hold up long enough for us to get there."

"Nothing's far from anything in San Francisco. And with the moonlight, we'll be fine."

Fucking BITCH!

The anger turned to rage, and he felt his face turn red. He faked another cough and grabbed for his water. But it was too late—her expression had changed.

He took a moment to supposedly catch his breath, while she watched him closely. No way he'd be able to push it now without putting her guard up. But what difference did it make, really? It wasn't ideal, but it would still tire her and give the hotel a chance to empty out. By the time they drove to the coast from North Beach, took the walk and then drove down to South San Francisco, it would be close enough to midnight. He could always spontaneously spark a romantic dance beside the ocean, and that would be enough. He'd suggest they stop for a drink on the way back, plenty of clubs open late in the city even on Wednesday, and he could probably even get another dance in then.

He made a show of regaining the power of speech. "That sounds perfect. I don't get many chances to see the ocean at night." He signaled for the check.

Her face relaxed and she laughed. "No, I don't imagine Omaha gives you too many opportunities for that. I couldn't live that far inland. I love all bodies of water, rivers, waterfalls, lakes, but the ocean is special. Looking out over the endless water just… moves me."

He smiled, relieved. Not the way he'd planned, but he'd covered well, and her romantic side was easing out.

He pushed out his chair and gave a small bow. "Then let us away to the seashore, m'lady."

Her smile broadened, and she rose from the table. "I'll drive, that way you'll get a chance to see the city."

A shadow crossed his face. "I'll drive, I don't mind. I prefer it."

Her eyes ran over him. "I insist. I've driven in the city before."

Bitch! You'll do as I say or I'll kill you right here!

He winced as the thought flashed through his head and he saw her eyes narrow. He took a deep breath and frowned. How had he not prepared for this possibility? No way was he going to risk leaving evidence behind in her car. And she'd seen the look on his face, knew something was wrong.

"I'm sorry, I have to come clean, and I'm a bit embarrassed. I have a phobia about riding as a passenger in cars, I seize up into a panic attack. Crazy, I know. I was in a severe accident when I was younger that killed my mother, and I just—can't. I have to drive."

She looked at him for a long moment, one nail tapping on the table. "Well. If phobias were rational, they wouldn't be phobias, would they? How about this. It'd be a pain to come back for one of the vehicles anyway, so why don't we each drive our own car?" She smiled, but her eyes were sharp.

"Of course, I should have thought of that myself." He kissed her hand. "Shall we go?"

He slipped her arm into the crook of his elbow and led her out of the restaurant while trying to drown out the voice in his head.

Keep it together, it's almost over.

Keep your eye on the kill.

CHAPTER FORTY-NINE

Jo pulled up the information on Serylda's IP address; it varied from log-in to log-in, with the same sort of pattern they'd seen with Porrthos/Otthello. She scrolled to the information about payment method. Serylda also used prepaid game cards that came from random locations across the country.

She stared at her screen.

Was Serylda just a paranoid gamer who didn't want Blizzard to have her information? From what Lopez and Horace had said, that paranoia was common, but so common that two of the five gamers they'd investigated would show this pattern? And if so, what real evidence did they have that this Otthello character was their killer, and not just another paranoid gamer?

She pulled up the chat transcripts and went over them, along with Otthello's other information. He'd been the only character deleted off Emily's friends list, but maybe they'd made a mistake by not getting information on all her friends. Maybe these other chats with Rimetra and Serylda were just tawdry attempts to lure them into video-game sex?

A chill ran through her. Lopez said some players had multiple accounts. This pattern was so similar to Otthello's, maybe this was some sort of trap Otthello had set to find out if the police were on to him? Had he created another account and pretended to be Serylda to see if the police would contact him? She checked the files. This account had only been in existence for six months, much less time than Otthello's account.

Shit. Maybe he knew the lady who owned the phone number. Maybe he'd paid her to notify him if they called?

She rubbed her eyes. Now who was getting paranoid?

If it were a trap, she'd already set it off and there was nothing she could do. The killer would disappear and probably alter his methods. They'd never find him, and countless more women would die.

But that scenario seemed unlikely. Much more possible that Serylda was an intended victim and happened to be paranoid about the information she gave to Blizzard. And Jo's most important priority was to move forward under the assumption that she was in danger, and continue trying to find her.

She called Lopez, asked her to start the paperwork to find out what they could about the rest of the players on Emily's friends list tonight. Then she thought about the printouts she'd made of the chat logs. She made her excuses to her mother and hurried out. She needed to go over them again, word by word, for even the smallest thing that she might have missed.

CHAPTER FIFTY

Martin followed Diana as she pulled into the Legion of Honor parking lot. The museum had long since closed, so they had no problem parking next to one another near the central fountain.

Martin surveyed the Greek Revival building aglow with hidden lights, and the cypress-lined view where the ocean met the bay. Many of the tree branches tilted away from the ocean, molded by the continual wind that blew off the water, and reminded him of neglected bonsai trees allowed to grow to full size. They added a ghostly element against the rapidly darkening sky, like creatures captured by a powerful wizard, forever frozen in the awkward posture of their attempted escape.

Diana gestured to the golf course to the right of the museum. "Back through the park there, the path connects with a trail. If we head south, it'll take us to the Sutro Baths and some picturesque romantic ocean views…" Her sultry voice trailed off, and she took his hand.

"Lead the way."

Their conversation lulled into a gentle rhythm of casual banter as they strolled. Once past the golf course, the path ran along the ocean; when they'd been walking about fifteen minutes it met up with a large tunnel. They joked about the darkness and huddled together as they moved through it. When they emerged from the other side, their view opened onto the ruins of the once-great Sutro Baths, set into the cliffs overlooking the Pacific Ocean. The moonlight shone off the series of skeletal pool foundations, presenting a serenity that juxtaposed the churning, roaring ocean beyond.

Diana pointed to the various structures. "I love these ruins. A century ago, this was a huge water park in a series of art nouveau buildings, with areas for heated pools, slides, even water trapezes. It must have been like one of the Seven Wonders before it burned down."

They took in the scene for a moment and Diana spoke again. "It's strange, isn't it? There's a beauty to it, but it's also so sad. Something great was here, something that made so many people happy. And then it was destroyed, ripped away with only a faint trace left as a reminder. Like the shadow of every person who swam and laughed here is watching us."

Martin pulled her back into his chest, so they were both staring out together. "I've never seen this sentimental side to you." He kissed her neck and ran his hands up and down her arms.

She laughed. "I suppose that was a little intense, wasn't it?"

"A little. But nice." He pulled her closer, one arm around her waist.

I should do it now.

They were alone on the end of the trail, and they hadn't seen a single person since they'd left the golf course. The way everything had gone wrong, it was so tempting to just do it, be done with it.

She wouldn't think twice if I loosened my tie…

He caught himself. No, this was how people got caught. And everything was back on track now; she was happy, relaxed. He stroked her cheek.

He gave a sensual chuckle, low in his throat, and kissed her hair. *So close to dying, and she has no idea.* He let the feeling of power surge, then sat with it, heart pulsing. *You live now because I choose to let you live. Because it pleases me to let you dance at my behest. I will not cheat myself. I will enjoy your death to the fullest.*

He nuzzled her ear and smiled.

After enjoying the view for a few more moments, Martin asked Diana if she was ready to start back. As they headed toward the tunnel, Martin tried to pick up the pace a bit in hopes of getting a few dances in before the swing club closed.

"Slow down, darling, these shoes aren't the best for walking on a path like this. If I twist my ankle, you'll have to carry me." She laughed.

He slowed and put his arm around her as they continued. They came out from the tunnel into moonlight that felt almost bright by comparison. The path bent toward the water, and they watched the moon glisten off the ocean as they continued along, leaving the tunnel out of sight behind them.

Diana stopped and pulled Martin close. She reached up to stroke his cheek, then looked into his eyes.

"I am so glad I found you. When we met, I wasn't sure about you at first. But I know now you are exactly the kind of man I'm looking for. Thank you for coming here with me." She lifted her chin and kissed him.

Martin returned the kiss, seized the opportunity to memorize the way her lips felt against his, warm and compliant, wanting him. He let himself savor her words. She was utterly enraptured by him, willing to do whatever he asked, and he'd been silly to doubt he could make it happen. She was simply a woman who liked things a certain way, especially when meeting a strange man for the first time. And that was fair enough—so many people weren't who they claimed to be online. He smiled at his wit, altering the position of the kiss. She smiled in response.

He breathed in the jasmine scent of her hair and let his mind linger over all the evening's difficulties, one at a time, allowing the adrenaline to take little stabs into him. Oh yes. This time it felt right—not like the last time—he could already feel his body responding. He'd been right to seek out the challenge, and to stick with it in the face of adversity.

He was imagining the feel of his tie cutting into her neck, enthralled with the picture in his mind's eye, when Diana plunged a syringe into his carotid artery, filled with enough black tar heroin to kill two men his size. She administered it quickly and effectively—his brain registered the prick but didn't know how to interpret it. Some sort of wasp or bee? He pulled back from the kiss and clasped his hand against his neck, eyes wide open.

It was far too dark for him to see her retract the syringe and slip it back into the bag in her purse. But he could see her features, contorted by a chilling moue. The expression terrified him, at least for the brief moment before the nearly pure heroin hit him and his consciousness imploded.

She paused long enough to snap two mental pictures of his face, the first filled with confusion, the second horrified realization. She braced her front foot with a slightly bent knee, then shoved her arms into his chest with all her strength. His eyes had already glazed over, and he put up no resistance as he fell backward over the railing.

She watched him topple, then disappear from view over the side of the cliff. She listened for the thud as he hit the rocks and bounced off them, then for the splash far below when he landed in the high-tide waters of the Pacific.

Diana knelt down and felt along the path until her hand found a rock the size of a walnut. She picked it up and put it into her jacket pocket. She pulled a scarf from her other pocket and wrapped it around her neck and mouth before continuing down the path, a seemingly sensible thing to do against the chill San Francisco wind picking up off the ocean.

CHAPTER FIFTY-ONE

Diana kept the scarf in place until she reached her rental car. There were no cameras in the parking lot, she knew, and it was unlikely any passerby would pay her any attention. But it was better to be safe than sorry.

She slid behind the wheel and started the car. She eased down the road to the main street, then headed toward the freeway out of San Francisco. She checked her watch: it was 10:30. The drive to Sacramento should only take two hours at the most, even with a detour well off the highway to fill up. She'd return the car, grab something to eat, and sleep on the flight home. She double-checked the timing in her head as she turned onto the highway and removed the scarf. She wouldn't be able to relax until she was home and able to clean up all the loose ends.

There was no question he was dead. If the fall on the rocks hadn't killed him instantly, the heroin would do the job within minutes—he'd either overdose or drown unconscious in the ocean. He'd wash up somewhere in a day or two, depending on where the currents took him. It didn't really matter when or where. After spending time in the ocean, the injection site would be difficult to see, and even if they did find it, the heroin would be nearly impossible to detect. Should luck fail her there, they would most likely attribute the death to an accidental or intentional overdose, or a tragic fall caused by heroin intoxication. The chance that the medical examiner would rule the death a homicide was negligible; every time she'd done this, the "accidental death" of the "out-of-town businessman" barely made the news.

CHAPTER FIFTY-TWO

Jo was still hunched over her desk poring through transcripts when Arnett and Lopez launched into her office the next morning, an expression of high alert on both faces. Arnett spoke without preamble.

"We just heard back about Otthello's Skype account. Bad news is, the information on his account, name, address, it's all different from the name and address on his *World of Warcraft* account, but it's still bullshit. Good news is, he had only one contact—established on the same day he asked Serylda to connect with him there, so dollars to doughnuts we've got her Skype ID. No real written chat, just the initial request to add him as a contact, and then a comment or two here and there to say hello before they called one another. But we do have a record of the calls, how long they lasted, all of that. They seem to be in contact quite often, almost every day, up until two days ago. And here's the thing. Her Skype account was deleted early yesterday."

"You mean his account was deleted."

"No. I mean hers."

What the hell? The information couldn't find a place to land in her brain. "Hold up a minute. They were talking regularly, then all of the sudden she deletes her account? How soon after their last call?"

Arnett consulted the file in his hand. "The next day."

Jo's mind raced. Were they too late? Had he killed her? It wasn't even two months since his last kill. But no, that didn't make sense.

A dead person can't cancel an account, and a loved one wouldn't bother for something like Skype. Was it a decoy account after all? "What about her *WoW* account? Is it still active?"

Lopez shook her head, expression grim. "Horace confirmed that her *WoW* account has been canceled, too. Both should be recoverable, but we wanted to let you know about the movement ASAP."

"Shit. We need to search for any strangled women matching his MO, now."

"On it. But it doesn't make sense," Arnett said, brows knit.

Jo nodded. "No, it doesn't. My thought is, maybe it's a decoy account, and I may have tripped the wire. But, as I'm thinking about it, the account would have had to be canceled before I made the call to the number on the account."

Lopez shook her head and waved her phone. "And it doesn't make sense, since Otthello's account hasn't been canceled."

"What?" Jo froze.

"There hasn't been any activity on it, but it's still active. Wouldn't he cancel that one too, if that's what this was about?"

Jo thought. "Unless he's confident we can't track him."

"But if he knows we're onto him, it's useless to him now. He's gotta know we're watching his conversations," Arnett said.

Lopez waved her hands and scowled. "Wait, we're getting ahead of ourselves. A decoy account makes no sense to me. I think it's more likely she picked up on something off about him, realized he was dangerous, and wanted to cut off any method of contact. I'd totally do that if some creeper were after me."

Jo considered. "That makes sense, but we can't afford to assume. We need to find out what we can from that Skype account."

CHAPTER FIFTY-THREE

Diana yawned as she flipped on the light in her entryway and slid the front dead bolt into place behind her. Cleopatra wandered out from the living room with sleepy eyes, and Diana reached down to pet her.

She dropped her keys into the bowl on the mantel, then hung her jacket and her hobo bag in the hall closet. She had no luggage; she'd been gone less than a day. She'd never had a hotel reservation at the Saville or anywhere else.

She took the rock out of her jacket pocket and padded into her bedroom. She pulled the bottom drawer out of the jewelry box on her bureau and gingerly placed it inside, next to the others already nestled there. Tomorrow, when she had time, she'd engrave it with his initials and the date.

She grabbed a Diet Coke out of the refrigerator and brought it to her study. When her desktop booted up, she deleted the decoy e-mail address and Skype account she had set up to use with Peter.

She'd already wiped down the syringe and needle and thrown them into the gutter outside a methadone clinic in Sacramento, close to where she'd picked up the heroin from her dealer that morning. She'd thrown the empty plastic bag that had held them into a garbage can at a Del Taco in L.A. on her way home from the airport.

She'd canceled her *World of Warcraft* account before she left. She dreaded having to start over with new characters every time she killed, but it really was the only completely safe way to be untraceable. She confirmed the final transaction and relaxed. She'd wait a week, then open up a new account. Or maybe she'd try *Guild Wars* this time, for a change of pace. Either way, this kill would stave off the nightmare for now. It would return eventually, but she'd have a few months' peace at least, and would treasure every blessed unbroken night's sleep.

The nightmare was always the same, more or less. It started with a girl, about eight, sitting on a hardwood floor in a fluffy pink princess dress, her bright hazel eyes fixed on the doll cradled in her arms. She rocked it and sang to it in a soothing voice, *Hush little baby, don't say a word…* A man appeared in the door behind her—the child froze as he lifted her up and threw her on the bed, her arms still fiercely gripping the doll. Diana never saw what happened next, but she heard the begging and the screams, and then the girl alone on the bed, sobbing, tangled in the skirt of her ethereal gown.

Then the girl sat up and screamed at Diana—"You didn't stop him! You let him hurt me! You didn't help me!" The girl's face twisted and morphed with rage and hatred, her mouth filled with pointed fangs, and she pulled a knife out from under the pillow behind her. She crawled toward Diana, slowly at first, then faster, her screams louder, shriller. Diana tried to flee, but in the way of dreams, her feet turned to lead, and the child caught up to her. She normally woke screaming just as the knife pierced her calf and felled her to the floor.

She'd lost count of how many therapists she'd seen, looking for any other way to get rid of the dreams. They told her she needed to heal her inner child, protect her the way Diana's mother had failed to protect Diana. Be the mother to herself that her own mother had failed to be. But her inner child didn't give a shit about bubble baths and the other types of "me time" they suggested. Because that damaged, raging little eight-year-old wanted revenge. She wanted the man who hurt her to pay, wanted to watch him die—and if she couldn't have him, she was happy with a stand-in. Any brother-in-crime that used married women and their children, who sent loving husbands plunging to their deaths, who never gave a thought to the lives and souls they destroyed as long as their selfish needs were filled. They were just as deserving of death.

So she hunted, and she killed. And for now, for a short time at least, the girl would let her sleep.

CHAPTER FIFTY-FOUR

Martin's body washed up the next day on Ocean Beach, contributing an element of surreal horror to the morning jog of a nearby resident, along with an element of utter delight to that of her German shepherd.

Detective Alan Guerrero surveyed the scene with a practiced eye and called in a team, but there wasn't much to see or document. The cold water had preserved the body fairly well, and because the victim had kept his wallet in a zippered internal coat pocket, identification was easy and fast. Martin Scherer, age thirty-two, from El Paso, Texas.

The investigation seemed open-and-shut to him at first. Suicides were not rare in any city, and the Golden Gate Bridge in particular was known for the high number of people who used it as their personal iFly. In the previous month alone, ten people had committed suicide by jumping from it, and several more tried but survived. The bodies that washed up on coastal beaches were a routine part of police life, even if this particular location was unusual. Most of those who weren't rushed out to sea by the tides washed up in Marin County, or around the China Beach area. Still—he shrugged—it all depended on which section of the bridge they'd jumped from, and the vagaries of the tides.

Guerrero contacted the El Paso police and gave them the information they needed to find out who, if anyone, might be waiting to hear from Martin Scherer. He gave instructions for a copy of the mandatory autopsy report to be sent to them. Then his thoughts turned to lunch, fully expecting that the paperwork he'd complete later in the day would be the last he'd hear of Scherer.

*

While Guerrero enjoyed his extra-large Giorgio's special on Clement and Third, a unit led by Detective Dan Swinyer went through Scherer's house looking for information about Scherer's next of kin. His house was obsessively neat and his personal records minimal. He had few paper-based records, but the bills they did find were paid and organized, and his checkbook reported a hefty bank balance. They found no indications of a wife or a girlfriend, or even extended family—no pictures, no address book, no personal correspondence. Swinyer instructed his team to bring the password-protected computers down to the station for the techs to look into.

"Swinyer, come take a look at this."

One of the investigators, Matt Frond, called him over to a small desk drawer he'd had to break into. Inside were six women's wedding rings, four simple bands, and two welded bridal sets.

Swinyer whistled. "Holy shit. What's this, six times a widower, and the sixth was too much to take? Hell, I admire him for holding out as long as he did."

"I don't think so. Take a look at the inscription on this band." Frond handed him a flashlight to shine into the drawer.

He leaned in and followed the inscription around with the beam. "Jeanine and Roger Hammond, June 13th 1998."

Roger Hammond, not Martin Scherer. That was hinky. And he could swear there was something about those names that was familiar.

"Do a search on those names, see what you come up with," he said.

"On it."

*

Jo continued to pore over the transcripts, praying the information about Serylda's accounts would come through in time to help the woman, if she existed. When her phone rang, she snatched it up without checking the caller ID.

"Fournier."

"This is Detective Dan Swinyer of the El Paso PD. I have some information I think might be related to a case you're working on, Jeanine Hammond's murder."

Jo set the phone on the desk. "I'm putting you on speaker. You have my full attention, Detective."

"Earlier today we got a call from San Francisco reporting the suicide of Martin Scherer, a resident of El Paso. When we investigated his residence, we found something strange. Six wedding rings in a locked drawer, one of them inscribed with the name Jeanine Hammond. When I plugged the name into the computer, your open homicide came up. The inscription matches her details, same spelling, with husband named Roger."

"We're on the next plane out."

CHAPTER FIFTY-FIVE

The hair on Jo's arms stood on end as they entered Scherer's house. The overwhelming smell of cleaning products and the icy, almost clinical feel was a bizarre cross between a badly staged model home and a hospital room. Nothing among the minimalist decor gave any insight into the person who lived there—no books, no DVDs, no diplomas on the wall, no family pictures. Nothing an inch out of place. Only the near-complete lack of dust kept her from wondering if it had ever been touched.

Arnett followed Jo into the study. The missing computers left the room without defined purpose, strangely like an abandoned office space.

"Matt Frond, Lieutenant Josette Fournier and Detective Bob Arnett of the Oakhurst County SPDU," Swinyer introduced them, and everyone shook hands. "We stopped the search once we realized this was related to your homicide. We've been waiting to bag and tag them so you could take a look."

Frond reached over and opened the drawer. He pulled the rings out one by one with forceps, photographed them from a variety of angles, then placed them into bags. After logging each one, he handed them to Jo. For all except Jeanine Hammond's, Jo took snaps with her phone and texted them out to New Orleans and Salt Lake City so the husbands could confirm ownership.

They finished the remaining search of the home quickly and found nothing else of interest. Scherer's lack of sentiment had that one benefit, at least.

Swinyer took them back to the police station to view the belongings found on the body.

"He had a zippered pocket in his overcoat—that's where we found his wallet. We also found these. Any idea why he'd be carrying these around?" He pointed to a pair of forceps and a long band of rubber.

Arnett barked a laugh. "I bet that's how he got Carson's ring off. Compressed the finger with the rubber. Jeweler did that for me once when I needed to get mine off, so he didn't have to cut it." He shook his head.

"Nothing else on him. If he had a cell phone or anything else, it's at the bottom of the ocean. Coat was fully buttoned up." He tossed the bag with the overcoat onto the table.

Jo picked it up and looked closely at the style and the buttons. They were a clear match with the security camera footage from Jeanine's hotel. The lab would test Scherer's DNA against the partial profile from Jeanine's dress, but it was already a fait accompli.

They had their killer.

*

Jo sat at her desk, staring out the window into the atrium. She wasn't satisfied, but she couldn't put her finger on why. She kept circling the details in her head, looking for peace.

Within hours, everything had come together. Investigators followed up on an abandoned car reported at the Legion of Honor museum in San Francisco; rental papers in the glove compartment were made out to Martin Scherer. The car had been rented at the Sacramento airport, and that took them directly to a round-trip Southwest flight from Houston to Sacramento for Martin Scherer, who hadn't made the return trip.

In light of the strange flight itinerary, Jo's team searched his name on flights and rental cars outside the greater Oakhurst, Salt

Lake City, and New Orleans areas, extending their search to airports that could be reached within half a day's drive. They found the corresponding reservations in Syracuse, Idaho Falls, and Mobile all within twenty-four hours of the respective victim's murder.

Beyond a shadow of a doubt, Martin Scherer had killed these women. In cold blood. Knowingly left behind husbands, children, parents, and friends to mourn them. He was a ruthless psychopath, and the world was a better place without him. Did it really matter how exactly he came to his end? The families had closure, he wouldn't kill again, and the taxpayers had been saved a considerable amount of money. What more justice could be done in the case, regardless?

But she couldn't shake it.

Why had Scherer been in San Francisco, and how did he end up in the ocean? Based on what they knew about his murders, everything indicated he'd been on this trip to kill—the flight out of Sacramento, the rental car, the large amount of cash. And the timing of the transcripts, the Skype calls—every indication pointed to Serylda as the intended victim.

But he was the one that ended up dead.

There were three possibilities, as far as she could see. The first was Scherer had met with some sort of random accident, or had been the victim of a random crime. That was possible, but Jo didn't like the coincidence that Serylda had canceled her accounts during the same time frame.

The theory that Scherer killed himself wasn't much more satisfying. Why the strange airport and the round-trip ticket? Maybe he hadn't planned to kill himself originally, and something changed during the trip? Maybe Serylda found him out, or escaped, and he figured it was only a matter of time before she went to the police? Killers made stupid mistakes all the time, and who knew what he told her if he thought she'd never see the light of day again? But why not just run, wouldn't it be smarter to disappear and start over? Surely his survival instinct would be stronger than that, and he certainly had the intelligence to transform his identity. And how did he get from the Legion of Honor, where his car was still parked, to the Golden Gate?

And there was the hat. Suicides didn't jump to their death with things like glasses and hats on, but they'd found no trace of the all-important fedora. Not *impossible* that he had it on when he jumped and it washed away. But it added to her unease.

The final possibility seemed most likely—that Scherer's attempt to kill Serylda had gone wrong somehow. They knew he took these women on dates—maybe they'd met up at the Legion and then she drove them to the Golden Gate for a romantic stroll. Maybe in a spontaneous moment he decided to throw her off the bridge instead of strangle her, and she somehow got away. Or maybe she picked up on something off about him, or asked him some questions she didn't like the answers to, and decided to run. Maybe he chased her, and there was a struggle. This was the only option that fit with the likely purpose of his trip, and with the account cancellations. If she'd accidentally killed him while defending herself, she wouldn't be eager to go to the police.

It made sense. It fit the facts.

So why couldn't she convince herself?

Arnett had no patience for her reservations. "Sure, something's strange about it all. But the asshole's dead. Who cares if it was an accident or if he killed himself?" he said.

"I know you better than that. You want to know the truth as much as I do."

Arnett let out an angry sigh. "I want a million dollars too. There are battles you can win and battles you can't. Two months ago, we were pissed because the Hammond case was going into cold storage and there was nothing we could do about it. We wanted justice, and closure for the family. We fought for it when nobody would help, and we got it. So we don't know every detail, so what?"

The FBI agreed. They refused to dedicate man-hours to tracing any of the IP addresses, despite Jo's additional request after the body and rings were found. If there had been another victim, she'd had a close escape, and there was no point in investigating further. In their opinion, it was just as likely that "Serylda" had been the decoy account Jo theorized, created to be sure that the police weren't on his tracks, and canceled when Jo's team started making phone calls. He could easily have faked the chat to himself and placed Skype calls from one to the other to make it look like a woman was in danger. And who knew—maybe when push came to shove he couldn't handle knowing the police were closing in, and killed himself. Regardless, there was zero reason to invest precious time and resources. This danger was over, and other people needed their help.

When she told Arnett the FBI had denied her request, he stared at her for a long moment. "I know what this is about."

"What's that?" Jo asked.

"You're pissed you didn't solve it. That something happened before we got there. I know you too well, Jo. You feel cheated."

He was right. She wasn't just uneasy, she was angry. Angry she hadn't seen the thing end by her own hand. But not just because she wasn't the one to solve it—she was angry at how hamstrung they'd been, how she'd had to leave most of the work to Arnett and Lopez, and how she hadn't been able to give the case the attention the women deserved. They'd been so close. If Rockney had let her keep on with the case, or if she'd been able to squeeze out more time, even just a few hours more—that would have made the difference. But no. And it was all her own fault—she'd damned herself to administrative hell when she took this job, turned her back on what she knew she was supposed to be doing. And she couldn't even remember why she'd taken it anymore. She'd almost managed to convince herself that she didn't miss boots-on-the-ground detective work that much, focused on learning how to be the most effective lieutenant possible, reduced the nagging to a small pull at the back of her mind. But this case had shattered that illusion. Even if she managed to become the best lieutenant in the history of the department, that wouldn't make her happy. She didn't just *want* to bring killers to justice, she *needed* to. By her own detection work, not by signing papers that allowed other people to conduct investigations.

Was that anger causing her to turn this into something it wasn't, make her cling to some strange hope there was more to it, something that needed her continued attention?

No. Those transcripts, they'd been too real. There had been an unnecessary complexity to it all for a decoy. Scherer had made mistakes with Serylda, and Serylda had become angry. She'd put him through his paces, made him work for it. Her responses were unpredictable, and there were times when he hadn't seemed to know quite how to respond. Jo shook her head—there were two distinct voices in those transcripts.

Her mind swirled with images. Jeanine, Emily, Aleta. They'd left behind so many loved ones, so many friends and family members whose lives would never be the same. She called up the faces of the ones she'd met—Paola. Teresa. Roger, who, like her uncle Michel, would likely never recover from the loss of his wife. Her fist clenched around the diamond at her neck. If the victim were someone Jo had loved, would a dead killer be enough? Was it enough for them?

Teresa. She bolted upright, the memory of Jeanine's niece prodding her. Teresa's small face tucked under her fiancé's large, angry one. Philip Begemack, with his history of restraining orders and controlling behavior.

One tragedy in the Hammond family was enough. There might be nothing she could do to clarify Scherer's death, but there was one thing she *could* do to help Jeanine's loved ones. Philip Begemack might not have been Jeanine's killer, but he wasn't a good man, either. And she could prevent Teresa Hammond from ending up the victim of an abusive husband, on an accelerating path to becoming a missing person or a wrecked corpse the police would only be able to assist after it was too late.

She reached down into her left desk drawer and flipped through the hanging folders until she found the restraining order paperwork against Begemack. She made copies on her desktop printer and slipped them into an envelope. Then she addressed the envelope to Roger Hammond and tossed the envelope onto her outgoing mail.

She turned back to her computer and pulled up a Word document. She drafted a letter resigning her position as lieutenant and asking to be reinstated as a detective.

To celebrate, she spent the evening reading everything she could find about suicides from the Golden Gate Bridge.

CHAPTER FIFTY-SIX

Diana was having a good day.

She finished the work she needed to submit and was gearing down for a relaxing evening.

Cocoa, I think.

She started the saucepan of milk heating, then slipped into her comfy fleece pajamas and a pair of fluffy socks. She padded back into the kitchen to be sure the milk didn't overheat. When it was warm enough, she gathered the ingredients and assembled the drink. She thought for a moment and then threw on some mini-marshmallows—what the hell.

Back in her office, she sang to herself while she loaded up *World of Warcraft* and logged on with her new avatar, Kalyka. She smiled as she typed the name. She'd thought about going with a spelling variation of Shiva, but decided that would be a bit too obvious. This was perfect.

Kalyka had logged out in the boonies, but her hearth was set in Dalaran, so she was back to the city in seconds. Diana pulled her legs up under her, sipped the chocolate, and scanned the chat channels. She was watching for anything a bit brash, a bit bombastic, but with an underlying intelligence. Something that cried out, "Look at me! I'm a man with a big ego who needs attention!" But there were also treasures to be found among the harder-to-detect trolls, who'd innocently start fights between other players, then sit back and watch, throwing fuel on the fire as needed. So, she approached it like a day fishing at the lake. You had to be patient, you had to be quiet, and you had to throw lots back because they were basically decent guys. But every once in a while, one would wave his wit and "charm" around like a metaphorical dick, the equivalent of a fish jumping into your boat.

She watched a few interesting exchanges, then cringed when a pathetic troll tried to shock everyone by making a joke about rape only being funny when it's committed by a clown. Several women threatened to have him banned, and the channel flooded as people banged out such insightful bons mots as "obvious troll is obvious." She sighed—some things never changed.

Her cocoa was almost gone when she saw something that interested her.

[2. Trade][Remoolus]: Girlfriend not in the mood? I have a tonic that makes Love Potion #9 look like butterbeer. Come to Remoolus & Company to get the potions for your motions. No charge if you provide your own mats; I pay you if I skill up.

She considered a moment, wondered what it was about playing a tauren that made otherwise intelligent people check their good sense at the door in exchange for cow-pun character names. She decided the pun wasn't egregious enough to place him in the unacceptable range—at least it had a hint of wit. She typed out a response.

To [Remoolus]: Clever. It's not every day in this game you find someone with wit, charm, and a full appreciation of Harry Potter references.
[Remoolus] whispers: I'm glad you enjoyed it. Believe it or not, I've had people actually ask me what Love Potion #9 is… >.<

To [Remoolus]: Oh, I have no problem believing that. The average age in this game is about 15—12 if you're going by mental age.
[Remoolus] whispers: LOL! So what are you doing in such a big city this late at night, little girl?

A smile spread across Diana's face. She was going to need another cup of cocoa.

A LETTER FROM
M.M. CHOUINARD

Thank you so much for taking the time to read *The Dancing Girls*. I hope you enjoyed reading it as much as I enjoyed writing it, and if you did, then you'll love my other Jo Fournier thrillers, *Taken to the Grave*, *Her Daughter's Cry*, and *The Other Mothers*. If you'd like to keep up-to-date with Jo Fournier or any of my other releases, please click the link below to sign up for my newsletter. Your e-mail will never be shared, and I'll only contact you when I have news about a new release.

mmchouinard.com

You can also connect with me via my website, Facebook, Goodreads, and Twitter. I'd love to hear from you.

The idea for a book about a serial killer who exploits internet anonymity has been wandering around my brain for years, as has the idea for a novel where the killer meets a potential victim who's more challenging than anticipated. One day those two ideas smashed into one another in my head like peanut butter into chocolate, and *The Dancing Girls* was born.

If you have the time and inclination to leave me a short, honest review, I'd very much appreciate it. Not only do I love getting your feedback, reviews help me gain the attention of new readers and allow me to bring you more books!

M.M.

mmchouinard.com

mmchouinardauthor

author/show/5998529.M_M_Chouinard

@m_m_chouinard

ACKNOWLEDGMENTS

Every book is a creation not just of its author, but of a tribe who breathe life into it. Heading that tribe is Leodora Darlington, who discovered it, believed in it, and helped polish it into what it is. The rest of the Bookouture team have also been essential in so many ways, including talking me off more than one ledge: Alexandra Holmes, Martina Arzu, Jane Eastgate, Nicky Gyopari and Ramesh Kumar all helped edit and produce it; Kim Nash and Noelle Holten tirelessly promoted it; Jules Macadam and Alex Crow helped market it; Ellen Gleeson made the audiobook a reality; and Leodora Darlington, Oliver Rhodes, Jenny Geras, Ruth Tross, Jessie Botterill and Natalie Butlin helmed the ship that transported the product to its readers; Maisie Lawrence and Peta Nightingale have helped steer it into new waters.

Also prominent in that tribe are those who beta read previous versions; their feedback allowed me to make crucial improvements, not just to this book, but to my writing skills generally. Particular thanks go to Dafina, Janette, and BSW, who did all that and so much more.

I've also now been lucky enough to have a second team, this one at Grand Central, lend their considerable talents to *The Dancing Girls* and bring it to a new audience. My heartfelt thanks go out to Tareth Mitch, production editor; Ivy Cheng, publicist; Alana Spendley, marketer; and most of all to Kirsiah McNamara (whose first name I fully intend to steal for a future novel).

Without my husband's support, this book would simply not exist. His daily sacrifices allow me to pursue my passion. He's the best, in every way!

My deepest heartfelt thanks go out to my readers. Thank you so much! If I make even one of you gasp, laugh, or tear up, I consider this a job well done.

And finally, thank you to my darling furbabies, who keep me warm and cozy while I write long into the night.

READING GROUP GUIDE

DISCUSSION QUESTIONS

1. At the opening of *The Dancing Girls*, we meet Jo Fournier as a newly promoted lieutenant. By the end of the book, she decides she no longer wants the job. What factors led her to take the promotion in the first place? Do you think she made the right decision? Why or why not?

2. What situational and psychological factors allowed Martin to manipulate his victims so effectively?

3. One of the book's themes is the difference between who people are and who they want to be. How does the online video-game setting explore this?

4. Emily and Martin have very different reactions to their stroll through the French Quarter. What do those reactions reflect about their two personalities? How did the reactions foreshadow each of their deaths?

5. Why did Emily stop struggling when Martin strangled her? What did you feel when she stopped struggling?

6. How did Martin's escalation play a role in his downfall? Was that inevitable?

7. How are Martin and Diana the same? How are they different? Is Martin a psychopath? Is Diana? Would Martin consider himself a bad person? Would Diana consider herself one? Why or why not?

8. Female empowerment and disempowerment are themes in this book. How do the women, including Jo, give away their power? How do they reclaim their power?

9. How did you feel about the way Martin was stopped? Do you think that counts as being brought to justice? Were you glad that Diana got away, or would you rather have seen her caught?

10. Jo's relationships with men, including her father, are complicated. How do her relationships with Karl and her father parallel her complicated feelings about her job?

11. When the book ends, Martin has been identified and is dead—he won't be killing again. What is it about Jo that makes it hard for her to be at peace with the case's resolution? How is this related to Marc's death?

12. Diana and Jo are both out to get Martin. How else are they alike?

13. *The Dancing Girls* is told from the perspective of the detective, the killer, and the victims. Which had the biggest emotional impact on you? Why?

A CONVERSATION WITH M.M. CHOUINARD

Q. *Being a detective is an incredibly difficult job. What kind of person or personality does someone need to have in order to take on this job?*

A. In my opinion, a detective needs problem-solving abilities, emotional intelligence, critical thinking skills, attention to detail, and tenacity. But I also think there's an increasing awareness in law enforcement that the traumas that detectives (and other police officers) experience are cumulative and can have negative consequences, so a willingness to understand your limits and recognize when you need support to remain psychologically healthy is also crucial. I've tried to reflect this struggle in Jo's character arc.

Q. *How did you create the character Lieutenant Jo Fournier?*

A. My first stab at writing a detective was a male character—I have no idea why. I shared the book with my critique group, and they found him to be a little too much like other detectives they'd seen before. So I did a fair amount of soul searching about what sort of detective I'd want to read that I hadn't already read. For me, that was a woman who'd been very successful in her career, but had found what she was "supposed" to do (take a promotion to lieutenant) wasn't making her happy; in other words, someone who had priorities other than career ambition. I also wanted someone who was fundamentally kind and empathetic, rather than the sort of person who gets what she wants through yelling, intimidation, and rudeness, which I see in a lot of fictional women police detectives. According to law enforcement I've spoken with, the hostile approach doesn't solve many crimes in the real world. And finally, I wanted my protagonist to be middle-aged, and to be dealing with the sort of questions many middle-aged women face, especially when trying to juggle career, relationships, family, and societal expectations.

Q. Why did you choose an online video game as your serial killers' hunting ground? Do you have personal experiences with World of Warcraft *or other online video games?*

A. I did play *World of Warcraft*, and that's a big part of what inspired this book. The social aspect of the game fascinated (and terrified) me because the virtual environment creates an illusory space that has a very compelling psychological reality, one that was often used by people looking to be something other than who/ what they truly were. And there's nothing wrong with that sort of escapism—except that not everybody in our world has good motives. So when I saw guild members and in-game friends start up relationships and then meet in person (in one case, a couple who met, fell in love, and ultimately got married!), I was always wary. All I could think was "how do you know he/she's not a serial killer?" And I'd always wanted to write a book about two serial killers who unwittingly find each other, so when that idea collided with the possibility of a serial killer who exploited the malleable psychological reality of online games, *The Dancing Girls* was born.

Q. *Is there any special research you did to make the details in your book feel real?*

A. So much research! I think the parts I enjoyed most of all were researching New Orleans and ballroom dancing. I've been to New Orleans and I loved it, so it was a blast to immerse myself in it again. And I have two left feet, so living vicariously through dancing tutorials was very fun.

Q. *Are there any personal inspirations that you drew from while writing this book?*

A: Jo's realization that the lieutenant job wasn't right for her was drawn from my own experience of climbing up a career ladder only to find I didn't want the job at the top of that ladder. And, more importantly, from my realization that it was okay to say "hey, this isn't right for me," and to not have that ambition. While my career type was different, my epiphany paralleled Jo's realization that just because you're a good detective and it fulfills you, that doesn't mean the promotion to lieutenant is going to be that much better—and, in fact, it may be the exact wrong step. Ambition for ambition's sake or because it's what people expect isn't always the right way to go. The important things are to understand yourself enough to know what's important to you, and to have the courage to act on that.

Q. *Is there someone, or multiple people, that you look to for help or feedback on your writing? Or do you prefer to work solo as you create the story?*

A. I have a critique group that I love that gives me amazing feedback, and a few trusted beta readers that have been incredibly helpful to me.

Q. What's one writing tip that you can give to readers and aspiring writers?

A: Keep writing. Samuel Beckett said, "Ever tried. Ever Failed. No matter. Try again. Fail again. Fail better." In writing, failure is a part of the path to success that you don't get to skip, because it's how your writing improves. You only learn to write a novel by writing a novel. So if you wrote a novel and nobody wants to publish it, write another one. Write a better one. Fail again, fail better, until you write the one that someone wants to publish.

Q. When did you first realize you wanted to be a writer? Do you have a specific writing process or do you just sit down and let it flow?

A: I can't remember a realization that I wanted to be a writer, I just always loved writing. I guess the first proof I have of my desire to be a writer is the story I got published in the local newspaper when I was eight.

In terms of process, I follow the principle that has been attributed to William Faulkner: "I only write when inspiration strikes. And I see to it inspiration strikes at nine every morning." I write every day (except for vacations!) whether the words are flowing or not. Sometimes the writing isn't great at first, but if I keep going, I warm up and things start going better. I can always go back and cut or rewrite the part that wasn't so great, but I can't revise a blank page.

Q. What do you like to do when you're not writing?

A: I love to read (of course). I also love genealogy, puzzles of any kind, cross stitch, paper crafts, nail art, and anything to do with Halloween.

Q. *What is one thing you want all of your readers to know about you?*

A: How much I appreciate every person who takes a chance on one of my books. Thank you so much!